A KNIFE IN THE BACK

Also by Alex Coombs

The Old Forge Café Mysteries

Murder on the Menu

Death in Nonna's Kitchen

The Hanlon PI Series

Silenced for Good

Missing for Good

Buried for Good

The DCI Hanlon Series

The Stolen Child

The Innocent Girl

The Missing Husband

The Silent Victims

A KNIFE IN THE BACK

ALEX COOMBS

NO EXIT PRESS

First published in the UK in 2024 by No Exit Press,
an imprint of Bedford Square Publishers Ltd,
London, UK

noexit.co.uk
@noexitpress

A CIP catalogue record for this book is available from
the British Library.

ISBN
978-1-915798-76-3 (Paperback)
978-1-915798-77-0 (eBook)

2 4 6 8 10 9 7 5 3 1

Typeset by Palimpsest Book Production Limited, Falkirk, Stirlingshire

Printed in Great Britain by CPI Group (UK) Ltd, Croydon CR0 4YY

For Tim Platt
Best friend

Chapter One

I hadn't been outside at 7 o'clock in the evening on a Thursday in years. Before, it was because I had been working in other people's restaurants. Now, it was because I had a kitchen of my own to run.

The outside world was the real world. The world I lived in most of the time was like the mythical world of Plato's cave, lit by fires and guessable only by representations of reality that in my case were the food orders that the ticket machine delivered at periodic intervals. Orders that I then had to turn into edible reality. But outside the kitchen walls, I knew that if you parked your car carefully – not by the side of the common which, as the many signs point out, is strictly forbidden – and strolled around Hampden Green, you'd think to yourself, 'What a peaceful place.'

It's what I had thought when I'd moved here.

A hypothetical, disinterested observer would note the green, with its fenced-off play area, a couple of mothers supervising their children before bed in the late summer, some small boys playing football at the mini goal-posts and maybe a dog walker or two, exercising their animals with

1

a fling-ball. It would seem like a nice place to raise a family or live a quiet life. The tasteful parish information notice-board (made of wood, a kind of walnut stained finish and a glass case; you had to have permission to put notices inside) gives details of Zumba classes and yoga in the village hall – run by a new yoga teacher, a woman this time. Regulars can be spotted sitting outside the local Three Bells pub having a quiet pint. And then there's my restaurant, the Old Forge Café.

In the calm, tranquil dining room that Thursday night, there were about twenty-five people, enjoying good food (at reasonable prices) efficiently and charmingly served by my young manager, Jess and her assistant waiter, Katie.

A peaceful place to eat in a peaceful Chiltern village. Until you go inside the kitchen...

Welcome to my world.

Heat from the stove, heat from the chargrill, heat from the hot plate, heat from the lights keeping the food warm on the pass, heat from the backs of the fridges, heat from the deep-fat fryers, heat and steam from the dishwasher...

'Cheque on!' I shouted to Francis over the kitchen fans. It was like a furnace in here. My jacket was sodden with perspiration and stuck to my skin. I wiped my forehead with the back of my sleeve.

'Two hake, one fillet steak medium rare, peppercorn sauce... no starter...'

Francis's large, red, sweaty face beamed at me from underneath his bandana that he'd taken to wearing in the kitchen, and he turned away to get the vegetable accompaniments ready.

And not just heat to contend with, but noise too. The roar of the extractor fans, which in this small space was like a jet taking off, the hiss and bubble of the deep-fat fryer, the clang of pans on the stove, the crash and bang of fridges as we frantically opened and slammed them shut, the dry crackle of the cheque machine as it printed out the new orders.

I added the cheque to the row of five that were already lined up in chronological order above the pass. At least this was an easy order to do.

I quickly finished plating the dish that I had just cooked, glanced at the clock, pulled a frying pan off the stove and balanced it on the cooker away from direct heat where it would keep warm until it was ready to be reheated before I sent it out.

'Service...' Jess, my manageress/waitress/confidante/friend/IT adviser, appeared, and I pointed at the pass. She was back from uni for the summer, thank God. Jess might be only twenty-two but she was by far the most mature person I knew, myself included. 'Two lamb, one smoked aubergine feuilleté. Thank you, Jess.'

'Thank you, Chef.'

She disappeared with the food, efficient as always. I turned to Francis as I took the cheque down and spiked it, and looked at the next three, to see they were all in hand. I opened my small locker fridge for mains and took out two pieces of hake and a steak fillet and put the piece of meat on the bars of the chargrill.

'Francis, get the red pepper relish out.' I liked the red pepper relish, simple to make (cheap to make, come to that), versatile, a real winner.

'We haven't got any, Chef!' came the shouted reply.

For a second, the world stood still as I digested the news, then I was back in action, mechanically turning the various pieces of meat on the chargrill, checking that the three small frying pans I had on the go with yet more meat inside were all to hand, making sure that the piece of turbot protected by tinfoil under the lights on the pass wasn't going over, getting too cooked. I was cooking fifteen meals simultaneously, and now this.

I turned to Francis who quailed under my gaze. I was very cross indeed. At 5 o'clock he had assured me that all the mise en place was done; well, that manifestly wasn't the case. You didn't run out of things in restaurants; it was unacceptable.

As was sending the hake out naked, minus its dressing as clearly stated on the menu, into the world.

I was tempted to bellow, 'What do you mean, we haven't got any…' adding a string of profanities, but what would have been the use?

One of the hallmarks of a good chef is being able to deal with crises and I am a good chef.

'Go out to the walk-in, get me a red pepper, an onion, a fennel bulb – and hurry up…' I snapped, suppressing the urge to scream at him. That would not be ladylike I told myself primly. If I'd been a man I might have said something like, 'You'll be wearing your effing nads for earrings if you do that again' – but I'm not a man.

Francis stood there rooted to the spot. Like he'd been hypnotised or glued to the floor.

I lost my ability to suppress my urges. There's a time and a place for everything. Now it was time to scream.

'Please, HURRY UP!'

It had no noticeable effect. He didn't leap into action; he ambled. There are times when I would dearly like to kill Francis.

Jess came into the kitchen and saw my expression, sensed the mood in the air.

'You okay, Charlie?' she asked.

'I'm savouring the moment, Jess,' I said through clenched teeth. 'I'm very much savouring the moment in a mindful way.'

Earlier that day I had been reading another article on mindfulness. Mindfulness had become my latest obsession. If I had some free time I would research it on the internet. Obviously, when I was cooking it wasn't a problem, I had laser focus on what I was doing, but I had noticed of late that when I was doing prep, or driving or running, my mind was becoming overwhelmed with negative thoughts. It was time to do something about it.

Whoever had written the article, I decided, had probably never worked in a commercial kitchen, but I was determined to take their comments on board, regardless. It was probably easier to be mindful if you work as a meditation teacher than a chef, but hey ho…

I crashed a pan on the stove to vent some mindfulness on metal rather than Francis's skull. It felt so good I did it again, but harder, repressing an urge to scream at the top of my voice.

Francis returned and handed me the vegetables.

He looked stricken, his plump, red face a mask of contrition. Contrition was no good to me. I gritted my teeth and tried to enjoy the Now.

The Now was far from enjoyable.

So, while I cooked fifteen meals, (Francis doing the vegetables, silently, miserably, like a kicked dog – now I felt guilty as well as angry, sometimes you just can't win) I frantically made a red pepper relish, buying time from the table by sending them some pâté and homemade parmesan and rosemary focaccia bread (chef's compliments).

The relish is supposed to gently cook for about three-quarters of an hour – I had it ready in ten minutes, softening the vegetables in the microwave before frying them, frantically cutting corners. More by luck than judgement, it ended up just fine, but by the end of the night I was a sweaty, angry twitchy mass of nerves enclosed in sodden chef's whites.

We sent the last cheque out and silence descended on the kitchen. I started turning the gas rings off on the cooker, shutting down the kitchen, tight-lipped with irritation.

'I'm sorry, Chef, I was as much use as a chocolate teaspoon…' Francis looked like he might cry, his lip trembling. He had taken his bandana off and his very blond hair was plastered to his head like he had been swimming.

Francis was huge, his chef's whites padded out with muscle.

'That's okay, Francis,' I said, patting him on the back (it was like stroking a horse), 'but please don't do it again.' I thought for a moment, reliving the sheer panic-stricken unpleasantness of those moments. 'Ever again,' I added.

'I won't... I promise.'

'Well, we'll say no more about it then.'

We cleaned the kitchen down, I sent Francis home, and Jessica and I sat in the small empty restaurant and had a beer. It was becoming a bit of a tradition really, and I was beginning to realise just how much I had come to rely on Jess's company since arriving in Hampden Green.

'You look terrible,' she remarked.

I looked at Jess. She didn't look terrible; she looked refreshed. I wondered how she continued to look full of energy after a long day and night waitressing. Perhaps she had this mindfulness thing down? Jess gave me a look of worried concern and pushed a hand through her dark hair that she fought a constant battle against frizz with. One of the few problems I don't have. My hair seems to enjoy being bathed in sweat. At least someone's happy.

Silver linings.

'I was thinking exactly the same thing this morning, while I was brushing my teeth,' I said. 'Perhaps I should start wearing more make-up.'

'Well, you'll need more than that,' she said as she drank some beer (thanks for the compliment, I thought) and looked at me with real concern. 'You're exhausted Charlie. How many hours have you worked this week?'

I did some mental arithmetic – fifteen hours a day for eight days – but I was too tired to do the sums. 'A lot.'

'Charlie,' she said, looking me in the eye, 'you simply can't go on like this – you need to hire another chef.'

I took a mouthful of beer. 'I can't afford to hire one – if I could, I would.'

Jessica looked unconvinced. 'You can't afford not to hire one. Working a hundred and twenty hours in a row' – Jess, unlike me, was good at maths – 'is not good for you.'

I smiled, rather bleakly. I knew that we were both right.

Jess drained her beer and stood up, reaching to pull on her jacket.

'I'll see you tomorrow at ten,' she said. 'Try and get an early night.'

I smiled. Fat chance. If you're a chef you haven't finished until the last cheque has been dealt with and then you have to clean the kitchen down, make a note of what needs to be done the following morning and also do your meat, fish and veg order. I don't think I've been to bed much before midnight in years.

'I will.'

She stood looking down at me, shaking her head. 'Get another chef. You're killing yourself.'

'If a miracle happens, I will.'

I watched as she let herself out.

Miracles never happen, I told myself sorrowfully.

Chapter Two

The following night was practically a carbon copy of the previous night. I felt like I had fallen into Groundhog Day. This time Francis had forgotten to make soup. He had a list – I had drawn it up and printed it out and laminated it – of all the things he had to do. It's called an MeP list, a mise en place list. Soup was the first item.

'Cheque on. Three vegetable soup of the day, three fillet steaks, all medium. New cheque, one duck, one hake, one salmon en croute,' called Jess. I don't like multiple cheques but I said nothing, there had to be a reason.

Francis hadn't moved.

'Francis?'

'I forgot the soup, Chef,' he said unhappily.

I stared at him in disbelief. How could he have been so stupid. And it was Friday as well, the busiest night of the week. I stood there for a moment as we both looked at each other. Time stood still.

I closed my eyes to blot out Francis's face. I listened to the ambient sounds of the kitchen, the fans, the faint murmur from the restaurant that lay beyond the swing doors, the sound of the gas and things cooking. I'd taken a further step on my spiritual quest by listening to a podcast on mindfulness and general lifehacks when I ran in the mornings. Today on my tempo run it had been on facing life's challenges, how they are an opportunity to grow. Well, I reflected to myself ruefully, as I re-opened my eyes, (no, unfortunately, this was not a bad dream, this was reality) here was a fantastic opportunity to grow.

I sprang frantically into action. I put the pre-prepared salmon in puff pastry in the oven, criss-crossed the duck skin with my chef's knife, seared it in a red hot frying pan and tossed it in the oven next to the salmon. I took the hake fillet out of the fridge, ready so I wouldn't forget it. Then I made a roast Mediterranean vegetable soup in about five minutes, fortunately I had a tub of roasted vegetables which were for a vegetarian special (quinoa with roasted vegetables, feta and mixed seeds) on tomorrow's menu.

'Blitz that now,' I told him as I banged the bowl down on the metal table in front of him. I recalled there were also some homemade parsnip crisps that I'd made. I got the soup ready while dealing with a couple of other cheques. I was pouring with sweat now, partly due to the heat of the kitchen but mainly the unexpected stress (having to make soup in the middle of service!). I managed not to swear or do anything rash.

A few minutes later I'd thrown in a couple of litres of veg stock, boiled it like crazy, re-blitzed it with a stick blender, wincing as droplets of boiling soup stung my face, checked the seasoning. How was the duck doing? I glanced at the clock on the wall, five minutes to go... The hake!

A small frying pan on, splash of oil... I carried the pan of soup over to Francis's station. Thank God he'd had the foresight to get three soup bowls and a ladle ready.

'Cream, Francis!'

'Chef.'

'Fill the bowls...' Back to the stove, hake on, back to Francis. I tipped some cream into the lid of the plastic bottle, leant over the first soup bowl.

'Swirl of cream, sprinkle of chopped parsley, three parsnip crisps on top as garnish, do the other two...' I lifted my voice, 'Service!'

Then back to the hake. Duck out, salmon could stay another minute. While I started plating this, I thought, I'm being remarkably calm. This was courtesy of Dr Melanie Thomas, the mindfulness woman. She was the creator of 'The Mindfulness Podcast with Melanie'. And also the author of 'Steps Towards Mindfulness – A Stoic Approach'. There was a plethora of mindfulness apps and books out there but I didn't have the time or inclination to research the subject. For now, she was my go-to woman.

The evening wore on. But I wasn't the only one having problems. Jess, out front, was getting increasingly annoyed with a table of one, a woman dining on her own.

So far, she had already sent back her starter, a prawn cocktail that I'd put on as a kind of whimsical retro joke and had proved wildly popular – face it, it's a nice thing to eat. It is comfort food at its very best. Table Seven had said, 'Not what I was expecting'! It was prawns in Marie-Rose sauce on a bed of leaves, what else could you possibly be expecting in a prawn cocktail, a margarita with a shrimp in it? She had said the wine was corked, which was not the case, and her panna cotta was 'insipid', followed by 'I should know, I go to Italy all the time'.

I felt like storming out and shouting, 'My boyfriend's Italian, he likes it, he says it's better than his mother's, you cretinous woman.' But I didn't.

Oh, and her fish was 'rubbery'.

I had never seen Jess so worked up. I tried to cheer her up with some of the mindfulness techniques I'd learnt.

'It's not the situation that causes us pain, Jess,' I said earnestly, 'it's how we react to it... Just look at me and the soup thing, I'm so over it...'

She leaned over the pass. 'Charlie, I love you, but any more of these bloody platitudes and I'm going home, okay...'

'Sorry, Jess.'

I watched as she left the kitchen like an angry cat. When we're disturbed it's our fault, not the other person's, I thought smugly. Maybe I should have shared that with her too. I had ordered a copy of Dr Thomas's book; I should have made it two.

Later that evening, after the last customer had left, I was having a drink of wine with Jess and savouring the tranquillity of my silent restaurant. I'd got my laptop open and was transcribing my scribbled notes on what we needed to order for the following day in terms of fruit and vegetables, and Jess was looking at something on her phone. I glanced over at her. Whatever she was reading was evidently amusing her, she was grinning broadly and occasionally her shoulders would twitch.

'What's amusing you?' I asked.

'Oh, nothing...'

'That is such an infuriating thing to say, Jessica.'

'What?'

She sighed, put her phone down and looked at me. 'Okay, it's an article by this woman lecturer in the *New Statesman* about what dicks male academics are. She sorts them into types, "Patronising Man-splainers, Screaming Queens and Mr Geeky – The Unitribes" as she calls them. It's hilariously accurate, you should go to Warwick...'

Warwick is where her uni is. I gather it has a famous (ish) castle too. She read me some of her article, I feigned interest, Jess saw through that immediately.

'You don't get it, do you?' she said.

'No, not really Jess. I guess you have to know that kind of background and I don't really. It's not my world.'

'No, I guess not, it's nothing like catering. Anyway, Charlie, you're kind of hard to intimidate.'

'Am I?' I said.

Jess laughed. 'Look, Charlie, the last person who tried to have a go at you, you half-blinded with a chilli... then there were those horrible thugs you beat up with a rolling pin.'

'Jess, you're making me sound psychotic,' I protested.

She stood up and stretched and put her phone away. ' I know you're not, you just have an adorable rough and tumble streak.' She smiled. 'Anyway, I'm off home, I'm going to go and watch Dr Young having a go at Jordan Peterson on YouTube.'

'You've lost me now,' I said. I didn't know who either of these people were.

She smiled as she shrugged herself into her jacket. 'It'll be like watching Tyson Fury fight Jake Paul,' she said, confidently. 'You know in advance who's going to win.' She walked over to the door. 'See you tomorrow.'

'Good night, Jess,' I said.

I watched her leave. Pretty, intelligent, confident, the world at her feet. Tyson Fury I knew, the others, well, they were hardly going to impinge on my world, were they?

On Saturday morning on my run, I was doing interval training and listening to my mindfulness guru, Dr Thomas. I couldn't do anything to alter my circumstances but I could do something to change the way I viewed them. That's what Dr Thomas told me. Today she had a special guest in the studio who was some kind of an expert on Stoicism. As I panted along one of the many footpaths around the village I nodded approvingly as he explained how we shouldn't get angry as it will only make the matter worse, but how we should plan our way out of things.

The word associated with anger in my mind was Francis.

I tried not to be angry with him. It was practically impossible. Forgetting the relish, omitting to make soup. Earlier in the week he'd managed to really screw up something I thought was impossible to ruin, garlic butter. He'd added a crazy amount of salt to it. 'Sorry Chef, I got distracted…' he'd mumbled, then he'd added, practically in tears, 'I'm as much use as a glass hammer.'

'That's okay,' I'd said, patting him on the shoulder, 'accidents happen.' Inside I was suppressing hysterical rage.

The thing was, he was great at washing up and he was

reliable. These are two prized assets in a kitchen porter. Generally, people who wash dishes for a living are not the most trustworthy individuals, and he was. It was just food that was his Achilles heel. That, unfortunately, is a real problem in a small restaurant.

I also owed him a considerable personal debt. Francis had, quite literally, saved my life. How can you possibly fire someone who has done that?

With the matter still unresolved, I wearily walked back across the common. There were a couple of runners jogging down the road. We waved at each other, I knew quite a few people in the village now. I saw a woman I knew as Pretty Mum, tall, willowy, good-looking, with her cockapoo and daughter in an expensive looking all-terrain buggy and Della, undoing the doors of her small van – 'Della's Dog Walking' – and releasing three of her charges, plus Della's own black cocker spaniel, on to the green, preparatory for their walk. She lived down the road from me, one of the few people who could say, like Jess and Francis, they had been in the village all their lives.

Later that evening, after service, I was in my local pub, the Three Bells, having a drink with Graeme Strickland the head chef at the King's Head, the Michelin starred restaurant in the village.

The King's Head had been a bog standard pub and these days such places find it hard to survive. Its owners had invested heavily and turned it into a sought-after restaurant. It became a destination place. The same could not be said of the Three Bells. If the Three Bells had been an animal, it would have been put down a while ago. But it was handy for both our establishments and we didn't care where we drank so long as it was away from a kitchen.

Strickland often ate at my place on his day off; I appreciated the compliment. Once you got used to his arrogance – he had quite a high opinion of himself, no faux-modesty there – he was a genuinely nice guy and insanely knowledgeable about food. He also freely gave me cookery advice and tips if I asked. This is kind of unusual in catering where chefs, understandably, tend to avoid sharing trade secrets.

I was venting about Francis and he interrupted me.

'Yeah, but Charlie, you know all this, you can't blame the guy for being thick, it's like complaining that your dog doesn't understand Shakespeare...' His eyes were slightly glazed, he'd obviously been doing coke in the toilets of the pub, it had made him philosophical. 'Francis is Francis and the dog's a dog, they're not going to change just because you get cross with them.'

Despite the drugs, he was right. Marcus Aurelius couldn't have put it better.

'So true, bestie,' I said. I changed the subject. 'How are things with you?'

'Oh, fine... Apart from this, it really annoyed me. I had this real bitch of a customer in the other day, moaning about this, that and the other. She had the turbot, said it was "rubbery".' He shook his head and drank some lager. 'What does that even mean?'

Rubbery? I thought. That reminded me of my own arsey customer. I told him about her.

'It has to be the same one,' he said decisively. 'Did you comp her meal?'

'Yes. I don't think we even charged her for the wine, she complained about that too.'

'It's definitely the same woman. She complained about the wine too. Has to be. I'm going to find out who she is, I bet all this is leading up to something.'

Strickland looked cross now. He was a small, neat man in his forties, my age, always immaculately dressed. He was also very good-looking, and he knew it. He had never made a pass at me though, he treated me purely as a good friend. I was happy with that. He also had a terrible temper.

'She'll claim that there's glass or something in her food, or say she got food poisoning, try and get some money out of us to hush it up…' He was very agitated now. 'I'm going through the CCTV tonight with Dan, after service,' he said. Dan was his restaurant manager. 'I'll send you her image. Show it to Jess, bet you it's the same person.'

'I think you're over-reacting.'

'Bet I'm not,' he said darkly. 'You're too trusting, that's your problem, Charlie.'

Tuesday morning came. I felt re-energised after my day off. I was closed on Mondays, my one day off a week. As I ran I reflected on what Strickland had said on the Saturday night. That was between listening to the importance of perception in life as explained in the mindfulness podcast. Melanie Thomas (I thought of her as Tranquillity Girl these days – I was going through all the old episodes, there were about a hundred I hadn't listened to) was making the point that we should narrow our focus down to what we have agency over. For example, I couldn't control the state

17

of the paths on which I ran, but I could make sure I was careful not to fall over any tree roots as I went. I couldn't make Francis into a chef, but I could limit the amount of damage he was able to inflict on food by hiring another chef.

Yes, I thought, with determination, that's what I would do. I would hire some help. I couldn't really afford it, but it would free me up to chase some outside catering for much needed extra money.

I was so pleased I had listened to Mel that morning, she had crystallised my intentions. I felt more in control now, not just of myself but my life.

When I got back to the restaurant, Francis came up to me.

'There's been a delivery for you, Chef.'

'The veg?'

'No,' he shook his head. 'It's from Amazon, I think it's a book.' His red face looked semi-astonished; Francis was not a great reader. He went over to where I keep the log books for writing down the fridge temperatures and came back with a small packet. I opened it.

Steps Towards Mindfulness – A Stoic Approach, it said on the jacket. I experienced a surge of excitement. I felt with Dr Thomas's book to help me I would start to really get somewhere.

'Can I have a look?' Francis said.

'Sure.' I handed him the book. I saw his lips move silently as he deciphered the title.

'What does Stoyk mean?' he asked.

'I'm not sure… how do you mean?'

18

'It says here,' he pointed to the word Stoic. 'Stoyk?'

'Oh, it's pronounced Stoic, two syllables, not one, sto-ic… it means…' well, that was hard to answer in a word.

Jess appeared through the swing doors that led to the restaurant.

'We'll discuss it later Francis,' I said.

My phone pinged, it was Strickland, there was a jpeg attachment to the message that said simply, 'found the bitch.'

I showed Jess my phone.

'Has he lost a dog?' she said innocently.

I explained the circumstances; Jess's face darkened. 'In that case I forgive him, I think he's found exactly the right word. Let's see her.'

I opened the attachment. There was a slim woman who looked to be in her fifties with short, dark hair with a flamboyant red streak in it and a combative expression on her face. Francis leaned over Jess's shoulder to take a look.

'That's definitely her,' Jess said, pulling a face. 'She's Table Seven all right. What's he going to do?'

'I have absolutely no idea, but I wouldn't like Graeme Strickland as an enemy, he's very obsessive. What's her name by the way, did you check?'

'Mel Craig.'

'Well, I'll remember that. We certainly don't want anything more to do with her, that's for sure. If she tries to book again, we're full. I suppose we should thank God she's not a food critic.'

Jess smiled. 'That's all we need.'

'If you don't like her,' Francis asked innocently, 'why have you bought her book?'

Jess and I looked at him in puzzlement.

'What do you mean?' I asked.

By way of reply he turned the book over. There on the jacket was a photo of the author. 'Oh, no,' I wailed to myself in anguish. 'Tranquillity Girl how could you!'

Dr Melanie Thomas and Mel Craig were one and the same.

Chapter Three

You wait years to meet one podcaster and then two come along at once. I was up at half past six for my run and I put my ear-buds in and looked at the podcasts stored on my phone. I rested my forefinger on the Zen-like icon of Dr Thomas's mindfulness app. Bitch, I thought and mindfully deleted it.

The podcast app suggested several other ones I might be interested in. Cooking? The podcast they suggested was done by non-professionals including a restaurant critic that I particularly detested. A wordy ignoramus, and if I see the word 'smorgasbord' (unless used by a Scandinavian) I feel like screaming. Ditto 'succulent', 'bivalve' and 'nestle'. So I rejected that suggestion. Then I saw one by a podcaster called Lance Thurston.

Lance was an anti-woke, right-wing broadcaster. I'd heard him described as a cut-price Joe Rogan (by Esther Bartlett, our local Wiccan witch, community leader and close personal friend) or 'that wanker', by Jess. The only reason he'd ever been mentioned in my hearing was because he lived relatively nearby. There are quite a few celebrities and well-known people who live in the Chilterns. The area is both pretty and accessible to London. Lance had eaten in my restaurant a couple of times but I'd been kind of underwhelmed. He was famous in a way that wasn't that famous; I guess he was a C list in the fame stakes, maybe rising to a B on occasion. The kind of level that might get you a place on Celebrity Big Brother or a night-club opening in Watford. He was well-known mainly because he was controversial. He'd provoked a hornet's nest of outrage with some possibly (he denied that they were) anti-gay sentiments expressed on air; this had of course, massively boosted his ratings. The Green movement too were frequently mocked. This had led to speculation from a Green spokesperson as to the size of Lance's penis. This had then, in turn led to condemnation of the penis remark by men's groups activists who pointed to issues of low self-esteem and embarrassment regarding male sexual dysfunction. All of this was meat and drink to Lance; controversy was the oxygen he needed.

More seriously for Lance was the hostility he had aroused locally from the Bucks SOBs. This acronym stood not for Sons of Bitches, but Save our Beeches. Bucks is famous for beech trees; the SOBs were an environmentalist protest group dedicated to saving woodland in general and trees in particular. They were led by a charismatic Timothée Chalamet lookalike called Roland Sylvanus. Jess had pointed out when I'd remarked on his weird name, Sylvanus, that it meant woods or something like it in Latin, and it was a safe assumption that it wasn't his real surname which was probably something prosaic like Dobbs or Smith.

Now the SOBs were not fearless keyboard warriors like the social media mob who seem very brave about expressing their outrage on the usual outlets; the SOBs did stuff.

For a start, they'd graffitied his sports car, a Ferrari, the fuel consumption of which Lance had controversially bragged about as being around twenty miles per gallon. Lance liked imperial units of measurement. Although mpg is standard in the UK, Lance's voice would linger lovingly over the word, 'gallon', like an ageing roué would lasciviously pronounce the words, 'suspender-belt' or 'negligée'. I had the impression that pounds and ounces, gallons, pints and quarts made Lance hot. Anyway, the SOBs sometimes congregated outside his house in fancy dress, protesting at his championing of fossil fuels. They pursued him at industry awards. Lance for his part excoriated them as sandal-wearing, bearded loons and left-wing thugs. They were sworn enemies.

Also on the sworn enemy list, a fairly lengthy one in Lance's case, (basically anyone to the left of GB News was, in his view, a metropolitan, leftie, woke, snowflake) was Jess's hero, Dr Susannah Young.

'I'm reading her book, it's called *Can Someone Tell That Bloody Woman to Shut Up!*. It's her collected journalism from 1980–2000,' Jess had mentioned earlier. Jess was prone to sudden enthusiasms about things, as we all are I suppose at that age. Taylor Swift was a constant, others came and went. Right now this Dr Young was her current fad.

'1980!' I marvelled. 'Was she some sort of child prodigy?'

Jess shook her head. 'She's a boomer, not that you'd know it, born 1960, but she started young, younger than me…' she said wistfully. 'She was a columnist for *Spare Rib* when she was my age.'

I was only half-listening, uninterested in Dr Young. 'Is that to do with barbecuing, spare ribs?'

'No, Charlie,' Jess said coldly, 'it was an iconic feminist magazine, nothing to do with barbecues.'

'Oh.'

Since Lance looked as if he were becoming a regular of sorts – he was booked in again – I thought that I'd give his views a listen in case Jess (not to mention Dr Young) had unfairly maligned him. Jess was only twenty-two after all and issues for her were very black and white. I was double her age, forty-four, and I've found, on the whole, life is more nuanced than I'd imagined when I was younger.

I put the ear-phones in, downloaded his latest episode and set off on my run.

'And another thing about electric cars,' sputtered Lance's guest, some guy from a motoring magazine, 'is that the batteries that power them weigh a ton, quite literally. The average electric car battery weighs around five hundred kilos, and an average electric car is thirty per cent heavier than its petrol counterpart.'

'But I guess they do save weight by being driven by people with emptier heads because of their smaller brains?' quipped Lance. 'I mean the people, the SOBs who damaged my car with spray paint, are noticeably stupid. They are also hypocrites…'

'Definitely,' his guest said. 'If they were so keen on the environment they would have keyed your car with their message, not used environmentally damaging spray paints.'

'Exactly,' Lance said, 'they use VOCs, that's Volatile Organic Compounds, dear listeners, which give you cancer, and hydrocarbons and they're terrible for the environment, but that's just it with the woke brigade, they don't really care about the environment. If they did you'd see them on public transport.' He paused for dramatic effect. 'Have you ever seen a young person on a bus in the countryside? Oh no... not them, the hypocrites, the milquetoasts, no, they won't get on a bus with the plebs and the poor and the old because they are too important saving the planet to actually do something useful. They've all got cars or use Ubers, it's okay when *they* do it, but not me... and have you ever seen a young person on a bike in the countryside? No. They've lost the use of their limbs through playing video games... they've atrophied.'

'It's Darwin in reverse,' said his guest.

'Exactly. Oh, by the way, SOBs,' Lance said, 'I got rid of the Ferrari after you damaged it, and I bought a car with even higher fuel consumption, just to spite you...'

'More than the Ferrari? What are you driving Lance, a traction engine?' asked the guest.

I'd had enough of the car stuff. I fast-forwarded it... Blah blah Ulez... blah blah, twenty minute neighbourhoods... Blah, blah, gay rights activists.

I stopped and put my running music on, that was far more inspiring than Lance. The weird thing was though that not only was he incredibly popular with his audience, there seemed to be a lot of them. Every Just Stop Oil protest brought a new peak in Lance's audience figures. Maybe he was secretly financing them.

I was now running near the Earl's house. The footpath ran through one of his many fields that lay next to Marlow House, which was the family home.

I saw two figures on the path ahead of me with a few dogs running ahead of them. At first I thought they must be professional dog walkers, like Della, since there seemed to be a fair number of animals, but as we drew nearer to each other I saw that it was Bryony and some kid of her own age that I didn't know. Bryony was early twenties like Jess, they'd been in the same year together at school. I slowed down and stopped to speak to her.

Bryony was the girlfriend of the aristocrat who owned much of the land and a fair number of properties for a couple of miles around where we were standing. Above the treeline in the distance I could see the grey tiles of the roof of the Earl's ancestral home standing proud above the landscape.

Bryony's short blonde hair shone in the early morning sun. She was wearing a tight T-shirt that clung to her perfect chest. You could see from quite some distance away that she was wearing nothing underneath. She was wearing baggy camouflage trousers and army boots. Her arms were a riot of tattoos. I knew them well, I particularly admired the tree with the snake coiled around representing the Adam and Eve story from the Bible and high on her right arm the Hebrew words 'the serpent beguiled me and I ate'. Together with the apple.

I smiled; I liked Bryony. Five dogs of various shapes and

sizes, animals that the Earl had rescued – he was big on animal welfare, frolicked around.

'Hi Bryony...'

'Hi Charlie...' She indicated the guy she was with. 'This is Roland.' Oh my God, I thought, the leader of the SOBs.

'Hi, nice to meet you,' he said. Roland was about my height and slim with a mop of dark, curly hair and intense blue eyes. He had quite a triangular face with high, pronounced cheekbones. He was strikingly good-looking. It was the face of a visionary or a poet. I couldn't imagine Roland fixing a washing machine, or working in a kitchen, come to that. So this is Lance Thurston's sworn enemy, I thought.

'Roland wanted to see the gardens. Unfortunately James is away in Sumatra at the moment.' I nodded. James was the Earl, Bryony's boyfriend, or sugar-daddy, depending which way you looked at it.

'Orangutans?' I asked.

She nodded. 'Yeah, the Sumatran orangutan, it's really endangered.'

The three of us fell silent, contemplating the plight of the orangutan. Roland was wearing slim-fit torn jeans; he had great legs I noticed. They were slim but looked muscular through the tight denim. Under the collar of his worn denim jacket he had seriously elegant trap muscles. His fingers were long and strong... I snapped myself out of this daydream.

'Anyway,' I said, 'I'd better get going.' I smiled at Roland. 'Nice to have met you. See you around Bryony.'

'Sure.'

I sped off across the field. As I did so I could smell the compost scent of weed as Bryony lit up a blunt and the aromatic smoke drifted across the grass. I wondered if Roland's interests were really about gardening or if they lay more in Bryony. He was achingly cute. If I was the Earl, I'd be seriously worried.

Chapter Four

'So how many will there be at this party?' I asked politely. I looked at the man sitting opposite me in my restaurant. It was nearly 10 o'clock and I was done for the evening. The place was almost empty apart from a few customers. Lance was shorter than I had imagined, with a bull-neck and very beefy biceps that he was showing off via a short-sleeved flowery shirt. Despite the muscles and the tattoos you could tell he was not the real McCoy when it came to scary masculinity. The key to knowing someone is a tough guy lies in their eyes and their demeanour, not in their physique. Looking at him, I could see someone who could pretend to be tough, but wasn't. Well, I'd heard the podcast, now I was meeting the real thing. And what I concluded was that here was someone who would talk the talk but fail to walk the walk.

Following his dinner, a mini beef Wellington, a mushroom sauce, rösti potato and green beans, a lemon mousse for dessert, he had, via Jess, asked me if I would be interested in catering for his birthday party on 30 August, in just over three weeks' time.

Yes I would. Very much so.

Now Lance Thurston scratched his shaved head.

'About a hundred and fifty guests,' he said, 'give or take.'

'A hundred and fifty,' I said, thoughtfully. 'And what did you have in mind?'

'A buffet.'

I nodded. 'Hot or cold?'

He looked at me like I was crazy. 'Does it matter?'

'Well, yes. For a start, if it's hot food we'll need proper plates, that'll add to the cost,' I pointed at the kitchen door. 'I can supply those, together with everything else that's needed. If it's cold food they can wander around with paper plates, should you wish to save money. Are they sitting down or what?'

It was increasingly obvious he hadn't thought this through. While he considered this I looked around my restaurant. There were just five people left eating, a table of three and a table of two. It had been quite a busy Wednesday evening, about twenty-five covers, but it had been a fairly easy service. The bookings had been nicely spaced out, giving me time to draw breath between one order and the next, nothing had gone wrong and there hadn't been any nasty surprises. The table of three had finished and they came over after they had paid their bill and thanked me.

One of them, a woman to my surprise, came back as her companions were getting ready to leave.

'Excuse me, are you Lance Thurston?' she asked.

'Yes I am.' He looked at her slightly warily, as did I. She didn't look like an eco-warrior, but you never can tell these days. This could obviously go one of two ways.

She smiled. 'I'm a huge fan, could I have a photo?'

Now he looked delighted. 'Sure.' She got her phone out and took a selfie of her and Lance. Then she thanked him and left.

'What a lovely woman,' he said to me. He then spent the next few minutes telling me how much his fans meant to him and how he tried to answer all their messages individually. It was rather touching, but I had to prod him into making a food decision. I had a kitchen to finish cleaning down.

Lance eventually plumped for sitting down and it would be hot food but with a buffet. I started going through a list of questions with him. Finally, we agreed on canapés, main courses and desserts. Wine was easy; I'd opened a house red and white as selected by Cassandra Jenkins, my wine supplier. They were both Italian.

'This is good, very good...' Lance murmured.

'It's a Bianchetta Genovese, from near Genoa in north west Italy. It's very light and refreshing isn't it?'

'Yeah, I'm happy with that, and the red?'

'It's a Rossese, a red wine, same area, Liguria. It's robust so it goes really well with the lentil and chickpea stew that we'll be having as the vegetarian option.'

'What is in that again?' he asked.

'Lentils and chickpeas.'

'Very funny, what else?'

'Tomatoes, red pepper, sweet potato, cumin, cinnamon, chilli... There's homemade harissa sauce to go with it, on the side, for those who like heat.'

'That sounds good.'

We decided on chicken and leek casserole as the other main and vol-au-vents, mini open sandwiches, bruschetta and arancini as amuse bouche.

'Well,' I said, closing my notebook, 'that's just about everything, I'll be in touch about a week before the party. Can I have your number?'

We exchanged mobile numbers and he thanked me and I watched his broad back leave the restaurant and climb into his taxi that was waiting outside.

'I can't stand that man,' Jess said as the taxi drove off. 'I don't know how you can bear to work for him.'

'Is that because of his behaviour or his politics?' I asked.

'His politics.' She conceded that he'd been polite and non-demanding.

'Did he leave a tip?'

Reluctantly she nodded. 'Yes he did.'

'Was it a good tip?'

Another nod. 'It was a very good tip,' she said begrudgingly.

I pressed home my point. 'Are you going to give it back, or donate it to charity, it being tainted money and all, from the grubby hands of that right-wing hate merchant?'

I knew damn well she was saving for a car. (Exactly, I heard Lance say in my imagination, what else would you expect).

'No, I'm keeping it.'

'Well, Jess,' I said, standing up, 'I guess that makes us both shills of the anti-woke, right-wing haters. I'm going to go and clean the kitchen down; I'll leave you to log on to 4chan.'

Francis was finishing the washing up as I cleaned down my area: the stove, the pass and work-surfaces. I turned the radio off and put Lance's podcast on. He and his guest were having a go at Dr Susannah Young.

Jess came in and frowned. Oh dear, I thought guiltily, this will be a red rag to a bull.

'Charlie, this is bordering on provocation. Please shut him up,' she said, sounding cross.

'They were discussing Susannah Young, Jess,' I said, turning Lance off. 'She'll probably be delighted by the publicity.' I was getting tired of Jess's hero worship of this academic.

'I'm sure she'll be thrilled,' Jess said. I nodded. ('Feminazi', Lance had called her). 'She's actually coming here next week and giving a talk.'

'What, here? In Hampden Green?' That was surprising. We were a nice village, but a village nevertheless. In my mind, based on Jess's adulation, I had built up Dr Young as a kind of academic/media superstar. I felt obscurely annoyed by Jess's adoration of the woman. I know it sounds ridiculous but I had almost taken it as a personal slight. Maybe it was because my further education had been in catering colleges, maybe I resented people with degrees. Or maybe I didn't? It was all very perplexing, maybe I needed a therapist. Anyway, regardless of my feelings, the question in my mind still remained. What was she doing here?

'Yeah,' Jess said, 'next Monday.'

It was hardly the Oxford Union. I said as much. I knew that the Hampden Green Society had a pull way beyond what might be expected of such a small place; people had relations or friends, who knew people… and so it went. The Six Degrees of Separation or whatever it's called. But I guessed from her reputation that Dr Young could normally pack out a sizeable venue. Mind you, the village hall is not some kind of shed, it's all light oak and high ceilings and polished floorboards and it can seat a couple of hundred people.

Jess explained. 'I was amazed too. Seemingly she's a friend of Esther Bartlett's and she's staying with her for a couple of days, so Lavinia Truscott asked if she wouldn't mind giving a talk and she agreed.'

'So you're going.' It wasn't a question. How could she miss this.

'I wish.' Jess looked woebegone. 'She's a hero of mine but the talk sold out virtually immediately.' She picked up the mop and bucket from the cleaning cupboard by the restaurant door to go and do the floor behind the counter in the dining area. She looked sadly at the cleaning implements. 'I feel like Cinderella being left behind.'

'I'm sorry, Jess.'

Jess disappeared back into the restaurant and I immediately picked up my phone and texted Esther. We were old friends now and if she could help, I knew that she would.

Five minutes later when Jess came back into the kitchen carrying her mop and bucket, I looked up at her from where I was squatting, tidying up my locker fridge and said, 'You shall go to the ball, Cinders! Get the pumpkin coach ready, saddle up the mice.'

'What!' Jess said, her face was ecstatic. 'You've got tickets for Dr Young?'

'I have indeed, Jess,' I said, proudly, 'I have indeed.'

Chapter Five

The speaker took a sip of water from the glass in front of her and bent closer to the microphone, the spotlight cast a golden glow on her hair.

'I'd like to thank you all for coming and to take this moment to suggest to those young misguided environmentalists protesting outside this hall that they take fewer foreign holidays, more public transport, stop showering every day and if they want to glue themselves to something, well why not McDonalds?' I thought to myself, this is eerily similar to Lance Thurston. 'They should be demonstrating against the patriarchy instead of trying to silence someone like me who tonight, among other things, would like to highlight the fact that sixty-two per cent of women killed in the UK are killed by their partners, and I, for one, passionately believe something should be done about it...'

She waited for the applause to die down. The hall was full and the atmosphere rapt. Dr Young then spoke for about an hour on her work and research. She was a good speaker, fiery, but also amusing. The audience loved her. She not only sounded good, she looked good too. The skin was still taut on her face and jawline, her figure still looked great, she could have easily passed for a woman twenty years her junior. Occasionally my mind would wander and I would speculate on what on earth she had done to provoke the SOBs led by Roland. There had been about twenty of them outside the hall, two of them dressed as Ents, holding a banner: 'The Trees of Priestfield Copse Say Shame on You Dr Young!' There was also an outsize coffin (open casket) containing a small, skeletal dead tree flanked by a figure dressed as the Grim Reaper with a skeleton mask. The sleeve had fallen back on the slim arm holding the handle of the scythe and I recognised the snake in the tree as belonging to Bryony. The cavalcade of protesters were led by Roland dressed as an old-style undertaker; he'd caught my eye and smiled at me. Roland looked very dashing in his top hat and frock coat. I had felt myself blushing unaccountably when our gazes met. Throughout her talk I kept wondering what Priestfield Copse was all about and what role Susannah Young had played in it.

She came to the end of her lecture and then closed with this dig at the man whose party I was catering for:

'And so the next time that you might feel inclined to tune in to a Lance Thurston podcast and listen to another homophobic, sexist rant and feel like nodding in approval, may I remind you that this is also the man who rails against "intellectual elites".' She leaned forward and scanned the attentive audience in front of her. 'Now' – pause for effect – 'maybe you could say I was biased. After all, I work in a university, I'm an intellectual, also, I'm one of a handful of well-paid women scientists – I'm part of an elite – but, ask yourselves, when you're examined by a doctor, operated on by a surgeon, when you buy a piece of software or get on board an aeroplane – who do you want to examine you, operate on you, have designed the program or pilot the plane. I strongly suspect that you would want that person to be one of the intellectual elite, basically not someone like Lance Thurston, dragging his hairy, onanistic knuckles along the ground and jeering at things he neither has the brains to understand, nor the balls to admit his ignorance. Good night!'

There was thunderous applause and Esther Bartlett, who had been sitting next to her on the podium, leaned forward and took the microphone.

'Ladies and gentlemen, I would like to thank you for coming and making this evening such a success and if you could express your appreciation once again for Dr Susannah Young…'

The two women on the stage sat back and smiled at each other while we, the audience, clapped enthusiastically.

'Refreshments are in the marquee, courtesy of the Old Forge Café,' Esther said as people got to their feet and headed out of the village hall where the talk had been held, to a gazebo outside where the food that I'd made earlier had been laid out.

Free tickets come at a cost.

The day after I sorted our tickets for the talk, I had sat down with Esther and discussed the catering. This was canapés and nibbles for 150 people, plus two glasses of wine, and elderflower spritz for the non-alcoholic alternative. I'd done all this at cost; the village hall kitchen had its own supply of plates and glassware, so at least I was spared that. I was curious to know more about the unlikely relationship between Esther and Jess's hero.

I knew Esther mainly through her work as head witch of SoBuNPag, that is, South Bucks Neo Pagans, a coven of white witches/pagans. She wore a variety of hats though, she was a local councillor, very active on the village committee and she also ran a book club and a wine society. She was as energetic as she was heavy, as high in kilojoules as she was in kilogrammes.

'Yeah, we were at St Anselm's together in Oxford, in the early eighties,' Esther had said. 'Oh, hang on a minute… I know, this'll help.'

She heaved her considerable bulk off the sofa she had been sitting on and went into another room, coming back a few minutes later with a large, white photo album, titled '1980–1985'.

'Roy's digitised all my old photos now,' she said. 'I'm all for progress, but y'know, it somehow lacks the warmth of this…' she tapped the cover of the album with a red-painted fingernail. 'Anyway, come over here and I'll show you.'

I crossed over to the sofa and sat next to her, her sofa sagging alarmingly under her weight so I was in danger of sliding down into the depression in the fabric and ending up rather too close for comfort.

She opened the book. I was transported back into a time that I was too young to remember but nevertheless somehow did. There, against the background of an Oxford college familiar from film and TV (thank you Inspector Morse and spin-off series) was a startlingly youthful Esther with long hair and a kind of peasant skirt. She had been pretty then, plump, true, but nothing like the plus size adult version next to me. In the picture with her was a very attractive blonde twenty-something year old wearing jeans and a silk shirt. She had the kind of figure that could cause car crashes from distracted male motorists. Her perfect breasts were highlighted rather than concealed by the thin, see-through fabric of her blouse. She had big hair and very red lips and dramatic eyeliner.

Esther laughed. 'Su was voted "Rear of the Year" and "Dishiest Fresher" at Oxford. That was 1978. There weren't so many women there then…'

'How did she feel about that?' I asked.

Esther smiled. 'She claimed to be outraged and insulted, but…' she gave me an arch look, 'I think she was secretly delighted… Su was always a great one for having her cake and eating it.'

More photos, a young, innocent looking Esther, caught frozen in time laughing at a party, sprawled on her back in a punt next to Dr Young, nipples once again prominent under a tight lacy shirt, the guy punting tall and good-looking.

'Tony, my then boyfriend,' she sighed. 'How I wept when we split up…' There was a lengthy pause while she lingered for a moment in the past. 'Bless you, Tony,' she whispered mainly to herself, 'they were good times.'

'Su was revered at college,' Esther continued. 'She was so glamorous, she had all these London friends, partied with the New Romantics and the post Punks, wrote for *Spare Rib*. She was tipped for greatness, we thought she'd be like Germaine Greer.'

She fell silent for a while, then resumed. 'But it never really happened, she never got the top jobs, I mean, yes, she's been successful, but not I think to her own satisfaction... she never got the glittering prizes.'

'So what does she do these days?' I asked, 'when not wowing the village halls of the Chilterns?'

The answer was journalism, radio, appearing as a guest on podcasts and occasionally on YouTube. She was also lecturing back at St Anselm's, their old alma mater.

'But I don't think it's going very well,' Esther said. 'She's having a row with the Master and a couple of colleagues. I know she's not happy there; I think that's what made her hook up with me again, a shoulder to cry on.'

So, now, back in the hall, Jess and I approached the stage. Jess had a copy of Dr Young' best known book, *The Equality Myth*, in her hand for the academic to sign. Esther came up to me. Today she was wearing a pink dress and a white hat so she looked like a huge pink blancmange, or a gigantic marshmallow.

I wondered what Dr Young made of witchcraft. I mentally compared her to the photos I had seen in Esther's photo album. She was still very attractive. She was slim, her blonde hair cut short, bespectacled, and wearing a tailored trouser suit. There were no prominent nipples or cleavage on display, but her figure was still excellent. Standing next to Esther emphasised her slender build. The two women looked like illustrations from a book my father had read to me when I was a kid, *Fattypuffs and Thinifers*.

To be honest, I wasn't as keen as Jess on Dr Young. Esther had introduced me to her before the talk, and when she'd found out I was a chef she'd just kind of grunted in a non-committal way and I saw her eyes flicker to find someone more important in the room to pay attention to. Then there was her journalism (I'd done a quick internet search) which paraded her zeal for social crusading and her caring credentials together with a vicious cruelty towards those who didn't share her views. Maybe what had really turned me off her was a searing critique of a restaurant in London that I'd once worked in. She'd slammed its prices as elitist and disgusting (more or less the same criticism she'd just mocked Lance for). Now, I knew the head chef who worked a seventy-hour week, fifty weeks a year, for much less money than I bet Dr Young earned. I also knew that the food only just broke even, any profit was made on the drinks. Well, I reflected, she wasn't to know this, but she could have found out, couldn't she?

Her particular bête-noire today had, of course, been Lance Thurston. He'd come under a great deal of flak in the previous hour from Dr Young who had thrown shade with gusto calling him, among other things, a Home Counties Andrew Tate, together with some unprintable unladylike expressions.

It had been funny and well-deserved, and Lance's opinions were certainly not mine. However, I had felt a bit guilty in a way because, after all, I was taking his money. I consoled myself with the thought that as a chef/restaurateur I was like a taxi driver, I accepted fares regardless. Besides, neither Oxford University, the *Guardian*, Channel Four nor the *New Statesman* – Dr Young's happy hunting grounds – would be bunging me any money in the foreseeable future.

Jess was clutching her book excitedly as she came over to join us. She'd got it signed. I wasn't quite so enthralled. Dr Young had given Jess what I felt was an unpleasantly evaluating look, her eyes lingering on Jess and I noticed her checking out her backside as she walked away. Now she was chatting to a crowd of admirers at the book table, darting the occasional glance in our direction.

'Well, that went well,' I said to Esther as we watched the doctor basking in the adoration of the worshippers.

'Sure did,' Esther said.

'She certainly gave it to Lance,' Jess said, her eyes shining. 'Wonder what he would say if he did hear any of it.'

'I can't imagine he'd be very happy,' Esther said.

I thought of what I had heard on the radio. 'No, he wouldn't,' I said thoughtfully. Lance was not going to take this lying down.

Later that night I was in my flat above the restaurant. It was a warm evening, the windows were open and I was enjoying a glass of Gewürztraminer that Cassandra had suggested. 'There's some great wines coming out of Germany at the moment, Charlie,' she'd said. I can remember thinking, I shall add this to the wine list and do some German food and recommend it as a pairing, Wiener Schnitzel with Bratkartoffeln – a kind of fried potato with onion and lardons – posh word for chopped up bits of bacon.

What else did I know that might work? My knowledge of German food was practically non-existent. Cakes, they were hot on cakes, and of course Wurst. I couldn't see Bratwurst selling well, certainly not Weisswurst. Or Currywurst, that weird hybrid that's so popular in Germany.

I turned my laptop on to note the Schnitzel idea down and idly logged on to Lance's podcast for that evening. Some podcasters like Andrew Huberman, whom Andrea, my boyfriend, was obsessed with, have a YouTube channel as well as the audio broadcast. Lance, who quite fancied himself (there's no accounting for taste) had one too. I was curious to see if he'd heard about Dr Young's attack on him.

I looked at the images on the screen in front of me. Lance, bull-necked, bald-headed, wearing a tight T-shirt the better to show off his bulging biceps, was talking to his guest, a well-known young (to my eyes) comedian.

'What women want from a man is leadership and discipline,' Lance said. Well, I thought, I beg to differ, but if a statement was going to be sweeping then Lance was very much your man. Bulls would be let loose in china shops, shibboleths assailed, statements swept, left-wing opinions outraged – that's what he was all about.

'My girlfriend just wants my body,' the younger comedian said, shaking his head sadly, 'she doesn't seem interested in my mind at all...'

'You may joke,' Lance said, nettled by this.

'Thank you,' said the comedian drily, 'it is my job, Lance...'

'Dude,' Lance said. Dude? I thought, Lance was from New Malden (I'd Googled him). He was speaking in a weary voice now. 'I get it in the neck from feminazi types all the time, only today I was called a knuckle-dragging ape by one of our so-called academics. Well, I have a message for you, Dr Young,' he flipped his middle finger at the camera, 'and I hope you die horribly like you obviously want me to.'

Unnecessary Lance, attack the argument, not the person. Her comments had obviously upset him, I imagined she'd be pleased by that. I'd had enough of him. I turned the podcast off. I wondered who had tipped Lance off about Dr Young's attack on him. I thought his own reply certainly lacked finesse.

I yawned and looked at the time. 9 o'clock. Bedtime for me on my day off. Tomorrow I'd have to be up at six if I wanted to get a run in before I started work. There was a huge amount of prep to do.

The following day Lance's wish came true.

Almost.

Chapter Six

I was peeling potatoes when I heard the sirens. At first I ignored them. Then Francis, who had been in one of the store rooms on the other side of the yard that the kitchen backs on to, burst into the kitchen, the door banging against the wall as he flung it open, the anti-fly chains that hung down from the top of the frame jangling, his eyes wide.

'Have you heard the news, Chef?'

'What news is that?' I asked, wincing at the racket, looking up from my large bowl of potatoes.

'My auntie just phoned me, the one who works at the police station, to see if I was all right.'

The words tumbled out of him excitedly.

'Why wouldn't you be all right, Francis?' I was mystified.

'There's been a shooting, Chef.'

'My God, where? Who?' I was alarmed now. I clutched my potato peeler tight, as if that was going to help.

'That woman that you and Jess went to see… the doctor woman…'

'Dr Young?' I frowned. What on earth was going on?

'That's the one, she's been shot!'

'Oh my days!' I said, nearly dropping the potato peeler in surprise. 'What happened?'

Francis poured out the story. Dr Young and Esther had been walking across a field that abutted on to the common, the village green. It is a sizeable field, bordered on one side by the common and some houses, on the far side by another field, on another by a farm and its outbuildings, at the bottom, a small, single-track road. The two women had been in the middle of the footpath that crossed the field when Dr Young suddenly collapsed. Esther Bartlett had stooped down to help her and seen that she'd been shot through the leg.

'There was blood everywhere!' Francis said with dramatic relish, as if he had been present.

'Is she okay?'

'Well, she was alive when they put her in an ambulance. What do you make of that?' He stared at me like an excited Labrador hoping for something from its owner. If he'd had a tail I could imagine him spinning on the spot trying to catch it.

'I have absolutely no idea,' I said, shaking my head. 'Poor woman, I hope she pulls through.'

'Well,' he said, goggle-eyed, eyebrows raised, 'I was as surprised as a nun who snogged the Pope!'

'Francis,' Jess said, in a warning voice, coming in behind him.

'I can say that, Jess,' protested Francis. 'I'm Catholic. Besides, it's not even rude!'

Just then Olivia, one of the part-time waitresses came in.

'Sorry to bother you, Chef,' she said to me, 'Esther Bartlett's just come in and wants a word.'

I immediately stopped what I was doing, washed my hands and went into the restaurant. Esther was sitting at a table. She was wearing baggy linen trousers and a top which had been a kind of taupe but now had russet smears on them like someone had dragged a paintbrush across. That, I assumed, was Dr Young's dried blood.

Standing behind her like a watchful guard was Della, her faithful dog sitting obediently to heel.

'I helped her over here,' Della said, by way of explanation for her presence in my restaurant, 'she looked as if she was going to faint.'

'Thank you, Della, dear,' Esther said, patting Della's hand. Today Della was wearing her dog-walking clothes, an old plaid shirt and army trousers. She had shoulder length brown/blonde hair streaked with grey and a squarish, emphatic jawline. She looked very no-nonsense.

'Esther!' I said, in alarm. 'Are you okay?'

'I'm fine...' She didn't look it. She was very pale and the good humour that she usually radiated like a forcefield was noticeably absent. She was breathing very heavily, her vast chest heaved and she fanned herself with one of my menus. The surplus flesh in her upper arms wobbled with the motion. I hoped she wasn't going to have some sort of heart attack.

'I know you're not open yet, Charlie, but I need to calm down before I go home, is that okay with you?'

'Of course,' I said. 'Can I get you anything?'

'Herbal tea,' she gasped, 'camomile if you've got it.' She closed her eyes and fanned herself some more.

'We do, I'll make it,' Olivia, who had followed me back into the restaurant, said and went behind the counter.

Esther said wearily, 'I've certainly had a bit of a shock.' She opened her eyes and gave me a wan smile.

'So, it's true,' I said, 'someone shot Dr Young?'

'I can't really believe it happened,' Esther said wonderingly. 'We were halfway across the field, when there was a bang and immediately Su collapsed. Luckily I had a belt on so I tied it round her leg... I carried her on to the common in my arms.'

Now there was an arresting image, I thought, Stanley Spenser would have loved it, a kind of Pieta on the Village Green. Esther carried on. 'Someone called an ambulance, thank Heavens, they were here very quickly. I'm going to go and visit her later in hospital.'

Della said, 'I think I'll head off now, Esther, now that I can see that you're okay.' She nodded to me. 'Nice to have met you in person, rather than just waving.'

'And you.' I watched her and her dog go. I turned my attention back to Esther.

'Do you think it was deliberate?' I asked.

'God yes,' Esther said, 'what else could it be?' I had, for some reason, been hoping that it might have been some kind of dreadful accident, a kid fooling around with a gun they thought was unloaded for example, but she was right, it would really stretch the imagination to come up with a convincing scenario. There was a lot of shooting round here, pheasants and such, but accidents were extremely rare.

'But who would want to shoot Dr Young?' I wondered

out loud, then I remembered the podcast that I'd been listening to the night before. Surely Lance Thurston wouldn't have done it?

Then I thought it could have been a deranged fan, a stan as Jess would call them. Someone at the meeting perhaps, either triggered by something that had been said, or slighted by their idol not responding to them. I thought of John Lennon and Mark Chapman, or Gianni Versace, or Joss Stone and her stalker. Lots of precedents.

'I spoke to Slattery,' Esther said. Olivia handed her the tea and she thanked her. I nodded. Slattery was our local policeman, you could see his house across the common if you looked out of my restaurant window. 'I have got to go and make an official statement later, when I'm feeling a bit better. It's been a bit of a nasty shock. Thank God Sue is so light and I'm so strong.'

She looked down with pride at her beefy arms. To be honest, I'd always thought of Esther as fat rather than strong, but maybe she was like a Sumo wrestler, or Big Daddy back in the day (my dad had been a fan of British wrestling). A brief roll-call of those forgotten men from Wolverhampton Civic Hall flitted through my mind. Presented on *World of Sport* by Dickie Davis. Giant Haystacks, Pat Roach, Adrian Street, Gorgeous George Gillette, all gone now.

'I don't know,' she said, 'who might have done it, but they had to be local, that's for sure. They had to be following us, or know that I always go on that walk every day with the dogs.'

'So that rules out embittered colleagues,' I said. It was

a shame. I didn't like the thought that it was someone in the village who was homicidal and armed. It would have been much better if it had been an Oxford don, or a journalist who had pulled the trigger.

Esther sipped her tea; colour was coming back to her face.

'I think the police should have a word with Lance Thurston,' she said echoing my previous thought. 'He's always going on about the importance of standing up for yourself et cetera and how dreadful women are, and she did have a go at him last night.'

'Well,' I said, standing up for my employer, 'maybe, but I've met him. I think he's all mouth and no trousers. I can't imagine he'd do anything like this.'

He wouldn't have had the balls for it in my view, but I kept this to myself.

Esther pulled a face. 'Well, I'm not saying it was him, but it'll do him no harm to be reminded by a police visit that words can have consequences. People like him encourage hate crimes, they egg people on even if they don't themselves believe their own hype,' she said. 'It could be one of those dreadful Intel people that drool over his podcast.'

I looked baffled; I *was* baffled. 'Intel?'

'You know, Intel, the ones with no friends?' she explained.

Now I was puzzled. 'The microprocessor people?' Surely not. I doubted Lance's podcast from leafy Bucks had much traction in Silicon Valley.

'No, don't be silly, the ones with no girlfriends who hate women.'

'Incels,' Olivia put in from behind the bar, 'I think that's who you mean Mrs Bartlett.'

'Thank you dear, yes.' She smiled gratefully at Olivia. 'Incels.'

'I guess you could be right,' I said, 'but at least Dr Young is okay. And so are you, thank God.'

'I feel much better now after the tea.'

'That was nice of Della to help you,' I said. 'Is she a friend?'

'Not really,' Esther said. 'But when her husband died a couple of years ago, cancer, it was quite nasty, a friend brought her along to some of our more public Pagan evenings. She thought it might help her.' She smiled. 'I don't think it did, Della's more of a church person, although she's a bit like the Earl, loves animals more than people. She adores the Earl. Della's very conservative, if not downright feudal. I like to think we witches transcend politics, but hey ho...'

She stood up. 'Anyway, thank you Charlie, and you, dear,' she said to Olivia. 'I think I'm ready to face the world now.' She turned to me. 'If you ask me, Lance has got a lot to answer for.'

Chapter Seven

Lance Thurston pointed with a strong, stubby finger:
'That's the marquee down there.'

I knew that he had a big house, but I wasn't prepared
for its grandiosity. It was at the edge of a village, Elmer's
Pond, about three miles from Hampden Green. There were
gates, a sweeping drive and behind it, long lawns and a
view over a valley. It was very impressive. We were standing
in his living room, it was only slightly smaller than my
restaurant, and looking out through the patio doors to a
broad sweep of grass beyond which the garden continued
towards a low hedge. Beyond that rose a row of trees that
had been carefully planted where the ground fell steeply
away so they didn't spoil the view. To the left of the lawn
was a sizeable garden office/shed.

When Jess had found out he'd invited me over to his
place to discuss the coming birthday party she'd immediately smelt a rat.

'Don't go alone, he'll hit on you,' she said.

'I can handle myself,' I said somewhat waspishly.

'He's freakishly strong. He posts all the time about how

much he can bench press and deadlift, he could tear you limb from limb.'

'I can lift weights,' I said haughtily.

'Can you bench press a hundred and seventy kg?'

'Well… now you mention it…' I know I had decided that he was harmless, but I'd often been wrong, particularly when it came to men. Maybe I should take precautions.

'If you are going, take Francis with you,' Jess suggested, 'just to be on the safe side.'

'Okay, Jess.'

She nodded approvingly then she carried on. 'Talking of sub-optimal people, I've been internet stalking Dr Melanie Thomas, aka Mel Craig.'

'Tell me more.'

'Well, she is basically a fraudster. The "Doctor" in her title is genuine' – here she paused – 'that is it's a genuine online purchase of an Honorary Doctor of Divinity from a Panamanian based' – her fingers sketched quotation marks – '"University." These doctorates cost sixty-eight US dollars.' She laughed. 'And they most certainly aren't very discriminating. I bought one for our dog, who is now officially Dr Siegfried Turner.'

'My God,' I said marvelling, 'you can really do that?'

Jess nodded. 'You really can.'

'So she's totally bogus.'

'Through and through. It gets even better. That podcast you were listening to, she had to close that down last year because she was done for plagiarising several writers on Stoicism. She just verbally cut and pasted chunks of their work and passed their arguments and ideas off as her own.

She was even using their words verbatim. She was told to desist, there was some sort of court order eventually issued against her. Thing is, the streaming service got to hear of it and shut her down. I'm surprised you managed to download anything, although maybe I should not be that surprised, she probably routed it through some less than scrupulous internet provider.'

'What about the book I bought?' I asked.

'Self-published again.'

'Anything else about her?'

Jess laughed. 'Yeah, she's a self-published fiction writer too. She goes in for kind of sub Stephen King/Anne Rice horror. The last one was called *Satan's Dark Mistress*. She publishes those under the name Mel Craig. That last book had rave reviews from Dr M Thomas, well-known psychotherapist and broadcaster.'

'She's got some nerve,' I marvelled.

'She has indeed.'

'Well,' I said, 'say what you like about Lance, he's genuine.'

'Yeah,' Jess sneered, 'a genuine dick.'

Now, in his enormous house, I evaluated Lance both as a dick and as a nuisance risk. He wasn't remotely threatening. When I had first met him I had dismissed him as all mouth and no trousers and nothing I had seen so far would make me admit I had been wrong. I recalled Esther thinking he could have shot Dr Young, I very much doubted it. Lance might have called for her execution on the podcast, but putting that into action was a very different thing. I certainly wasn't afraid of him, so when Francis asked me, 'Do you mind if I stretch my legs, Charlie?', I looked at Lance and said, 'You don't mind if my assistant goes for a walk round your garden, do you?'

'No, fine by me.'

'Off you go, Francis.'

'Thank you, Chef,' he said, reverting back to kitchen etiquette. He walked away happily through the patio doors to explore the garden. I watched him like a concerned parent keeping a wary eye on a precocious toddler. There's something about Francis that makes me want to mother him. It's not just me, Jess, his cousin, is similarly afflicted.

'Is he special needs?' Lance asked me condescendingly.

'No,' I said, shortly. I wasn't having Francis mocked by anyone, much less Lance who, face it, was nothing more than an idiotic podcaster airing his opinions like a loud-mouthed guy down the pub. The fact he earned shed-loads of money to talk bollocks was neither here nor there.

Lance rubbed his stubbled chin and stretched. When I'd met him at my restaurant he'd been wearing a shirt and chinos, today he was wearing a tight T-shirt the better to show off his jacked physique. I think he was trying to draw attention to his pectoral muscles. He kept twitching them, it was obviously meant to be alluring but was the polar opposite.

'Have you got a boyfriend, Charlie?' he asked in an offhand way, as if he were just making conversation. His left boob twitched. His nipples strained the fabric – not a good look in a gentleman. I noticed he casually tightened the muscles on his arm so they swelled up. If this was supposed to excite me it was certainly a non-starter. Perversely it made me think of Roland. I suddenly realised I rather fancied him. I pushed the thought from my mind. I think it was an adverse reaction to Lance's wafts of testosterone. At least I hoped it was that.

'We're not here to discuss my social life, Lance,' I said coldly. 'It's your party that's on the agenda…'

He held his hands up in a placatory manner. 'Whoa… sorry, Charlie, didn't realise you were so sensitive about it.' This was a highly annoying thing to say, and of course, he knew it. I decided to say nothing. The silence prolonged itself.

'Okay,' he said, buckling first, 'I apologise, I was just making conversation… So we know what we're having for food for the party.'

'We do,' I said, 'but I'd like to go over it again so there are no misunderstandings and I also want to establish the exact time you want me to send dinner out. Later we'll go over to the marquee so I can see where I'll be setting up the food stations. By the way, why is the marquee up now?'

'The company has got a labour shortage. They can't put it up when I want it cos they're committed to other events. Well, that's what they told me. I'm not being billed for long term use anyway. I quite like it, it's fun having a gigantic tent in your garden.'

We went through the food again, Lance asking the odd intelligent question. Occasionally I would catch glimpses of Francis ambling around outside like a happy but distracted dog. When Lance and I finished, I said, 'Let's take a look at your kitchen now so I know where I'll be working on the day.'

'Sure,' he said, with a slightly exasperated glance at Francis who had rejoined us. 'We'll have a mini grand tour.'

He led us out of the lounge into the spacious hall with a grand staircase sweeping upstairs.

'This used to be the dining room,' he said, leading us through a doorway, 'but I've had it converted into a gym.'

We walked into the large airy room where racks of dumb-bells and a kind of multi-gym, looking as they do like an instrument of torture from some hi-tech middle ages, contrasted with the Regency style wall paper and moulded ceiling cornices.

There was also a bench press set up with a bar and several plates on either end. It looked heavy.

'My speciality,' said Lance modestly. He sat on the end of the bench then slid underneath and pushed upwards.

His face turned a kind of beetroot red and the bar slowly rose and fell and rose again, his gym tits looking like twin hot-water bottles, as he completed his bench press. Veins were standing out in his forehead as he cranked out a second rep. I knew he was doing this to impress me but honestly it was kind of hard to think of anything less guaranteed to float my boat. A third one and then the bar clanked down on its rests. He sat up. 'Impressive, eh?'

He stood up. There were several metal barbells standing erect in a kind of holder. Francis was inspecting them. He reached out an exploratory hand then there was an almighty crash as somehow he managed to knock them over. 'Oops,' he said, smiling guiltily. Lance looked at him, annoyed. I could see he felt that Francis had stolen his thunder. He was obviously unaware that there was no thunder to be stolen.

'Why don't you come over here, big boy, and show us what you can do?' Lance said nastily, pointing at the bench press.

'You don't have to, Francis,' I said quickly.

'Let's see what you're made of,' Lance insisted.

Francis shrugged and took his place on the bench. He lay back and grinned at me and Lance as he grasped the bar and pushed upwards. Up and down it travelled as if it were light as air. I watched in delighted awe. I obviously knew that he was strong but I had no idea of his strength in terms of ability to move a load. Well, now I did. He had obviously at least three times the strength of Lance, and then some.

Lance's face was a study to behold. It reminded me of the Evil Queen in Snow White when she confidently asks the mirror who is the fairest of them all, expecting the answer she doesn't get.

Francis completed his tenth rep and replaced the bar gently, then sat up. He beamed at both of us. Then he immediately forgot the bench press, pointed a finger and asked, 'Why have you got a chest freezer in the corner?'

It was a very Francis thing to do, lose track completely of what he was doing and change the subject. Mind you, Lance was only too pleased to discuss something other than weight-lifting after his humiliation at the hands of someone he'd earlier anathematized as 'special needs'.

'Come and have a look.' He waved us over imperiously to view his freezer, a bog standard industrial spec freezer, complete with hasp for a padlock so you could lock it. To keep pilfering hands from your frozen goods.

Next to the freezer was a large grey metal cupboard with a keypad. It looked kind of incongruous with the gym equipment.

'What's in there?' I asked.

'Guns.'

'Guns?'

'Yes, it's a gun safe. I shoot.' He shook his head at me for being so slow on the uptake. He banged the top of the freezer with a meaty fist to bring my attention back to the matter in hand.

'I had a guest on my podcast a while ago, Dr Laine... you do listen to it don't you?' he asked.

'Sometimes,' I said, 'when I get the chance.'

Francis and I exchanged guilty looks, of course we didn't, we had got better things to do, but he'd started talking again, probably unaware of the possibility of a world in which people had absolutely no interest in him, his guests or his opinions.

'Anyway, Dr Paul Laine is an expert on cold therapy,' he paused, 'and the benefits of cold exposure on a regular basis are phenomenal: better immune health, mitochondrial repair and cellular rejuvenation.' He carried on in this vein for some time, like a salesman for Cold Therapy while Francis and I both tuned out. Then he opened the lid.

The freezer was full of water.

'I switch it on when I go to bed,' he said, 'then I get into it first thing, there's some ice formed on the top, so I break that and hop in for five minutes, it's miraculous.'

Thank God we weren't here at eight in the morning otherwise he'd have probably insisted that we give it a go. I wondered if Francis could cope with it, it wouldn't surprise me at all if he did.

As if reading my mind he looked at me meaningfully and said, 'Why don't you come round tomorrow and give it a go? I bet you look great in a bikini.'

'I do,' I said, nodding, 'I look absolutely fantastic. However, that is absolutely not going to happen until my summer holiday next year, and you won't be there Lance, so I'll pass on the kind offer.'

'Oh, I wouldn't be too sure,' he smiled, 'I can be very persuasive.'

'Let's go and look at the kitchen, Lance,' I said, ending his aquatic chat up line.

We walked into the kitchen and the first thing I noticed was a woman I knew well, cleaning the outside of an enormous American-style fridge.

'Hello, Della,' Lance said, sounding faintly surprised, 'I thought you were out. I didn't hear your car.'

'I came on my bicycle,' she said. Unlike today's effete, milquetoast youth according to Lance and Dr Young I thought. She looked at Francis and me and smiled.

'Hi, Charlie,' she said, 'I'm Lance's housekeeper.'

'Nice to meet you again,' I said, 'I didn't know you worked for Lance.'

She nodded. 'As you can see.'

Lance was looking very impatient at this amicable village chit-chat. Della must have noticed. 'Well, I'll get out of your way,' she said. She turned to Lance. 'I'll be in tomorrow about ten,' she said to him, 'I'll be doing the upstairs bedrooms tomorrow.'

'Thank you, Della,' he said.

She smiled again. 'Nice to have met you again, Charlie. I've been to your place a couple of times, I liked it.'

'Thank you,' I said. Always nice to get a compliment. She disappeared out of the kitchen.

Lance looked thoughtful. 'She's a fantastic cleaner,' he said, 'they're so hard to find. They're normally thick as two short planks, or light-fingered or they've got a drink problem.'

I nodded. I could sympathise. The same could be said of kitchen porters, it's partly why I cherished Francis.

I walked around his kitchen which, as is often the case in rich people's houses, looked remarkably unused. I guess it's because they eat out a lot or have people like Della to clean up after them. Aside from its size, it was conventional and unremarkable. I opened the fridge that she had been cleaning out of curiosity. It had hardly any food in, some cheese and a jar of olives, but was well-stocked with protein drinks and white wine.

For me the most important thing was adequate work surface space, and there was plenty of that. I took a closer look at his stove, that was suitable too.

'Yes,' I said, 'that all looks fine.'

'Do you want to come and see my studio, where the magic happens?' he asked, with a hint of eagerness.

I didn't, but he obviously wanted to show it off, so I relented. 'Okay.'

He led Francis and me out of the kitchen and into another

room that overlooked the front garden and the drive. There was a desk with a kind of boom microphone on a swivel, a laptop and a couple of screens, another smaller microphone and some fancy looking computer equipment. On the walls hung a dozen or so framed photographs of celebs, media types and famous people who had been on the podcast. I even recognised some of them without needing to ask.

Out of curiosity I asked, 'Do you know a podcaster called Melanie Thomas?'

'It rings a bell...' He frowned. 'Quite a loud one actually... I know so many people, Charlie, that's the problem. Give me another clue.'

'She sometimes uses the name of Melanie Craig.'

His face darkened. 'Oh God yes, yes I do. I must have blanked her from my memory. She sued me over a podcast that I did a couple of years ago, she said that I had defamed her, I didn't even know who she was... She was calling herself Dr Melanie Thomas back then and giving out sex advice. Some of it mentioned me, saying I was a narcissist, I seem to remember. Well, I said something like, takes one to know one and then I made some joke about her looking like a bulldog licking piss off a nettle, then bang! I get this lawyer's letter. Defamation of character. My agent did some digging, they were a no win, no fee bunch of shysters, he said I should just settle out of court, so I did, cost me five k.'

'Seriously?'

'Seriously. That woman is bad news, believe me.' Then he laughed. 'But I kind of got my own back. I did some digging of my own and a group called TherapyWhistleBlowers got in touch with me to ask what I knew about her. So I added my grievances to a long list they already had, but because I was famous it encouraged more people to come forward. I think it put paid to her "therapy/podcasting" career. So, he who laughs last, as they say.'

As Francis and I left his house, I began to get a very ominous feeling about Melanie Craig.

Chapter Eight

The following evening I was checking messages on my phone during a lull in service. I had put into practice the first (currently only) Teutonic food idea so far to go with the Gewürztraminer. It was quarter past nine and I had just sent the last mains course of the day, a breaded veal escalope with red cabbage and German-style fried potatoes (Jess had pointed out that if I called them Bratkartoffeln on the menu, nobody would have a clue what they were) and, from the vegetarian section of the menu, a cauliflower cheese with Parmentier potatoes (they are cubed, deep fried potatoes, like chips in the form of a dice) when I got a message from Lance.

'Really could do with talking to you, can you come over?'

I frowned. Personally, I really could do without talking to Lance – particularly in his house, alone.

Equally, I was intrigued as to why he wanted to speak to me.

Jess came into the kitchen,

'Cheque on – two Eton mess and a white chocolate mousse with gooseberry compote please.'

I repeated the order back to Jess as I put the ticket on the cheque grabber on the pass, the metal counter that separates the kitchen per se from the area where the waiting staff take the food.

'Francis,' I said, with deep misgivings, 'can you do this?'

'Yes, Chef,' he said.

I picked up my phone. 'I'll be in the Three Bells at 10.30pm,' I texted back. That would do. Neutral ground.

'I'll be there, thanks,' came the reply. I frowned, I wondered what he wanted.

I glanced down at what Francis was doing. I sighed deeply.

'No, Francis, not like that...'

I got to the pub earlier than I expected, at 10 o'clock. It was very conveniently situated a couple of hundred metres or so across the common from my restaurant.

I raised my glass of white wine to my lips. This was unusual for me, the wine here was notoriously terrible. But tonight I felt like mixing it up, experimenting with drinks for a change.

The Three Bells was looking exceptionally empty tonight. It was a very functional pub, nothing was wasted in an attempt to brighten the place up. Its threadbare carpet, bright overhead lighting and heavy furniture, the kind that could never get broken in a pub fight, was the antithesis of a welcoming hostelry. I drank a mouthful of wine and repressed the reflexive shudder. It was even worse than I remembered, but I wasn't going to let that deter me, I'm often stupidly stubborn. Chefs can drink anything, I told myself sternly. I reminded myself again that bottled lager was the only safe drink in the place besides spirits.

Behind the bar stood Malcolm, the landlord, thin with a very red face and a moth-eaten, grey cardigan, nothing would prise him out of this garment, not even extreme heat. He surveyed his pub expressionlessly. Then the door opened and Bryony came in. She was wearing a skater dress that clung tightly to her curves, and Doc Martens. Her face lit up when she saw me. She came over and asked if I wanted a drink.

'Pils, please, Bryony.' I'd changed my mind about not drinking lager. I'd suspected the wine was going to be bad, but not that bad.

She returned with the drinks. Then the door opened again and a gaggle of young people came in, local kids in the eighteen to twenty-five age group. They'd be here for one of Malcolm's famous nightly lock-ins. Bryony waved at them, she'd been to school with some of them.

'So how did you meet Roland?' I asked. My question came out of nowhere, it took me by surprise. It wasn't like I had been thinking of him, it just popped out. Bryony didn't seem all that surprised, but then she was quite high, in a world of her own.

'At a demo that James and I were in, outside the Ecuadorian Embassy in London, demanding better protection for the Galapagos. He recognised James and they got talking. James likes him.'

'What's his story?'

'He's from round here, Wycombe. Went to RGS, then Oxford... he's a bright kid.'

'Which college?' I asked, no idea why; I don't know anything about Oxford colleges.

'St Anselm's. He did PPE there…'

'What's that?'

Bryony shrugged. 'I have no idea, one of the Ps is Politics, I know that because he said to me, "I started SOBs because I didn't want to just study politics, I want to shape politics".'

'Shape politics?' I queried.

She shrugged again. 'That's what he said… shape politics… who knows what that means… He comes round a lot, he likes to talk to James about activism.'

I bet he does, I thought as I looked at Bryony's pneumatic body straining against the thin fabric of her dress.

'He's very good-looking isn't he?' I said to her.

She shrugged. 'I guess…'

One of the girls among the youngsters playing pool waved at Bryony to come and join them. She nodded back in acknowledgement. I liked Bryony and didn't want to see her hurt by the extravagantly attractive Roland.

'I think you should be careful with Roland, Bryony…' I said in a warning voice that I hoped didn't sound naggy or preachy.

'Why?' she asked, standing up.

'Because he fancies you?'

'He doesn't fancy me, Charlie,' she said, looking down at me, 'it's you he fancies… now if you'll excuse me…' She wandered off to join her friends at the pool table.

While I was digesting this bombshell, (a kaleidoscope of emotion: shocked, flattered, flustered, alarmed and, deep down, delighted) Lance came in. He was carrying a small, logoed sports bag in one hand, which surprised me. He was hardly on his way back from the gym, he'd already got one of those at home.

He looked around, as if startled by what he had discovered behind the heavy door with its stained-glass panels. I doubted he'd been in a scuzzy boozer for many a year. He walked over to me.

'Hi Charlie, want a drink?'

'No, I'm fine, thanks.'

I watched him as he went over to the bar, swaggered over might have better described the way he moved, as if he were determined to semaphore to a non-existent audience how alpha male he was. Nobody looked at him in his floral fitted shirt, tasselled loafers and his too-tight, bum-clenching chinos. When he reached the bar he turned around to face his audience. I saw his face fall as he realised he didn't have one. He came back to my table with a gin and tonic.

'Would you believe they don't have artisanal gin!'

'You amaze me,' I said, drily.

'Is this your local?' he looked around disparagingly. 'Jesus, what a dump.'

I shrugged. 'Well, it suits me,' I said. Although what he said was undeniably true, the Three Bells was a dump and then some, I wondered if part of his hostility was that nobody had looked at him when he had walked in. It was obvious that Lance liked being famous and resented it when nobody reacted. It made it even more unlikely in my opinion that he'd taken a pot-shot at Dr Young. He would have

69

been delighted to be the target of her ire. I think Lance would have agreed with Oscar Wilde that there's only one thing worse than being talked about and that's not being talked about.

'So why did you want to see me?' I asked.

'This thing with that woman who was shot…'

'Dr Young?' I said, raising my eyebrows.

'That's her,' he said, angrily, frowning. 'Do people really think I shot her?'

I was surprised by the question. 'I suppose some do, particularly after you said that you wanted her to die horribly, on air. That does sound like you might like to kill her,' I reminded him. 'You can hardly blame people if they thought you might actually follow through on a promise.'

He made a dismissive gesture. 'Yeah, but I didn't mean it.'

I raised my eyebrows in lieu of stating the obvious – that he shouldn't have said it then.

'Well, why are you asking me anyway?' I said. 'I don't get out much, I'm stuck in a kitchen most of the time, how would I know what people are thinking?'

He persevered. 'Is it true that the woman Young was staying with is a witch?'

I nodded. 'She certainly is, in fact, she's the head of a coven.'

'A what?' He obviously hadn't the word before.

'A coven of witches,' I said. 'That's the technical term for a team of witches. Coven.'

'Is she a good witch?' he asked. I looked at him, increasingly puzzled by his questions. They were beginning to appear slightly unhinged.

'Are you feeling all right, Lance? You seem a bit out of sorts?'

'I'm fine,' he snapped.

I shrugged and tried to answer his question. 'Do you mean, is she good at being a witch? Or do you mean is she a "good" witch, that is, a white witch? What is it with all these witch questions, Lance...' then a growing suspicion, 'you're not doing one of your hatchet podcasts on her, are you? She's a good friend of mine.'

He shook his head. 'No. Definitely not.'

'Promise?'

'I promise.' His voice had the ring of sincerity.

'Well, what then...'

He opened his sports bag. 'I found this in the garden this afternoon.'

He brought out a large glass jar and handed it to me. Inside was a doll, a kind of Action Man figure like young boys have but with a T-shirt on which someone had Sharpied 'Lance'. Nails had been driven into his eyes and mouth and heart and wrapped around his neck was a length of black cloth. It was deeply sinister.

'What on earth is this?' I asked. The more I looked at it, the more it gave me the creeps.

'I think it's called a poppet jar,' he said, 'you make it to curse someone.'

'Well,' I said, looking at the Action Man figure, 'he's got more hair than you, maybe yours will grow back – and he's slimmer too, you might lose some weight.'

'This is no laughing matter, Charlie.' He looked very worried. Oh my God, I thought, he's scared.

'Please put it away, Charlie, it really gives me the creeps.' I put it back in the bag and he looked relieved. 'So, do you think it was Esther who did that?'

'No,' I said, shaking my head, 'I really don't think so.'

'Are you sure?'

'Definitely. Esther is far too nice to try and curse someone. She is just not that sort of witch.'

'Well who, then?' he asked me plaintively.

'I haven't the foggiest idea. Tell you what, Lance, give me that and I'll take it to show Esther. She might know who did it, might recognise their handiwork, or if not I can always ask her to lift the curse, if you like.'

'Would you mind?' he asked hopefully.

'Not at all. You might have to pay her some money.'

'I'll do that.' He looked pathetically grateful. 'I'll do whatever it takes.'

He took the jar out of his bag and gave it to me.

'Oh, where did you find it?' I asked.

'Does it matter?'

'I don't know, but it's the sort of question that Esther might ask. These things can be important, you know, like the devil often appears at crossroads, that sort of thing.'

'It was in the flower bed by the left side of my house.'

'See, the left side, that's the sinister side…'

'Under a hydrangea. Do you think that's significant?' he asked in a worried tone. 'I mean a hydrangea…'

'I don't know, you can make them change colour, hydrangeas… something to do with acid and alkaline soil.' Where's Monty Don when you need him?

'Maybe that's important?'

'I don't know, Lance. I'll ask.' Then I wondered. 'Was it hidden? Like, buried or something?'

He shook his head. 'It was just placed there, like it was meant to be found. I guess whoever did it wanted to frighten me as well as curse me.'

He gave a wan smile. Well, I thought, half of their plan had certainly worked.

The door opened and a couple of youngsters walked in. They weren't local kids. I recognised them as chefs from Graeme Strickland's place. They had just finished work and were almost fizzing with adrenaline and probably drugs. They nodded politely to me as they walked by. They ignored Lance.

'Don't they know who I am?' he said, plaintively. I laughed. I thought he was joking, then noticed that he looked hurt. It was as I had suspected earlier. He really did believe he was famous outside the podcast world. He obviously didn't know chefs, they wouldn't have known who the Prime Minister was if it came to that.

Then the door opened again, some villagers, keen to be on time for Malcolm's lock-in, followed by a man, neither a youngster nor a chef.

He walked over to our table and stood staring coldly down at us from his great height.

He was a commanding presence. He was very tall and had grey hair and a grey moustache. His eyes were grey too and they bore down at us with an almost ferocious coldness. He was wearing a two-piece casual suit, it looked expensive. I knew that it would be Savile Row, made-to-measure. This was Earl Hampden, or the Earl of Hampden

Green. I was never sure how these titles really worked, nor did I particularly care. We were old acquaintances. I suppose grudging respect would best describe our feelings towards one another. So, I knew him fairly well and I knew, right now, that he was furious.

'What in hell's name do you think you're up to, Thurston?' he demanded.

Lance may have been fearless and hyper-masculine on his podcasts; faced with a genuinely angry, ferocious man bigger than he was, he displayed a disappointing lack of virility.

'What do you mean?' he blustered. He looked badly frightened. For all he knew the Earl was Dr Young's boyfriend or husband, come to avenge her. I wondered what was going on. It was very unlike the Earl to get angry over anything other than animals. I wondered if maybe Lance had said he liked bull-fighting or bear-baiting, or made a joke about manatees, they were one of the Earl's current passions, not up there with orangutans, but top five. Dissing any of those would have been fighting talk to the Earl.

The Earl's fist had gathered a handful of what I decided was probably Paul Smith fabric and he hauled Lance upwards. With reflexes honed in the kitchen I managed to grab our glasses as the table was tilted forward by Lance's body.

'You disgusting murderer,' hissed the Earl. He shook Lance like an angry child might a doll. I reflected that dolls and Lance were becoming a bit of a living metaphor this evening.

'I'm innocent,' squealed Lance. 'I didn't shoot her!'

The Earl let go of him and Lance dropped back against the banquette. He sprawled there limply, gazing up at his attacker, as much get up and go, maybe less, in him as the poppet doll.

'What are you on about, you moron?' the Earl demanded, frowning. He obviously wasn't here about Dr Young. Don't say anything, Lance, I willed telepathically, it's a rhetorical question.

'You touch those trees and I'll bury you, that's a promise,' the Earl said, menacingly. 'Good night Charlie,' he added to me, then turned on his heel and stalked out of the pub. He was so angry he hadn't even noticed his girlfriend playing pool. Bryony, for her part, had ignored the whole thing.

I handed the visibly shaken Lance his drink. The pub had fallen silent when the Earl had grabbed Lance in the way that happens when there's a pub fight or the promise of one. Now everyone started suddenly talking again and pretending they hadn't been staring at us.

'Trees?' I said to Lance.

He said quietly, 'I was going to get those beeches at the bottom of the garden felled.'

'But they've been there forever!' I protested. 'Why do you want to do that?'

'I've got a helicopter,' he said defiantly.

'A helicopter!'

'Yeah, and I need to build a concrete pad for it. You know the kind of thing, for it to land on and take off. God knows how he found out.'

I shook my head disbelievingly, stood up, picked up the poppet doll and turned to go. Before I did I said, warningly, 'This is Bucks, Lance, people take beeches very seriously indeed.'

Chapter Nine

Time passed. Dr Young recovered and was discharged from hospital. Before I knew what was happening nearly a week had gone by since I'd seen Lance in the pub. As I'd told him I would, I dropped the creepy doll round at Esther's who promised to have a look at it.

It was Monday, I set my alarm ultra-early. I left my restaurant and ran slowly, listening to music and thinking about the week that had gone by and the week that was to come. I thought about Dr Young and the attempt on her life; that got me to musing once again about Lance. I was kind of surprised no one had tried to kill him. Both he and Dr Young shared something in that they were both professional irritants. It was hard to tell who I found the more annoying, provocative Lance or sanctimonious Dr Young. Personally, I felt they were two sides of the same coin. I ran another kilometre thinking about the two of them and their symbiotic relationship and their similarities. While they obviously disliked each other intensely they shared quite a few characteristics. They were highly egotistical, selfish. Lance was prepared to sacrifice the beautiful, old trees for his ridiculous helicopter. Dr Young was prepared to stick the knife into people (the attack on my old chef still rankled) if it would further her career or make her a buck or two. And they both had an audience of irony-free, worryingly fanatical supporters.

I jogged on and started thinking about Roland Sylvanus, the eco-activist. He too was a public irritant, but unlike Lance and Dr Young, but – and at this point I had to reluctantly acknowledge how shallow I was being – he was extremely attractive. There, I thought to myself (and ridiculously I could feel myself blushing) there, I've said it now, I really fancied Roland. I should have known long before that moment. From the first time I had clapped eyes on him not far from here in the field with Bryony, I knew I had wanted him. And not in an ecologically friendly, vegetarian, touchy-feely, agape kind of way, but in a snarling, carnivorous, red in tooth and claw, frenzy. The next three kilometres raced by as I day-dreamed about him in an R certificate fantasy.

Then I pulled myself together, this couldn't be healthy, and thought about food and Lance's party. That brought me back down to earth with a bump. Cooking and food preparation never fails to centre me when I get distracted by trivia. I had created a huge amount of work for myself by agreeing to do the catering, but fortunately I didn't need to worry about my own place as I had an agency chef booked to cover for me while I spent time doing the prep for the party. Even with someone minding the store so to speak, there would be a hell of a lot to do.

I checked my running watch on my right wrist, I was

running seven minute kilometres which seemed fast to me but probably wasn't. By the time I arrived back at the Old Forge Café car park I was dripping with sweat. I thought to myself, I spend my entire life bathed in sweat, either working in the kitchen or exercising. I wondered if it was good for me.

There was a car there that I didn't recognise, a sleek, black Mercedes sports car with tinted windows. For a moment I wondered if it was Lance's, then I dismissed the thought. The Merc was flashy, undoubtedly, but it lacked Lance's brutal, in your face unsubtlety. I didn't know what he drove these days, but a kind of muscle truck or another sports car of the sort targeted by the SOBs would be more his style, something to get people's attention. Then I thought maybe it was the Earl. Lance had made a nasty enemy there, that was for sure.

The driver's door opened and Anna Bruce, mystic extraordinaire, stepped out.

Chapter Ten

'Hello, Charlie,' Anna said, in her habitual cool, measured tones.

'Hi Anna,' I said, highly self-conscious of my muddy, stained running tights, my long sleeved grey running top now a dark grey around my neck, throat and armpits from sweat.

Anna Bruce didn't look hot, sweaty and flustered. She looked cool, composed, immaculately made-up and relaxed. She was wearing expensive looking blue trousers and ballet flats. She had a man's white shirt on and a string of pearls that stood out on the tanned skin of her neck. Her short, white hair, as ever, looked immaculate. In her ears she wore sapphire earrings. I just knew that they would be real stones, she was that kind of woman. There was nothing fake or cheap about Anna.

I wondered what she wanted. Anna was a psychic. That makes her sound flaky or new-age, she was neither. Her client base was mainly corporate – hard-headed businessmen seeking to get an edge in deals, hirings, firings or whatever else they did in their FTSE 100 or Fortune 500 worlds. And they paid extravagantly well for her services, Anna was far from cheap. She had helped me a couple of times, dug me out of the shit, as at least one of my former head chefs would have put it. She had never charged me either, not that I could have ever afforded her. I fell into the category of pro bono.

'Would you like a coffee?' I asked. One of the perks of owning a restaurant.

She shook her head. 'I haven't got time, I'm driving to Folkestone to catch the shuttle to France.'

'Lovely,' I said. 'Holiday?'

She shook her head. 'Business in Nantes.'

Silence fell. She hesitated and I said, with an air of enforced jollity, like you do when there's an awkward pause in the conversation, 'So to what do I owe the pleasure?'

'I came to tell you that you're in danger, Charlie,' she said, her face serious.

Well, that wasn't what I was expecting on a Monday morning, out of the blue. But I guess that's the way with bad news, it often comes unawares. The call from your boss, 'Could I have a quiet word with you please...' the policeman at the door. The unexpected phone call at two in the morning.

'Oh,' was my reaction, then, as always, make light of it, 'a dissatisfied customer?'

'It's no joke, Charlie, I'm afraid,' she said. 'I won't go into the ins and outs, they are trade secrets I suppose, but the omens are not good. Someone means you harm, serious harm.'

'Do you know who?'

She shook her head. 'No, but it's a woman, and she harbours evil thoughts against you.'

'Oh my God,' I said. Anna had always proved completely accurate in her predictions, uncannily so. I was now seriously rattled. 'Could you be a little bit more specific?'

'No.' She opened her car door. 'I've delivered the warning, I can't do any more. The rest is up to you.'

That was so Anna Bruce. She didn't sugar-coat pills and she didn't pull punches. She had delivered the message, the rest was up to me.

'That's not very reassuring.' I wanted to scream, what am I supposed to do? HELP ME!

'I didn't come to reassure you,' she said, 'I came to put you on your guard.' Her face softened. 'You're brave, Charlie, resourceful and capable... and now you're forewarned.'

'Thank you,' I said faintly. 'When are you back?'

'In a couple of weeks or so, maybe more, maybe less, hopefully I'll see you then. Take care,' she admonished and got into her car. The door closed with that lovely expensive clunk that Mercedes have and the car swept out of my car park. She didn't look back.

I didn't like the sound of that 'hopefully'. She could have chosen a different adverb. 'Definitely' would have been good. Maybe an 'absolutely'.

I slowly walked across the car park to the rear entrance of my restaurant. Monday had certainly got off to a grim start. Still, the week could surely only get better.

Chapter Eleven

Later in the week, I was still processing what Anna had told me. Nothing untoward had happened. I wasn't sure what I could do about her warning so I pushed it to the back of my mind. I had more pressing work concerns. Saturday night I would be doing the catering for Lance's party. I had arranged for an agency chef to come and work with me on Thursday night. I'd show him the menu in action then and we'd have the Friday working together so he could go solo with me advising and doing the starters and veg before working the Saturday night on his own.

The agency I was using was called ChefPlace. They were a small outfit and their rates, although still high, were more reasonable than their rivals'. I'd used them once or twice before and they'd been both efficient and reliable. I had no worries on that score.

You choose your agency chef by ability. I'd booked a chef at the level of sous chef and upwards, that is, someone experienced, who could work independently and who could cope with cooking multiple main courses at once. In a place like mine you need the ability to cook thirty to forty main courses in a couple of hours, on time and to spec. They were going to send me a guy who worked for them called Dan whom I'd employed a couple of times; he was fine.

Then at 10 o'clock at night on Thursday I got a call from Richard, the guy who owned ChefPlace. I saw the caller id and I picked up with trepidation. At that hour it was not going to be good news.

'Hi Richard, what's up?' My voice brittle and cheerful in that way you are when you're expecting the worst.

'Bad news Charlie, thought I'd better phone personally.'

My heart sank. 'There's a problem?'

'Dan broke his arm, playing football earlier. He can't do tomorrow or Friday or Saturday, he'll be out of action for a fortnight.'

'God, I'm sorry to hear that, can you send someone else?'

'I've got no one free, Charlie.' He sounded genuinely distraught. He was a nice guy Richard, he knew the depth of the shit he'd just dropped me in. 'You know we're small, I've only got three on my books who could do you, and the others are busy. I'm sorry…'

I took a deep breath. 'Well, thanks for letting me know, Richard.'

'Sorry again…'

'It's not your fault, Richard, these things happen.'

I hung up. I tilted my head back and let out a silent scream. I felt like the Edward Munch woman in the painting. But not so chipper.

I carried on mechanically cleaning down my section of the kitchen, spraying the work-surfaces with anti-bacterial spray and wiping them down. The radio was playing something by Tame Impala. Francis was sending out the last dessert order, a cheese plate (locally sourced cheeses), homemade chutney and a pear and blueberry cake which was actually a bit of a disaster – the fruit had sunk to the bottom as it was cooking and had given it a kind of slimy quality to its base. I'd got around this by making a fruits of the forest coulis and serving it with a piped swirl of Chantilly cream. So now it looked stunning on the plate and the coulis disguised the texture; it had turned into a real winner of a dish. Snatching triumph from disaster.

If only the problem of a lack of a chef could be so easily addressed. I wondered if Graeme Strickland would lend me his sous. I knew he wouldn't. For a nano-second I wondered if I went round and burst into tears might help, I was practically there already.

My phone rang again. For a delirious moment I thought it might be Richard, telling me that it was that he'd found someone to cover for me. It wasn't, it was Graeme Strickland. I took the call, hoping he might help me out somehow.

'Hi, Graeme.'

'Charlie. Have you heard anything more from that Mel Craig woman?'

'No.'

'Me neither, but one of my chefs saw her the other day, she's actually living in the bloody village, can you believe that!'

'What!'

He laughed humourlessly. 'I told you that woman was

bad news... I just wanted to warn you. Don't let her into your place, she is barred from mine...'

'Er, Graeme,' I said in a kind of wheedling way, hoping to borrow a chef.

'Sorry, Charlie, gotta go, we're crazily busy here, the team's gonna be working till stupid o'clock tonight and this morning to get everything ready for the weekend...You take care.'

He ended the call. I stared at the phone.

Damn.

Thursday dawned. I was up early at six and went for a five k run. I set an uncomfortably fast pace, relishing the pain as it stopped me thinking about this afternoon. I would have no choice but to call all the bookings for Saturday, all seventeen of them, and cancel them. It was awful. But it was a trade-off that had to be made. I couldn't cancel Lance's party. There were no good options left to me. To add to my woes, I had a mountain of prep to do for the day ahead and that was without the work needed for the coming party.

'Be strong, Charlie,' I told myself.

I got back to the restaurant at just before seven and stood outside for a moment in the road, checking my time. It was good, at least something was going well. Not that that was any consolation quite frankly. I slipped in through the gate to the backyard.

Something was different. I did a double take, like a dog sniffing the air at an uncertain scent. There were the wheelie bins, in their usual places. The twin outside storehouses looked the same. There was the little seating area we used surrounded by the earthenware pots in which I grew herbs. Then I stared uncomprehendingly at the two suitcases that were now standing outside the kitchen door.

I walked over to them. Who did they belong to?

I felt a pang of fear. Was this the event that Anna had warned me against? Was there some maniacal woman hiding in my dry-store about to leap out at me? If so, why had she brought luggage?

The suitcases weren't old, but they were scuffed and worn. They didn't look like they belonged to a woman, they were indefinably masculine. They certainly weren't Andrea's, my boyfriend's. His would have been much more stylish.

Then, right on cue, the owner of the cases appeared, emerging from the dry-store in one of the outhouses.

'Hello, Charlie,' he said.

I stared in disbelief.

'Hello…' I said faintly. Thank God, I thought, it's only you.

Chapter Twelve

'Hello, Murdo,' I said faintly. Murdo was a young, twenty-something year old kid whom I had worked with a year previously. He was a nice guy, tall, gangly, pale, Scottish and ginger. His long, skinny limbs were a riot of colour from the large number of tattoos that covered his skin. He had a sweet nature but his Achilles heel was a heavy drug problem. On the plus side, he was also a very good chef.

I was somewhat surprised to see him, if only because he still owed me a thousand pounds that I'd given him to pay off a drug dealer. I also wondered what the suitcases might be doing. My initial thought, uncharitably, suspiciously, was that history was repeating itself and that he was in hock to the tune of several grand to some London coke dealer and wanted to hide out at my place, and maybe borrow some more money.

I wiped the sweat off my forehead on the sleeve of my running vest.

'Hi, Charlie.' He grinned at me.

'You're looking well,' I said, and I meant it. His eyes were bright and not through chemical agency. To be honest,

I was mildly astonished that Murdo was not high on some drug or another since he obviously was not at work.

'Thank you. That's because I'm clean and sober these days.'

'Well, I'm pleased to hear it,' I said, not really believing him. 'What are you doing in this area?'

Of course, what I really meant was, what are you doing by my bins outside my restaurant. And explain those suitcases.

'Well, I wanted a word...'

That sounded faintly ominous. I unlocked the back door and ushered him in.

'There's a kettle there,' I said, 'make yourself some tea or coffee and I'll be down in a minute. I need to go and change.'

I went upstairs, pulled my running clothes off, showered, changed into my chef's whites and came downstairs. Murdo had made himself a cup of tea and was looking at my mise en place list, that is all the jobs I had to do before we opened at twelve. It was a very long list.

'I've got to crack on with this, Murdo,' I said. I was beginning to feel slightly irritated with him now. I had things to do and no time to chit-chat. 'You can talk to me while I'm working.'

I started chopping vegetables for a quiche.

Murdo said, 'I've just finished a six month contract at La Petite Coupole in London.'

'Very nice,' I said. It was a Michelin-starred French restaurant, much talked about, particularly in the industry.

'Yeah, I was working there as a chef de partie.'

'You've come up in the world,' I said admiringly. The cooking at La Petite Coupole was defiantly old-school and by repute so was the way the kitchen was run. It was not a place for the faint-hearted.

'Aye, it was tough, mind... but anyway, here's the important thing. I've given up drugs, I'm working a twelve-step programme... nae mair boking my guts up first thing of a morning.'

'That's good, well done you.' I put a frying pan on and started sautéing some red onions. He looked at me and smiled. I bit my tongue and sighed.

'Murdo, I'm very busy... could you get to the point?'

'Do you want me to make some shortcrust pastry?' he asked, he'd obviously taken on board the MEP list.

'That would be helpful, about five hundred grams flour...'

He washed his hands, put on an apron that was hanging up by the door and started weighing the flour and butter. Thank God, I thought to myself, at least that's one job done. I didn't need to worry about checking Murdo's work, he was better than I was in many respects.

'Part of a twelve-step programme is making amends to those we've wronged,' he said.

'That's nice.' I started cracking eggs into a bowl for the quiche. Murdo was working the butter and flour together to make a mix the texture of fine breadcrumbs.

'I want to apologise for my behaviour, Charlie...'

'That's fine, there's no need...' Some money would be nice, I thought, now you come to mention it. But I doubted Murdo had any, even though he wasn't shoving it up his nose or down into his lungs. Or so he said. You never know with addicts. I wasn't sure of how much I really believed of the clean and sober claims.

He shook his head. 'There's every need, not just for you, but for me. Anyway, look, I've got a job lined up on a cruise ship in a month or two. I haven't got any money so I can't repay you in cash, but I can repay you in time. If you want, I'm perfectly happy to work for you for free for the next three weeks, just give me food and a place to sleep.'

OMG, talk about the answer to a prayer.

'When can you start, Murdo?' I asked, anxiously.

'Now?' he said, grinning.

I tried to control the look of relief that was spreading over my face.

'Murdo, that would be fantastic.'

'There is just one drawback, Charlie,' he said, looking serious.

'What's that?'

'You have to listen to my music.'

'Murdo, I would be delighted. I can't tell you how much I've missed Cannibal Corpse.'

'I knew you'd come around to them, Charlie.' He walked over to my radio and took his phone out of his pocket. Murdo was a huge devotee of the genre of music known as Death Metal. 'What's your Wi-Fi password?'

I gave it to him and he synced his phone with the speaker. He turned up the volume as the crashing chords thundered through the kitchen. There was no mistaking it for Taylor Swift, that was for sure.

And as the singer came in on the track 'Blood Blind', Murdo turned to me happily. 'Just like old times, Charlie!'

I thought of the old times he was referring to and shuddered.

'I devoutly hope not, Murdo,' I shouted.

People had died in the old times; I didn't want to revisit them.

Chapter Thirteen

Murdo, aside from the music, was a dream to work with. He was good, fast on his feet and he had that innate sense of timing that all really good chefs have. You might have, for example, on one single order various items. On this hypothetical order, a chicken breast – cooking time twenty minutes, a duck breast – cooking time fifteen minutes, and a sea bass – cooking time, under five minutes. All have to be on the pass (the metal holding area in a kitchen where lights and the hot metal surface keep the food warm until it's delivered to the table) simultaneously. So, you do one, then the other and then the other. If you screw up one, you screw up the other two. And the customer won't be happy. Now, so far, so good.

But remember, when that order (or cheque as it is known) comes in, there are already maybe three or four other meals cooking. And, in a place like mine, there's only one of you. So as well as cooking the food, you have to plate it and you have to make sure that it goes out with its vegetable garnishes and accompaniments. And that's just the main courses, you're also doing starters and desserts. It's not an easy job.

So he worked Thursday lunch and dinner with me, shadowing me and helping out, then on Friday we swapped roles and he did the mains and I helped him out. Back in the day, we'd have said I was his bitch, but nomenclature has moved on.

Murdo made very few mistakes. You could see that his Michelin star training at the Petite Coupole had really made a difference. Everything was plated beautifully, even though he sometimes wasn't sure what the accompanying sauces, garnishes and vegetables were. Luckily I was there to help and the menu had been designed by me to be relatively straightforward. Francis was there to assist on veg and starters. In fairness to him, he had made great strides; he had gone from unbelievably bad, to relatively bad. If only he were as good at cooking as weightlifting.

We finished the service and went and sat outside the kitchen on our upturned beer crates. Murdo vaped away and drank a Coke. I don't think he'd ever been much of a drinker but he'd made up for that with the enthusiastic drug consumption of a true dope fiend. I marvelled at the change as I drank a glass of wine and Francis sat beaming at us, drinking the Asahi lager I kept as his special treat.

'That went well, Murdo,' I said, 'so you'll be okay tomorrow will you?'

'Aye, Charlie,' he said smiling, 'it'll be pish easy, dinnae worry your heid.'

Saturday, the day of the party dawned. I was up at five in the morning doing the final prep for the food. The bruschetta were going to be topped with chopped, seasoned tomatoes, basil and garlic. Others had whipped goat's cheese, lemon zest and rocket. There were some with mushrooms and thyme as well. By six I'd prepped all these toppings; the bread I would slice and finish in the oven at Lance's.

I moved on to the vol-au-vents. I'd baked off three hundred of them on Friday. I made a large quantity of cheese sauce, about three litres, and later when he arrived, I would get Francis to stuff a hundred with prawns, a hundred with mushrooms and a hundred with chopped ham. All of these would be bound with cheese sauce before going into the pastry cases. I put the three different fillings in three steel bowls for later, next to the pan full of sauce. Even Francis would be hard pushed to cock that up, but I'd be keeping a beady eye on him, just in case.

I made myself a well-earned espresso, checked the time, half past seven, and moved on to the sandwiches. I had a lot to make. I clingfilmed a steel prep table then covered it in 75 slices of sourdough bread. I arranged them in a pleasing grid formation and then, working left to right, top to bottom, like a swift automaton, speedily buttered them with a palette knife, then horseradish, then rocket and then pink, thinly sliced roast beef. Then I clingfilmed them and sliced through the twin layers of wrapping with my razor-sharp carving knife, bundling them up and refrigerating them, ready for the evening. I did the same with rye bread and smoked salmon. I find making large quantities of sand-wiches, 150 in this case, very therapeutic, hypnotically relaxing. It's more fun when there are two of you, circling an enormous prep table with countless slices of bread while one person spreads using a palette knife and a container of softened butter and the other follows, laying out whatever ingredient goes on top, a kind of intricate culinary ballet.

I checked the clock. Half past eight.

Then the arancini. I'd made quite a lot of mushroom risotto for a special on Thursday and Friday. To cook a risotto from scratch takes, give or take, twenty to thirty minutes. In a restaurant like mine you par-cook it, so when you get an order you can do it in about ten to fifteen minutes. I had added the stock to my par-cooked risotto earlier before I made the sandwiches and it had cooked through and cooled enough for me to handle it. I hand-rolled it into small balls, covered them in a gloopy mix of flour and water and then bread-crumbed them. These I would deep-fry later at the party. Great finger food, they'd go out with the vol-au-vents.

At half past nine, by the time Murdo rocked down the stairs from where he'd been sleeping in the spare room in my flat above the restaurant, I was sweating off three kilos of diced chicken and a similar amount of leeks in a large pan, ready to make the casserole.

'That for your party?' Murdo said, peering into the pan.

'Yeah, I've just got the veg option to do. I should be all done by eleven, then I'll help you with the restaurant prep. I should have time to make the desserts. There's a mise en place list for you up there. Francis will be in at ten, he'll do the easy stuff. Then later he'll be going with me to the party.'

I looked at him anxiously, 'Are you sure you'll be okay on your own?'

He smiled. 'Oh, aye, nae bother.'

I was relieved to hear that. 'And a friend of Francis will be in to help with the washing-up.'

Murdo nodded and looked at the to-do list, it was fairly daunting. Friday night had been busy and we had to get everything restocked by lunchtime. There had been no time to do any prep then and I hadn't wanted Murdo to work straight through to eleven at night.

He looked at the list, raised his eyebrows, turned to me and grinned. 'Better crack on then.' He walked over to the radio. 'This absolutely calls for something retro to go with your food,' he said, eyeing my vol-au-vents. 'It's definitely time for some Sisters of Mercy then.'

I got to Lance's about four. As I rounded the final bend before his house I saw that his party had attracted some unwanted guests. In the road at the bottom of Lance's drive were about twenty demonstrators from the SOBs. The last time I had seen them they had been demonstrating against Dr Young, now here they were demonstrating against Lance. The fate of Lance and Dr Young was becoming strangely intertwined.

'Oooh, crikey,' Francis said to me from the passenger seat, 'they're not happy campers are they!'

Death and his coffin weren't there today, but the Ents were, fresh out of Fangorn, and this time they had a new banner, a helicopter with a big red X through it and the slogan, 'Buzz off Thurston! Save Our Beeches!' They were led, naturally, by Roland. He was wearing shorts and a plain white T-shirt. I slowed my car and stopped and he came over. I lowered my window and he leaned in. 'It's Charlie isn't it?'

'It is.' His hands were resting on the window frame of the car door and I noticed on his left forearm he had a tattoo of a youthful Pan with his head thrown back in ecstasy, long curly hair flowing from his head and the curled ram's horns. It was very well done and I found it disturbingly sexual. On his right bicep was the Green Man, again it was exquisitely done. Roland's body, unlike Lance's was not packed with redundant, bulky muscle, it was slender and boyish, but with the build of a gymnast.

Bryony's comment, he fancies you, was not just lurking at the back of my mind, it was thundering through it on horseback. A neighing kind of horse, with very loud, insistent hooves.

'Well,' I said, 'nice seeing you again. I've got work to do.'

Pan had hooves didn't he? Be still my beating heart! I told myself sternly. It was up to all sorts behind my ribs.

'Hope to see you soon,' he said. I didn't really trust myself to speak. I smiled tightly, nodded, put the car in gear and headed up the drive towards the house.

Outside the front door, Francis and I unpacked my old Volvo. It was an amazingly useful car for outside catering jobs, you could get so much inside it. It looked a bit shit compared to the Maserati next to it though.

Lance wasn't around; Della, his housekeeper was though.

'Can I give you two a hand?' she asked.

'That would be great.'

We carried the food inside. Della was sturdily built, she was no Francis but she made light of her heavy burdens. She also had a reassuring, no-nonsense presence. I was glad she was working with me. Her presence was very calming.

'I'll be helping you this evening,' she said. 'Lance is paying me to waitress.'

'Oh really.' That was good news. I was going to use Francis to carry food out to the guests. He'd be fine putting food out on the tables in the expensive-looking marquee that was currently occupying a sizeable part of the garden but I was relieved that someone responsible would be going around with trays of vol-au-vents and arancini.

'That's great,' I said.

'Just to confirm, I've got a couple of girls helping me, so we'll be circulating with drinks and nibbles and we can point people in the right direction when it comes to food. What is the food by the way?' she politely enquired.

I told her what the menu for the evening was.

'I like the sound of the lentil and chickpea stew,' she said, 'not the chicken.'

'Oh, really,' I said, slightly aggrieved, I don't like unasked for criticism. What was wrong with chicken and leek?

'I'm a vegetarian,' she said, primly, 'I don't approve of eating meat. It's wrong on so many levels, unethical, and it's very damaging to the environment.'

I recalled that Lance was not known for his vegetarian sympathies. He'd done a podcast on why we should arrest vegetarians, I think mainly on the grounds that they were

103

intolerant. Which was, obviously, kind of hypocritical of him.

'Well, Della, there are some very good plant-based options on the menu at the Old Forge Café and I'm sure you'd enjoy eating there.'

She smiled. 'I know,' she said. 'I've eaten there before, I told you.'

'Sorry.' I felt like I had let her down in some way. I'd forgotten she'd told me.

'I forgot…' I gestured vaguely around me, 'what with one thing and another…'

'That's okay. It must be hard running a business, it's a man's world after all.'

'I'm not so sure of that.'

'I am,' she said firmly with an enigmatic smile. I hadn't got a clue what to make of this so I just shrugged vaguely.

She picked up the big, shiny, steel dishes that I would use to hold the hot food in. They're kept warm by liquid chafing fuel which comes in a small tin, it looks like a can of paint. It has a wick which you light and it burns slowly with a rather pleasing lazy blue flame for several hours. I'd brought a dozen of these with me, more than I'd need, but, with Francis around, accidents happen.

I suddenly thought, I'd better not let him anywhere near those, he might burn the marquee down. 'Ooopsi!' I could imagine him saying as a fiery inferno engulfed Lance's party.

'Where shall I put these?' she asked.

'Those can go out to the marquee.'

'And the fuel? In the marquee too? Or leave them here?'

I didn't want them in the kitchen, there was enough going on in there already.

'Put them in Lance's weight room, they won't be in anyone's way in there.'

'Okay.'

I started carrying the rest of the food into the kitchen.

I started work in Lance's kitchen and through the window I had a good view of the garden and the doomed trees that ran along its borders at the end where his proposed helipad would be situated. Quite why anyone would want a bloody helicopter baffled me. Rich men's toys, I suppose. It's a man's world, as Della would have said.

I started unwrapping the sandwiches and laying them out artistically on the large, silver oval display plates on top of paper doilies. Then I garnished them with some rocket. I had put the oven on a low heat earlier and now I put the first batch of vol au vents into the oven to warm through. I could hear the rumble of R&B music from the huge speakers inside the marquee as the DJ tested his sound system for later.

I looked out of the window and saw Luke Skywalker hand in hand with Marie Antoinette while Captain Jack Sparrow chatted to Della outside the tent. For a nano-second I questioned my eyes or my sanity and wondered if my one and only acid trip from twenty-five years ago had come back to haunt me. Then I realised that of course, it was a fancy dress party. Gandalf walked past with a can of Stella, talking animatedly to the Wicked Witch of the West. That reminded me of the poppet doll.

Idly I wondered if the curse that had been put upon Lance had originated from SoBuNPag, the South Bucks Neo Pagans as Esther's group were known. As I had told him, I very much doubted it. For a moment I considered the possibility that the Earl, angered by the proposed tree felling, had paid one of the witches to put a spell on Lance. He certainly had enough money to afford it. I laughed, as if he'd do that. I remembered once he had told me, in all seriousness, that if anyone threatened him with violence – which had happened once or twice in his life I was sure, he'd hire some heavies to deal with it. If the Earl meant Lance some harm, Lance would be nursing more concrete injuries than a nebulous curse. Lance would be in A&E.

In my opinion he would be wise to take the Earl seriously as an enemy. The Earl had a lot of friends, a lot of power in the county and a great deal of money. And he was utterly ruthless. It wouldn't surprise me if he was funding the SOBs. They must need money, quite a lot had obviously gone just into the costumes, not to mention the very Lance-specific banner. The Ents were very lifelike. I wished Roland had dressed up as the undertaker again, maybe he'd got a costume for later – dressed in his shorts and a T-shirt he looked as if he were about to slip into one.

'Shall I start taking some food out now, Chef?'

Francis was champing at the bit. He was wearing a dark suit that must have been bought for him a few years previously when he was the same height as he was now, but less bulky. Tonight he packed out the material of the suit, the huge muscles of his arms and shoulders bulging through the fabric. Fortunately there was no need to fasten the jacket, it simply would not have met. He looked a little like the Incredible Hulk mid-transformation, but not so angry and not so green.

I filled a tray with assorted canapés and sent him out. 'Don't linger in one place Francis, you always get some greedy bastard trying to wolf down as much as possible if you do...'

'Got it, Chef. How do I look?'

'Incredibly smart, Francis.'

I watched him proudly out of the window as he walked around among the swelling number of guests in their costumes, circulating as instructed, and I filled another tray which I gave to Della, who was making good on her promise to help me, to take to the girls.

The clock on the wall now read 6.30, food service time was between seven and eight. I warmed the hot food up in the large pans on the stove and went over to the marquee, checked that we had enough plates and cutlery and then grabbed Francis to help carry the food. The large pans were weightless in his hands. We filled one dish with the chicken and leek, one with the lentils and chickpea stew; the other two contained brown rice and new potatoes. I also set out harissa sauce, tabbouleh and merguez sausages.

'Show time!' I said.

'What shall I do now, Chef?' asked Francis.

'Just lurk, inconspicuously, and when things get low come and see me in the kitchen and we'll top it up.'

'Got it.'

I walked back to the kitchen.

I poured myself half a glass of wine and looked out of

the window at the garden. It was half seven now and still fully light, the party was in full swing. Most of the guests were in the marquee but a few had brought their food outside. The quality of the costumes was extremely high; most people had made a real effort.

Francis came back a few times and I would fill up a pan and give it to him to replenish what was there. I could see Count Dracula out on the lawn eating a plate of food with some Roman emperor, a French maid and Catwoman.

I checked what food was left in the pans. Most of it was gone, and I thought I may as well put the rest out. I picked up the pan containing the stew and walked across the grass to the marquee. Inside it was noisy. The DJ was playing low-key club classics at a fairly low volume and overlying the rumble of the music were a hundred odd people talking and eating.

'Nice costume,' a drunk Robin from Batman said to me, apropos my chef's whites. He was smelling strongly of weed. He must have been impressed by the fidelity of my fancy dress down to accessorising it with a pan of chicken and leek stew.

I filled up the Gastronorm chafing dish, gave it a stir to check that it wasn't catching on the bottom of the steel container and burning. It seemed fine. I checked the two fuel cells underneath. They still had plenty of liquid but I thought I'd move them to the ends of the container and add a third one in the middle.

Guests in the marquee wandered around. I was bumped into by a drunken Zeus clutching a tin foil thunderbolt and then, as I was bent over the table I felt a tug on the pony tail where my hair was tied back. I turned around in annoyance. There was some woman dressed as an Oriental harem girl with baggy trousers and a veil covering her face.

'What do you think you're playing at!' I said angrily.

'I'm so sorry,' she said apologetically, 'I thought you were Tilly.'

'Well, I'm not Tilly,' I said irritably. 'I'm Charlie, I'm a chef and I'm working, so keep your hands off me.'

'My apologies again...' she disappeared back into the crowd.

I finished what I was doing, straightened up, turned and bumped into Lance.

He was almost unrecognisable as a hippie from circa 1970. He was wearing a long-haired wig, a kaftan and psychedelic loon pants with silver high heel boots. He had a peace sign necklace around his neck and a fat blunt in one hand which he was puffing away at. His eyes were hidden behind octagonal mirror shades.

In fact, I don't think I would have recognised him if he hadn't spoken to me first.

'Hi, Charlie, great food...'

I peered at him, saw my face reflected in the shades. 'Is that you Lance?'

We were joined by the Boy Wonder and then Rupert Bear. The Caped Crusader's sidekick greeted the birthday boy. 'Hi Lance, baby...'

'Cool, Robin...' They high fived. Lance passed him the blunt and Robin took a deep drag on it appreciatively.

Lance grinned at me. 'Yeah, baby, far out... want to practise some free love?'

'No, Lance, I can't say I do,' I replied.

'Square,' he said.

'This chick ain't for balling, Lance,' I said firmly. 'Dig it!' That was the extent of my sixties patois, more than I'd expected. I stared at the ill-assorted trio. Give me strength! It really was beginning to feel like an acid trip, a bad one at that.

'Hey, chill out baby,' Robin said, moving very close to me in an invasion of my personal space.

I lost my temper. 'Less of the baby, Boy Wonder.' I jabbed him hard in the solar plexus with two fingers. It probably looked playful but it wasn't, I knew it would hurt. He stepped back hurriedly. 'Now fuck off back to the Batcave.' I said.

I turned to Lance. 'I'm just going to get more chafer fuel, any more "banter" Lance,' I said in a warning tone, 'and there'll be trouble, okay?'

'Sorry, Charlie.'

I walked off to the house without looking back. There was a side door by the kitchen and I went in, leaving it open. I went through the kitchen and into the hall.

There were a few party guests inside the house: Bo Peep, Genghis Khan and a Jewish guy with one of those hats and ringlets. That was interesting. If he was actually a Hasidic Jew was that fancy dress or just normal? And if he wasn't, was that racist? Who knows?

I stopped this speculation and went into the gym room where Della and I had left the fuel.

I looked around the room. There was the gym equipment as I had seen it last. It was an impressive collection, the neat racks of dumb-bells and kettlebells, the weights for the barbells in increments from two and a half to twenty kilos. A squat rack and a bench press and a pull-up bar. And there was the chest freezer full of water that Lance firmly believed would grant him health and prolong his life.

Its green light was on. It was plugged in, evidently busy. I walked over to it and opened the lid and looked inside. It must have been on for a while, a layer of ice had formed on the top. I thought about how horrible it would be to climb inside and shuddered. You wouldn't get me doing that, that was for sure.

I closed the lid and walked over to the table with the chafing fuel on when I became aware that the door to the gym had opened. I looked round and saw Rupert Bear standing there. He was wearing his trademark clothing of mustard yellow check trousers, matching scarf and red jumper. His mouth was stitched in a friendly grin. Somewhat incongruously he was holding a baseball bat.

He walked towards me.

'Can I help you?' I said. He nodded and then too fast for me to realise what was happening he swung the bat and I received the most powerful blow I have ever experienced in my life to my stomach. Its force was tremendous. It drove all the breath out of me and I pitched forward on to my knees. There was another huge blow to the back of my neck but I had hunched forward and the blow meant for my head bounced off the bunched up muscles of the top of my shoulders, but it was enough to nearly knock me cold.

Fighting to breathe, I had been badly winded, and dazed, I was aware of his paws pulling me to my feet. He half dragged me across the floor, then lifted the lid of the freezer and I started to struggle against his grasp, but I was moving very feebly. He hoisted me upright, propped me against the freezer and then he bundled me backwards into the icy waters.

The dramatic drop in temperature was like nothing I had ever felt in forty-four years. It was almost heart-stopping. For a nano-second my body couldn't differentiate if the water was hot or freezing, it seared into me like liquid fire. Then the icy cold bit. It revived me almost instantly, but far too late to do anything about it. I struggled to get out but was pushed down deeper. My head went under. For a moment I thought he was going to drown me. My lungs were bursting. But then I felt the pressure on my shoulders release.

My head cleared the water and I took a huge breath as I gasped dramatically and then the lid slammed down on top of me. I was in complete darkness. I put my palms against the lid and pushed up, but that achieved nothing. The bastard bear was probably sitting on the lid.

Fear now almost superseded cold. That gives an indication of how terrified I was, it was unbelievably cold. I rested my nose against the plastic underneath the lid, at least I could breathe easily. I had maybe five centimetres, plenty of room, I wasn't going to drown, I could survive but only if I kept my head above the icy water. But how long would it be before I passed out?

And then I heard an ominous sound.

I had noticed before that the freezer was a commercial one and it had a hasp so it could be secured with a padlock to keep the wandering hands of kitchen staff off the frozen goods inside. There had been no padlock on it a moment ago. Now I heard a familiar click. I've padlocked enough things in a kitchen to know that sound well.

I pushed frantically upwards. The lid didn't move.

I wasn't just trapped inside. I was locked in.

Chapter Fourteen

Inside the freezer, cold was overtaking fear. I fought back panic and considered my options. That certainly didn't take long, they were severely limited. The temperature of the water was terrible, far worse than I could have imagined.

I tried to bang on the lid of the freezer but my efforts were useless. My clothes were clinging to me, weighing me down, hampering movement, and the sound of my knuckles hitting the plastic would be inaudible unless you were standing really close by and listening hard. It was like being in a terrible dream where you can't move. And the cold was searing, so bad at times it felt like unbearable heat.

I took a deep breath and squirming round so my back was against the lid, tried pushing upwards. That didn't work either. I fought my way back to lying on my back with my mouth open and tried breathing quickly, bellows breath like I'd learnt in yoga. It was supposed to warm you up, fat chance against the icy water, it was like bringing a cucumber to a knife fight.

How long could I survive in the icy darkness? Five

minutes maybe before things started to shut down. The worst thing was that now I was hardly conscious of the cold, and lying partly floating in the freezing darkness, I could feel myself beginning to lose consciousness. I would blink and think, where am I? My brain was shutting down. When I did finally black out, I would drown. Then with the freezer running all night I would be encased in a solid block of ice by the time someone opened the lid.

That horrible image prodded me into action but my movements were feeble, and getting weaker. As were my thoughts.

Then I was dimly conscious of a voice penetrating the lid of the freezer. 'Chef? Are you in there?'

Francis!

I felt a jolt of new energy run through me and I slammed my hands upwards with as much force as possible. I shouted his name.

'Don't go away!' I heard him say. 'I'll get you out.'

Part of me thought, easier said than done.

In the Old Forge Café I have a couple of freezers, one upright, one chest, in one of the outhouses. There is other stuff in there, a crowbar, tools; it would have been the work of seconds to find something to prise or smash open the freezer. In Lance's house there would be tools, but where? By the time Francis had located them, it could well be too late.

I heard a noise, two noises. One of Francis straining, 'huuuupppppppp!', the other of buckling and cracking plastic, then with an almighty crash light burst on to my face as bright as if I were staring into the sun and I was aware of Francis reaching in and hauling me out as if I was light as a child.

I lay on the floor of the gym staring up at the ceiling and Francis's face looking down at me. I was shaking uncontrollably both from cold and, I guess, shock.

Relief and gratitude at still being alive washed over me. I wasn't dead... I could hardly believe it, and cold as I was, trembling on the cellar floor, it was bliss not to be trapped in the icy clutch of the freezer.

I was alive... I was alive...

'What's going on?' A woman's voice. I looked up, it was Della. Her face was one of huge concern, she looked terrified...

'Oh my God! Charlie! Are you okay?'

I was trembling uncontrollably. 'Yeah, I'm fine...'

'What happened?' Francis said. He was still very red in the face from the effort of tearing the padlocked lid off the freezer. It was now lying on the floor. He must have not only splintered the plastic from where the hasp had been and torn a jagged rent in the side of the freezer, he'd then in his angry desperation ripped the whole cover off, like you might do with an annoying piece of cardboard packaging, and tossed it across the room. I noticed with a surge of affection that his suit jacket, Hulk-like, had ripped down the seams under his right arm. I also noticed that the freezer was still plugged in. It would be ridiculous to have survived freezing only to be electrocuted.

'Della, could you unplug the freezer please.' She did so. I got slowly to my feet and said to Francis, 'Thank you

Francis. Tomorrow we're going shopping and I'm going to buy you a new suit.'

He beamed at me with delight. 'Thank you, Chef.'

At that moment the door to the gym opened and Lance and Robin burst in.

'Jesus Christ, what's happened?' Lance said, pulling off his mirrored shades.

I looked at them both. 'Where was Batman when I needed him?' I demanded.

Chapter Fifteen

Francis drove me back to the Old Forge Café, my teeth chattering, occasionally uncontrollably shaking, and I walked into the kitchen wearing my sodden clothes. The friend of Francis's who had stepped in to do the washing up, I vaguely knew from the pub, a nice kid, stared at my entrance in amazement. Murdo was busy single-handedly doing all the cooking. We'd got about fifty booked in and although it was early in the evening, quarter past seven, things were just heating up. Murdo's back was to me and he hadn't heard me coming in over the roar of the fans.

Jess came in from the restaurant at that moment with an order, saw me and I noticed her eyes widening in horror.

'Oh my God, Charlie, what happened?'

Murdo turned around, saw me and stared, his face a pantomime expression of shock and surprise.

'Someone put Chef in a freezer full of water!' Francis explained, which added to the general mystification. Briefly I explained.

'Jesus,' Murdo remarked, 'you could be deid!'

'Well,' I said, 'that was certainly somebody's plan.'

Murdo put a lamb rump with its garnish of a mini shepherd's pie and hispi cabbage out under the pass; the rosemary jus came in a small steel jug. I may have narrowly survived death, but cooking still went on, which I found strangely comforting.

'Service...' called Murdo. Katie bustled into the kitchen, stopped dead in her tracks. My new wet look was certainly turning heads.

'I'll tell you later,' Jess said.

Murdo pointed at the pass. 'Table 23, Katie, and come back for the Gilt-head bream...' he said.

God, it was wonderfully warm in the kitchen, warm and safe. I suddenly felt very emotional, all these people around me whom I could trust implicitly: Jess, Murdo, Francis, Katie...

'That food looks great, Murdo,' I said approvingly. 'I'll just go and have a quick shower and change and I'll be down to help.'

'Are you sure? After what you've been through?' He shook his head disbelievingly.

'Definitely...' The comforting heat of the kitchen enveloped and cocooned me.

'There's no place I'd rather be more...' And it was true.

'Cheque on,' said Katie, reappearing after Table 23 had been dealt with, leaning over the pass, 'four fillet steaks, all well done... no garnish, just fries.'

'Fucking Scots,' said Murdo, cheerfully.

'How did you know!' Katie said, round-eyed at Murdo's clairvoyance.

'I ken mah fellow-countrymen,' he said with a smile.

I went upstairs, showered and changed, then ran back into the kitchen. It was lucky for Murdo that I found the stress of the kitchen therapeutic. The truth was, I did. Here, everyone in the place was Team Charlie, from Jess to the two waitresses under her, the kitchen staff of Murdo and Francis – even a third of the customers who were locals that I knew and who had supported me from the beginning, were all on my side. So long as I stayed here in my warm, snug refuge – albeit working like a maniac, I was safe from harm.

The evening passed in a pleasant haze of work. I just did starters and desserts, I left the heavy lifting, and all thinking, to Murdo.

About ten in the evening came that point I loved where we had sent the last orders out and an unusual air of tranquillity hit the kitchen. Murdo and I smiled at each other, both drained physically and mentally after the long, hard battle of service. I nearly offered him a drink but then remembered that he had given up the drugs and the alcohol.

'Would you like a tea?' I suggested.

'Aye, camomile if you have it.' I silently marvelled at this. I think up to this point I hadn't really believed in Murdo's sobriety but here we were. I was impressed.

'We most certainly do,' I replied.

I left him to start clearing down the main part of the kitchen. Francis would normally have dealt with any desserts but he had returned to the party and was still clearing up at Lance's. Jess had volunteered to step into the breach.

I walked out into the bar area of the restaurant and

surveyed my small kingdom with an unusual degree of pleasure. It felt marvellous to be alive. That's a huge benefit of having your life threatened, it really makes you appreciate being able to walk upon this Earth. I could easily be in a morgue somewhere or worse, turning slowly into a human popsicle. I knew that the feeling wouldn't last, of course, there's only so long that you can wake up in the morning and think, 'Thank God I'm not locked in a freezer full of ice', but just for now I was savouring the smell of the coffee from the Gaggia machine and the sensation of sweat trickling from my neck to my back, naked and warm under my chef's jacket. It was a great feeling, not one I usually enjoyed, but I did tonight.

I took our teas back into the kitchen. I could have done with a glass of Sancerre or ten but I didn't want to tempt Murdo – not that when he was drinking and drugging he'd shown any interest in wine, he had been more of a lager boy.

We sat down on beer crates outside the kitchen in the small yard and chatted about the evening, then the gate to the road outside opened and Andrea walked in.

Chapter Sixteen

I lay next to Andrea in bed staring up at the ceiling. It felt particularly nice to be beside him considering I could well be lying in a morgue, or even at the bottom of Lance's freezer encased in ice like an experimental Damien Hirst artwork that critics would doubtless applaud, saying he was really pushing the boundaries with *Frozen Chef #1*.

Who the hell was the person in the Rupert Bear costume who had thrown me in that freezer? My mind went over and over the incident. Why? Who in God's name would want me dead?

Andrea shifted his position beside me. It had, of course, been Jess who had called him the moment she had heard about the incident and Andrea had immediately left the party he was at. His company were sponsoring a di Chirico exhibition and he'd been at a private viewing for major clients earlier in the evening. I was flattered. If the boot had been on the other foot, if it had been him inside a freezer on a Saturday night, he would have had to wait until service was over before I rushed to be at his side. That's catering for you. Or maybe I'm just flinty-hearted.

My left hand idly stroked his naked body. He was, like me, in his forties. He was slim, he had a swimmer's body, good shoulders and pecs, there was silver in his thick, dark hair now but he was still very good-looking in that north Italian way that certainly floats my boat.

'So who the hell would want to kill you?' he wondered, echoing my own thoughts.

'I have absolutely no idea, unless I inadvertently upset one of Rupert Bear's chums...'

What was the badger called? He always seemed untrustworthy. Bill Badger, I remembered. If it was going to be anyone it would be that shifty badger, I'd never liked him.

Andrea propped himself up on one elbow. 'This is no laughing matter Charlie...'

'I know, I know...' I yawned. 'I have absolutely no idea though and thinking about it isn't going to change that, is it?'

'I suppose not.'

'Now, Andrea... since you're here...'

I rolled on top of him and we made love again. Afterwards I got up and set my alarm for seven. I have to leave it on the far side of the room as otherwise I just mute it and go back to sleep. I planned to have a bit of a lie in, then I'd go for a long run, about ten k before I started the prep for Sunday lunch.

As I got back into bed he said to me, 'Look, Charlie, I've been thinking about you and me.' Oh God, I thought, you really pick your moments, don't you, Andrea. I had just escaped death, I was not in the mood for a serious discussion about relationships.

'Why don't you move up to London and come and live with me?' he asked. 'The flat's more than big enough for the two of us, we can go out in the evenings like we used to... we can be together.'

This was not what I wanted to hear.

I sat up in alarm and looked around me. 'I already have somewhere to live... in case you hadn't noticed...' I waved my arms indicating my room and by extension my business. God, how I hate being patronised.

'I know, I know...' he held his hands up in a pleading way, 'but you could get a full-time chef in, you could manage it from a distance... I'd pay any shortfall... look at it this way, a lot of top chefs have more than one restaurant.'

I thought, what a terrible, terrible idea. And what about my friendships here? Jess, Esther Bartlett, where would I be without the witches of Hampden Green, Francis, Bryony. No way.

I yawned again. 'Sorry, it's been a long day.' I didn't want an argument. 'We'll talk about this tomorrow, I'm too tired right now, I love you.'

'And I love you. That's why I want to be with you seven days a week, not just the odd weekend.'

'Good night, Andrea,' I said, firmly, shutting him up.

I rolled over on my side and thought to myself, 'I'm going nowhere, baby.' Then exhaustion hit me like a wave and I fell asleep.

Chapter Seventeen

On the Sunday we didn't discuss Andrea's offer. That's not to say I didn't think about it. And seriously. He had a large, two bedroom flat with a roof terrace in Clerkenwell near the City of London, the financial district. It was a lovely apartment, beautifully furnished; Andrea had taste. His dad had been a fan of Italian futurist art and had bought quite a few paintings and sculptures when the market for such things had been non-existent. Things had changed, tastes had changed, and now a couple of million pounds worth of art hung on his walls. If this wasn't enough, he had his parents' old house in Le Marche in Italy and a great job doing god knows what in finance. He earned a lot of money. The Old Forge Café made enough to afford a full-time chef if they moved into the flat above the restaurant as part of their salary. Andrea could make up any shortfall if need be, and I could easily keep an eye on things two or three days a week.

I could do anything I wanted to during the day, he'd be at work or away on business, in the evenings we could eat out, go to the theatre, do whatever.

I would be a kind of kept woman. A dream life?

Sod that for a game of soldiers, as my dad would have said (well, he'd have used the f word). I like my independence. I wasn't born Mrs di Stefano and I shall die as Ms Hunter. Mind you, trapped in the freezer I would have bitten my hand off at the wrist to be a kept woman in Clerkenwell. Alive and well, it wasn't so tempting.

Anyway, I wasn't going to do it.

Life and the universe then rewarded me for my principled stance with the metaphorical equivalent of a bucket of cold sick tipped over me. Two days later on Tuesday morning, I received a letter from Mel Craig aka Dr Melanie Thomas, Mindfulness Woman. She claimed that she had found not one but three hairs in her food when she had eaten at the Old Forge Café on Friday, 2 August. There was one of said hairs taped to a sheet of blank paper enclosed with the letter. A day later she had come down with acute vomiting and diarrhoea. She had kept a stool sample and sent it off to be analysed at a private healthcare company and the report had confirmed that her sample had contained traces of salmonella. A copy of the report was attached.

She did not wish to take me to court for compensation, but in view of the trauma inflicted on her by the experience, the horror and distress from the hair incident, the unsympathetic attitude of the waitress who had humiliated her, the hurt and misery of the needless food poisoning which had to have been the result of poor hygiene plus a week's loss of earnings (she was self-employed) while she recovered, she felt that she was due some compensation from the owner of the Old Forge Café. She would be prepared to accept £5,500 payable by BACS to account number such and such within ten working days from dispatch of the letter. If this was not done she would have no option but to seek legal redress via her solicitors who were very experienced in this area. She also pointed out that the fines involved for poisoning trusting members of the public were frequently well above the figure that she was asking for and I might also want to be spared the torrent of negative publicity that would doubtless be raised by the case going to the courts.

Yours faithfully

Mel Craig

I thought of Strickland's call from a few nights ago. The fact she was living in the village somehow made all this worse. She was like an evil witch out of a Grimm's fairy tale. First she came in disguise to my house, then she sent me a poison apple, or in this case, a letter dripping with poison, and now, like the witch, she had an evil cottage just up the road.

'The evil bitch,' Jess said, handing me back the letter. 'This is outrageous.'

I felt a wave of misery wash over me. Evil was the word. It was all so untrue yet all so highly plausible. It was all so cleverly done, you had to admire it in a way.

I was looking at the hair attached to the piece of paper. My hair is shoulder length, the hair looked about right. My hair is brownish red, going grey at the roots (I have it dyed these days). This hair was my colour and had a tell-tale grey root. I believed it was mine. How the hell had she got hold of it? I always tie my hair back in the kitchen and I wear a hat, a skull cap.

Jess had found Craig's booking on the system, the report said that she had shown symptoms the following day and salmonella had been found in her stool sample.

'Well,' I said glumly, 'the time matches; it's eight to seventy-two hours after eating affected food, I seem to remember.'

'What causes it?' Jess asked.

'Several things. Undercooked fish being one. Oh God, she said her fish was rubbery... don't you remember?' I was kind of alarmed now.

Jess nodded her head. 'She did say that, but you always check your fish is cooked through, don't you?'

That was true. I always press the blade of a knife in, you can feel if it's uncooked easily enough.

'Or,' I said, 'faecal contamination, like if you don't wash your hands after you've been to the loo.'

I knew it couldn't be either of those two things. I was pretty fastidious.

'How did she get the hair?' Jess wondered, 'if it's yours?'

Then it came to me.

'The party!'

'What, Lance's party, where you were attacked?'

'Yeah.'

'But I don't get it?' Jess's face was a picture of confusion. 'You mean she tried to drown you or freeze you, to get some hair?'

'No, Jess, before...' I told her what had happened when I was putting out the fuel for the buffet. 'It must have been her at the party. Dressed up as a bloody belly dancer or harem girl or whatever.'

'It has to be that. Let's speak to Lance about it. He might know something.'

'I'm going over there later to collect my stuff that I left behind on Saturday. We'll speak to him about it then.' Then a thought struck me. 'Jess, when you did that deep dive on Mel Craig, or Dr Thomas as she was calling herself, did you visit a website called TherapyWhistleBlowers? The one that Lance mentioned.'

'Yes I did. Why?'

'Could you find it for me, I just want to look at something.'

'Sure, my laptop's in the restaurant, I'll just go and get it.'

She disappeared and returned with the laptop open and the page ready. I looked at the home page. The site had been set up by the parents of two kids who had been the victims of a rogue therapist. John of Guildford, as he styled himself, like some mediaeval chronicler, had claimed that St Teresa had come to him in a vision and commanded him to heal the sick, and also recommend he charge £200 an hour for doing so. At least one girl had died as a result of John's dubious (let's not mince words, fraudulent) healing ministry. He was currently banged up for fraud and rape.

So, there was Mel, with a brief resumé of her fake doctorate, her conviction for plagiarism and a list of contributors who had supplied information leading to her being outed on the site. I was interested to note that as well as Lance's name appearing, there was also Dr Susannah Young who was listed as a victim of said plagiarism. Unusual to find these two linked in a common cause and probably both unaware of the fact too.

At 4 o'clock we arrived at Lance's house. Della let us in. Her dog jumped up at me joyously. I patted her appreciatively. Della obviously loved animals.

Today she was wearing jeans and a T-shirt with a PETA slogan under an unbuttoned striped man's shirt. I wondered how old she was and guessed she was in her sixties, but she looked quite lean and fit. Vegetarians often do, it's a lifestyle thing I suppose, except for the ones who work in health food stores who generally look wan and ill.

'How are you feeling?' she asked, holding my arm and looking at me anxiously.

'A lot better than when I left on Saturday night, thank you.'

'That was unbelievable,' she said, shaking her head. 'Thank goodness you had that nice boy with you to rescue you.'

'Indeed,' I said, I was anxious to drop the topic of my ice bath. 'Is Lance around?'

'He's in the living room,' she said. 'You know the way.'

Jess and I walked into the living room. Lance was sitting on the sofa looking pale and subdued. He brightened up when we walked in.

'Charlie…' he said, 'and…?'

'This is Jess,' I said, 'my manager.'

'Of course,' he said, 'I remember you now, from when I ate in your restaurant a while ago.'

132

He had perked up a good deal when he saw Jess. She was a good looking girl, with a stunning figure. This was obviously not lost on Lance.

'Can I get you anything?' he asked. 'Drink of something... ? Charlie, thank you so much for your amazing behaviour the other night... it was incredible.'

I hadn't called for an ambulance or the police. Or more pertinently, gone to the press. 'Maniac Killer Bear Attacks Woman Chef at Podcaster's Birthday Party'. I think that's what he meant was so amazing.

I couldn't see the point, I could imagine how the police interview would have gone:

'Can you give us a description of your attacker, madam?'

'Yeah, medium height, covered in brown hair, wearing yellow check trousers, matching scarf and a red jumper. Very distinctive ears.'

All the police would have done would have been to wreck his birthday party; I'd been hired to enhance it. The blows from the baseball bat hadn't harmed me. My dad had been a semi-pro boxer when I had been growing up and he earned extra money with Uncle Cliff as a bouncer in night clubs. So I'd been brought up to regard hard knocks both literally and metaphorically as par for the course.

'That's okay,' I said.

'You must be tough as old boots,' he said. That was a dubious compliment if ever there was one.

'I had a letter from Melanie Craig, Lance,' I said.

He pulled a face. 'That won't have been nice, I imagine.'

'No it wasn't,' Jess said, 'we think she was here at the party.'

Lance looked horrified. 'You're joking. Surely not. I didn't invite her.'

'Lance, I'm sure you didn't. She must have gate-crashed, you wouldn't have registered her,' I said. 'You were out of your nut on weed, you were pissed, you wouldn't have noticed if aliens had landed.'

'That's probably true,' he admitted.

Jess sketched in what we thought had happened.

'So can I get access to the images from your smart doorbell?' Jess asked.

'I don't know,' Lance looked suitably clueless, 'can you?'

'Yes,' Jess said, simply.

'Fair enough,' Lance said.

'I'll need the passwords for your Wi-Fi and for the smart system.'

'Okay. They're in the study, follow me.'

The three of us trooped through the house to his study.

'Can I use your pc?' Jess asked. 'I'll download the files to a memory stick and go through them at home.'

'Sure,' he said, switching it on, 'I'll just find the password for the doorbell.'

He went to his password manager. 'I'm very security conscious, particularly of passwords.'

He scrolled through the list of accounts until he came to his camera security and wrote a string of letters, numbers and characters on a Post-It note and gave it to Jess.

'There you go. You can connect the laptop to my other screens.'

We left Jess to get on with it and returned to the living room. Lance paid me and gave me a more than reasonable bonus in cash as a kind of thank you for not having turned his big event into a crime scene. I remembered my promise to Francis to get him a new suit. The money would more than cover it. Lance was a generous guy.

'Thank you,' I said, and I meant it. He made a kind of dismissive, aw shucks gesture.

'Let's go outside,' he said, 'it's a lovely afternoon.'

We sat on his terrace and looked out over the lawn. The marquee was gone. The trees at the bottom of the garden looked majestic.

'So are you going ahead with your helipad plans?' I asked, hoping he wasn't. I was with Roland on the importance of protecting trees.

Della brought us out tea, dainty salmon sandwiches (okay, it was tinned salmon but strangely I prefer that on a sandwich) and there was some nice looking chocolate cake under a mesh dome to keep flies or wasps off. She had put everything on a trolley, which she had pushed out to the terrace and I was enjoying the sensation of being waited on.

'I made the cake specially for you,' Della said. 'I hope you like it, it's always a bit intimidating cooking for a chef.'

'It looks lovely,' I said, 'thank you.'

Lance bit into a sandwich. 'Of course. I've got the builders coming in a fortnight.'

I looked at the row of trees at the end of his garden. They were beeches, I'm not very good at trees but I've learned to recognise them since moving to Bucks. There were seven of them, very tall, their leaves a soft green, they had very few side branches until the very top where they exploded into interweaving foliage. Their trunks were smooth and somehow gracious.

'Seems a pity to chop them down,' I said. That was an understatement. He was going to fell these majestic trees to lay a circular slab of concrete so his stupid helicopter could land on it. I could understand the SOBs' and the Earl's fury.

Lance shrugged and gestured with his half-eaten sandwich. 'Well, I've got to move quickly or the council might slap a TPO on them.'

'TPO?'

'A Tree Preservation Order.'

'Oh, I see.' I thought about that. It wouldn't surprise me if the Earl applied for one of those. Those were his fields that Lance's garden backed on to. And what the Earl wanted, the Earl usually got, by hook or by crook. The Earl had a lot of power locally and he would have no compunction whatsoever in abusing his authority if it came to a question of ecology. He'd know whom to bribe or threaten and you'd be a brave man or woman to stand up to him.

Personally, I rather hoped that he would get a TPO put on the trees. I didn't know the Earl that well and our paths rarely crossed, but the next time I saw Bryony, which I often did while running, and she was often dog-walking, I would most certainly suggest it to her.

In the meantime, I rather treacherously accepted a piece of cake from Lance and as I was biting into the moist, chocolate sponge, Jess appeared.

'Success,' she said.

'Well done,' I congratulated her.

'So, you've found the bitch,' was Lance's contribution. Jess let this pass. Normally she would have said something about derogatory language like that, but, face it, Mel Craig was a bitch.

Jess's fingers stroked some keys of the laptop, swivelled it round and the three of us gazed at the image from the doorbell's camera. There was the driveway. There was a field opposite and Lance had paid the farmer (one of the Earl's tenant farmers) to allow parking in it, so his driveway was vehicle free apart from his Maserati and my Volvo. Then up the drive came the belly dancer. She was wearing a turquoise jewelled bustier-style top, a matching belly dancer style skirt/bottom and a kind of diaphanous, turquoise chiffon cloak, or shawl. She was wearing golden gladiator sandals. A turquoise veil covered her face apart from her eyes. Her head was covered by a headscarf that matched her veil but as she approached the door I caught a glimpse of a tell-tale streak of red in the dark hair that was momentarily visible.

'That's her,' I said, confidently.

'Is that Mel Craig?' wondered Lance. All you could see of her face was her eyes.

'That's definitely her,' I said.

'Well,' Jess said, 'now we know how she got hold of some of your hair.'

I nodded. 'I'm not sure that will be enough, though. Her presence at the party, even as a gate-crasher, doesn't prove that she got my hair here.'

'That's true,' Lance said, 'but it's a start. Aside from Mel Craig, though, what I can't understand is Rupert the Bear attacking you. I don't know who the hell it was, but someone tried to kill you, Charlie, that was no prank. I think you should maybe report it to the police.'

'In spite of the adverse publicity this might get you?' I was amazed he suggested it.

Lance shrugged. 'They say there is no such thing as bad publicity…'

'You're right,' Jess said. 'I've told her that, she doesn't listen.'

'Well,' I remarked, 'I don't think there's much point; after all, they wouldn't be able to do much to protect me anyway. No,' I said standing up and stretching, 'Melanie Craig is the main threat to my peace of mind. Come on Jess, let's leave Lance to getting his next podcast ready.'

We said our goodbyes, were seen out by Lance, Della was out somewhere, presumably walking her dog, and climbed into my car.

As is often the case in life, when you think about someone hard enough, there they are. I'm sure there's a technical term for it – like it's a kind of confirmation bias. Or possibly it does have significance, a synchronicity, a meaningful coincidence as Jung would have said. Driving into Hampden Green we both saw, in the distance near where the children's swings are, a by now familiar figure.

I braked and stopped the car. Jess had seen her too.

'That's her, isn't it?' she said.

We both watched as she marched away from us, the streak of red in her dark hair clearly visible in the late afternoon sun. She had to have walked past the Old Forge

Café to be where she was. We were closed at this time, but I imagined her staring vindictively at the building. Like a malicious witch. Like one of the characters in her (no doubt) crappy supernatural novels. I bet those plots had been filched from other, forgotten horror stories. She obviously had a history of plagiarism, why stop with philosophy and mindfulness? Why not fiction too? No wonder the ideas in her podcasts had been good, they weren't hers, they'd been stolen from other people.

'What did she want? What do you think?' I asked Jess.

She shook her head. 'God knows. Maybe she had a walk around the car park trying to trip over so she could sue you for that too. She's so hateful…'

If looks could kill, she'd have toppled over then and there. But she didn't. We watched her together as she opened the gate to the field where Dr Young had been shot and disappeared from our sight. I found it hard to bear the thought that she actually lived in this village. It was our village and Mel Craig had polluted it with her lies and her blackmail. It was adding insult to injury.

'Whatever she was up to, it won't have been good,' I said to Jess.

'So true, bestie,' she agreed.

I pulled into my car park, both of us wondering what further torments Mel Craig had in mind for me.

Chapter Eighteen

The following morning I took Francis shopping for his new suit. It was much harder than I had imagined. Francis was not tall, but he was ridiculously stocky and a jacket that buttoned up around him was simply much too tight in the arms and too long in the body. The same problem with his legs which were like oil drums of muscle.

'We'll have to leave it for now, Francis,' I said and to sweeten the blow I took him to a branch of German Doner Kebab where he had some enormous doner about the size of his head, which seemed to delight him. Bless Francis, he was easily satisfied.

Later, when I got back, I worked with Murdo in the kitchen. I would have him for a few more days, then he would have worked off his debt to me and would be on the move. He'd said three weeks when he arrived, he had now given me a finish date of around 20 September. We'd discussed this. 'Are you sure you can't afford me, Charlie? I'm prepared to work for minimum wage if you give me board and lodging, plus tips.' Kitchen and front of house get the tips divided between them. I don't take any, so it mounts up. The problem was, I still couldn't afford Murdo even on minimum wage. So I was making the most of my last few days with him.

We were working away with music in the background, not Beech Tree FM, my radio station of choice, oh no, we were listening to 'Empire in Ruin' by Pantheon, and the subject of the local witches came up. Murdo was fascinated. He asked me, apropos the witches, 'But what do they do exactly?'

'I think they worship the Great Mother in all her aspects, well, Esther's group certainly do… but others worship other things… I guess…' I was quite hazy on the details. 'They celebrate the solstices and the equinoxes and there are some other sacred days as well. Esther often hires me to do the catering for those events.' That was the limit of my knowledge. 'They're quite eco-friendly… quite Green,' I added, lamely.

'Aye, but ken, are they really witches, like, do they do witchy things?'

'Well, I guess they will do things like ask the help of the gods for practical things, like, job applications or the weather… I remember Esther doing some sort of ritual to ensure rain for her garden last year. Why do you ask?'

'Just curious really, they don't curse people?' I immediately thought of Lance and the poppet.

'Esther wouldn't, that's for sure. I've never seen her angry.'

'Never?' Murdo looked disbelieving.

'Never.' I said firmly. It was true, Esther was unfailingly cheerful.

About half an hour before service began, I went over to my dry-store to get some more flour. There is a small bin of it in the kitchen and a huge bin of it in the outhouse. I walked out into the small cobbled yard at the back of the kitchen, stretched and looked around. It was a very pleasant place. I had herbs for the kitchen growing in planters: mint, parsley, a rosemary bush, and opposite the kitchen door I had the old brick outhouses, one for the freezers and one where I kept tinned goods, oil, stuff like that. I walked into the dry-store and stopped in horror.

Hanging from one of the shelves was a small, Rupert Bear doll. His paws were holding a very sharp looking pair of surgical scissors, the kind with long, sinister blades. The incongruity of it all, the wicked looking steel held by the normally benign bear was very disconcerting. It would have been upsetting to anyone, but to someone who had nearly been killed by Rupert, it was horrific. Naturally he was wearing his trademark clothing. He looked as if he were about to spring into demonic life, wielding the scissors.

It was a terrible kind of death threat. Immediately I was transported back to Lance's house, back to the baseball bat attack and the freezer.

I actually felt like throwing up. My heart was thundering. I backed away, took a bin bag from the shelf (there was a shelf that contained cleaning stuff), opened it wide and, holding the plastic sides wide apart, put him inside. I didn't want to touch him, I would have somehow felt contaminated.

Once he was safely in the bag I carried him out to the wheelie bin and threw him in. Someone was clearly sending me a message: I know where you work, I know where you live and I'm coming for you. You didn't have to have Anna Bruce's psychic chops or Esther's occult knowledge to divine who was behind this. It was straight out of one of her (no doubt) crappy horror novels.

What the hell had I done to deserve Mel Craig?

It was no mystery as to how she had got in. I was convinced it was her. First she'd eaten in my place, planning her attack. Then she'd moved to the village (admittedly I didn't know which way round this was – it didn't matter) Then she'd got my hair, then she'd blackmailed me, and now she was waging some kind of terrible psychological warfare.

I suddenly had an image in my mind of Mel Craig as an artist, a painter, adding a detail on the canvas, stepping back, evaluating what she had done, and then adding another brushstroke. The title of the picture, reflecting her psychotic behaviour: 'A Knife in the Back'.

I guessed she'd planted the doll there the day before. The gate to the yard was normally unlocked so the deliverymen could get in easily. I sighed; I'd have to review security.

She'd certainly got some balls sneaking onto my property to leave this ursine voodoo doll, but I knew she had cojones from her gate-crashing Lance's party and grabbing my pony tail. It's what made her so bloody formidable.

The Rupert Bear doll had rattled me. Part of my brain said, suddenly, loud and clear, 'Pay her off.' If she was capable of this, God knows what else she might have been up to. While she obviously wasn't Rupert Bear himself, why kill the goose that lays the golden eggs? With me dead there would be no money forthcoming. Had she seen Rupert try and kill me? Or had she somehow learned in some arcane manner from Lance or Della what had happened?

Not only was there that bothering me, the doll operated on a more visceral level. It made me more sympathetic to Lance's fright at the poppet doll. That reminded me, I'd called round to see Esther a while ago, bringing the voodoo doll thing with me to see if she could shed any light on it. After the latest Rupert Bear outrage I decided to pop in to see if she had any feedback for me on Lance's doll and to vent about my own experience with voodoo style happenings. I felt like seeing a close ally as well after the bear scare. I needed all the reassurance I could get.

'I am so angry it's not true.' Esther's face was beetroot red, she was shaking with rage. 'That bloody woman, I cannot believe it.'

I had never seen her in a temper before, I was certainly seeing her in a temper now. She was almost hyperventilating and her many chins were wobbling. I hadn't expected to find her in such a fearsome mood.

'What bloody woman?' I asked. Part of me thought, Mel Craig?

'Susannah Bloody Young.'

'Dr Young? Why, what's she done?'

By way of an answer, Esther handed me the copy of the left of centre Sunday newspaper that she read. It had been some years since I had actually handled a physical newspaper. I get the trade press sent to my phone and that's all the reading that I have time for. Maybe I should pay more attention to the news, all I know about the world is it's bloody awful, as per usual.

Anyway, 'The Witches of Eastwick', ran the headline – only Eastwick was crossed out and Hampden Green substituted written in felt-tip pen. An effect done by the newspaper. The photo of a (relatively) youthful Cher was contrasted with an unflattering photo of Esther. The byline was 'Susannah Young'.

I read the article. It was horrible, almost unbelievable. Nothing in it was actually false, but Esther and her friends were well and truly mocked. Coming from a friend it was bad enough, coming from someone who had saved her life, it was a stunning piece of nastiness. I read it again. Running through the article like lettering through a stick of rock, was a kind of visceral hatred of life in the countryside, where people who had lived there, in some cases for generations, were vilified as ignorant, superstitious bigoted characters. Esther, who had after all been a university friend of the author, was portrayed as a kind of stupid, insular fatso and her husband, Roy, who had served with distinction in the army and had received a medal for war work rescuing Bosnian Muslim children, as a knuckle-dragging, jingoistic thug. Even her dogs were pilloried.

I handed her back the paper. 'I'm so sorry.'

'And to think I saved her life…' Esther shook her head, 'and I organised that ceremony of healing for her.'

I knew what she was talking about. She had organised one for me a year or so ago when an ex-lover of mine had tried (and obviously failed) to kill me. The main purpose of it, as Esther had explained, was to draw a line under the event, helping you to come to terms with it – otherwise the trauma could well linger and poison the rest of your life. I am no psychologist, but that seemed perfectly reasonable to me and the ceremony involving twenty-seven (three is a significant pagan number, as is nine, so the multiplication has occult significance) women chanting and moving in perfect graceful unison was surprisingly moving. They had had to bring in NoBWic, the North Bucks Wiccans, to make up the numbers; she'd obviously gone to a lot of trouble for me. I had certainly felt a great deal better for it. Susannah Young's description of it was a travesty.

'Maybe it's because you saved her life,' I reflected. 'No good deed goes unpunished.'

'Maybe.' Esther's voice was gloomy. 'Roy's furious. I hope he doesn't shoot her. I wish whoever did do it had been a better shot. Up a couple of feet, bingo! Anyway, Charlie, what did you want to talk to me about?'

'The doll that Lance gave me.'

Esther nodded and said, 'Hang on a minute, I'll go and fetch it.'

She left the room and came back with it a couple of minutes later.

'Here we go. Well, as you suspected, it's a poppet doll. It's not one of ours, if that was what you wanted to know.'

'I didn't think it was for one moment. What can you tell me about it?'

'Well, obviously it's sympathetic magic.' She explained, 'You would baptise the doll, ideally in water you'd stolen from an actual baptism, with the name of the person that

147

you wanted to hurt, thus creating a psychic bond, then you would do what whoever made this has done, drive nails into the doll to symbolise hurt, saying a spell as you did so. This would vocalise and concentrate the message.'

'And the cloth?'

'Probably soaked with the blood of whoever laid the curse. You'd cut your finger or something, or use menstrual blood if you're a pre-menopausal witch.'

'Why? What would that do?'

'Human blood is very powerful, Charlie.'

Earlier that day I'd made chicken liver pâté; there was a lot of blood on the vacu-packs of the livers. 'What about the blood you'd get in the chicken livers for chicken liver pâté?' I asked idly.

Esther rolled her eyes. 'No, Charlie, that would not work at all – nor for that matter would beetroot juice if you were a vegan witch.'

'Would this thing really work?'

'Oh, yes,' Esther said, firmly. 'Well, up to a point. This one is kind of amateur. I'd have added some soil from a freshly dug grave and another couple of touches which I won't tell you about, but which are absent.'

'You're sure it's from an amateur?'

'Absolutely.'

'How do you know?' I didn't particularly care, I just wanted to know if the perpetrator was in Esther's coven, or if they were an outsider.

Esther asked me, 'Could you tell from a fine-dining plate of food if it had come from a Michelin-starred restaurant or from a non-professional?'

'Definitely.'

'Well, then.'

We both considered the poppet doll. It certainly gave me the creeps. I toyed with the idea of bringing up the Rupert Bear doll, but decided not to. That wasn't done with sympathetic magic in mind, that had been done to intimidate me, like a brick through the window.

'Who's this Lance anyway?' Esther asked.

'He's a podcaster. Lance Thurston; haven't you heard of him?'

'Oh God, of course I have, I just didn't realise he was the intended victim, I didn't make the connection. Was he the one who Susannah made such a song and dance over when she gave that talk?'

'The one and only. You don't think she did it?'

'After that article,' she said, glaring, brows knitted, still fuming, 'I very much doubt it... How is Lance?' She looked at the doll, at the nails through his eyes. 'Has he been having migraines?'

'He certainly had a headache after his party, but I think that was a hangover. You really think he should be worried?'

'I would be, if I were him...' she handed me the doll back, 'face it, someone really does not like him. Lance has got a bad enemy somewhere in the village.'

I stood up to go, Esther got up too. Then she suddenly flung her arms around me and crushed me against her. I was surprised by the strength of her arms. Hidden under all that flab was a powerful physique. I felt her body shaking as she sobbed. I held her close and patted her on the back. Jesus Christ, I thought, what's going on.

'I'm sorry, Charlie,' she moaned, her voice muffled as her head was buried in the fabric of my shirt. 'I'm sorry...'

'It's okay, it's okay...' I said soothingly. I felt like crying too, Esther's distress was contagious.

'I'm so upset...'

She pulled her head away from my body, her face wet with tears. From somewhere she produced a tissue and blew her nose.

'What is it, Esther, darling?'

'I'm sorry, it's just that fucking bitch.'

'There, there...'

'Back at uni,' she said, bitterly, 'I was the ugly friend... that's why she hung out with me, that and I had a car and she couldn't drive, so I was like her chauffeur. Then, you remember Tony...' I did, the guy in the photo. 'She slept with him, not because she fancied him, but just to humiliate me... she left just enough clues so I would find out...' She sat down heavily. 'And I was a complicit victim, I let her do this to me because I was such a people pleaser. When she got back in touch with me, I thought maybe she had changed, maybe she wanted to kind of atone for her past behaviour... but the leopard doesn't change its spots.' She blew her nose again. 'And now it's started all over again. The betrayal, the contempt... I hate her so much, Charlie.'

'Oh, Esther, I'm so sorry.'

It was hard to know what to say, how to comfort her. It was just awful to see the calm, competent, unflappable Esther reduced to this.

Then she smiled wanly at me. 'The thing is Charlie, I really do hate her, and I'm frightened of what I might do.'

Chapter Nineteen

Whatever bad things Esther had to say about Dr Young there was no faulting the latter's courage. Being shot hadn't deterred her from revisiting the village hall. A week after I had my conversation about the poppet doll, while I was running back across the common to my restaurant, I saw there was a notice on the wooden board on the common to the effect that Dr Young would be delivering a lecture on patriarchy and superstition in the village hall. Tickets were available from the village hall website. It was a fair bet that Esther wouldn't be organising this one. The village hall committee were either unaware of the situation vis-à-vis Esther and the Doctor or there was someone on that committee who seriously disliked Esther; I inclined to the latter view. Village feuds were poisonous, like rifts in the solid ground suddenly opening up and spewing out noxious matter that had been buried deep for ages.

Anyway, I wasn't impressed. The bloody nerve of the woman, I thought. Then this was immediately followed by the suspicion that she was doing this to further torment Esther, rubbing salt into the wound she'd re-opened.

'Have you seen the news,' Jess said, she was very excited. 'Susannah's here again. I'm going; would you like a ticket? It's so brave of her to come back and confront her demons, they say there's going to be a TV crew as well… The academic they couldn't silence.'

I looked up from the work table; I was preparing Hasselback potatoes. You have to cut through most of the potato, say 90 per cent of the way with a knife at about five millimetre intervals. I use new potatoes and rest them in a dessertspoon while I make the incisions. That way you don't go all the way through the potato, the lip of the spoon's edge catching the blade of the knife before you cut too far.

'No, Jess,' I said, coldly, 'I'm not. She was horrible to Esther Bartlett, and in print too, so loads of people saw. It was nasty of her. And unnecessary.'

'Maybe,' Jess said with the callousness of youth. I could see that Esther and her pagan friends cut no ice with Jess's generation, whereas Dr Young did. 'But Esther's stuck in the past, with her stupid beliefs…'

I bit my tongue. Esther certainly did believe in the reality of Celtic gods and goddesses but that was her business. There was no point in getting into an argument with Jess about it. I was saddened though that she had taken Dr Young's side in the argument. Jess plainly thought that the speech in the hall was to make a point that she couldn't be silenced. I firmly believed that it was to further hurt Esther.

I carried on with my potatoes and then I suddenly had an idea. I suppose that it was the mention of Esther that triggered it.

When Jess came back into the kitchen I asked her, 'Could you do me a favour?'

'Sure.' I think she felt that she had overstepped the mark with her comments about Esther and wanted to show willing, to smooth things over between us.

'Could you go online and see if there's anyone locally who does DNA testing?'

'Yeah, why?'

'That poppet doll that Lance gave me, Esther said the piece of cloth in it was probably soaked in the blood of whoever laid the curse on him. We could find out who it was from the DNA in the blood.'

Jess looked at me sceptically. 'Well, we could if we had access to the police DNA library, which we don't, and if that person had a police record. Or we could find out who it was if we went around and politely asked all of Lance's acquaintances to give us DNA samples and then you paid for them all to be processed and then compared. I don't think it's the best idea that you've ever had, Charlie.'

I felt very deflated. For a moment or two I had been convinced that I was on to something, now it seemed I wasn't.

'Oh, well,' I said. And forgot all about it.

A while later Jess came in with the mail. I took a break from my prep, sat down in my office and opened the post. One of the letters was an official looking document. I opened it and it was a summons to appear at the Aylesbury court on the twelfth of October, in just over a month's time, to hear the case of non-payment of claims for compensation.

Damn. I hadn't forgotten about the wretched woman and her attempt to defraud me, I had just kind of pushed it to the back of my mind.

The letter showed me just how far she was prepared to push things. I guess she was desperate these days for money. She couldn't podcast any more, no reputable publisher would touch her with a barge pole after her plagiarism history, and the horror novels were selling really (gratifyingly) badly. Their position in the Amazon league tables was several million below the number one slot. Jess had explained to me that although the algorithm used by the media giant was shrouded in mystery, Mel Craig's sales were tiny to the point of non-existence. But this very desperation of hers was making her correspondingly more dangerous. She'd taken a risk with the Rupert Bear doll (inspired no doubt by her horror story imagination) and now she was risking things further with the legal threat. It was a gamble, but obviously worth it in her mind.

I sighed to myself. The sisterhood were very much letting me down, I thought. First there was Mel Craig and her extortion attempt, now there was Dr Young and her vendetta against Esther. Doubtless Lance would have an opinion on the fickleness and general awfulness of womankind. Jess came in and found me staring glumly at the letter. I handed it to her and she read it.

'Bitch,' she muttered, angrily, then looked up. 'Well, I'm sure you'll win.'

'Well, I'm not. The thing is, I bet she's done this lots of times, it's all very slick what she's done. If only we could find out.'

'We could hack into her computer,' Jess said quietly.

I looked at her sharply. She smiled and raised a questioning shapely black eyebrow. I had seen Jess break into a laptop before but that was when we actually had it in the kitchen. She had inserted a program on a memory stick into it via the port.

'I don't want to break into her house, Jess, there's enough going on in my life without being arrested for burglary.'

Jess shook her head. 'We don't need to break in to do it.'

'Really?' I said eagerly. 'Tell me more.'

So that evening found us parked near Mel Craig's house in a white van belonging to Francis's dad. She was staying in a semi-detached house on the edge of the village that was used for short term lets. Like many places Airbnb had taken root even here. We sat next to each other in the back surrounded by gardening tools and implements, the van smelt not unpleasantly of soil, while Jess booted up her laptop.

'Okay,' she said, 'first, let's have a look at the Wi-Fi networks nearby...'

Her fingers moved over the keys and then a list of other networks appeared. 'This looks like hers. Now,' she looked at me, 'what we're going to do is a de-authentication attack. We're going to interrupt her connection and when the pc tries to log back in, we'll capture her password. Okay, here goes.'

We looked at the screen, the strings of numbers and the acronyms meant nothing to me. She moved the cursor and clicked away. 'C'mon, c'mon... yesss, that's it...

disconnected... now it's trying to re-establish the connection... now, here we go... Bingo! Got you.'

She turned to me. 'This is her Wi-Fi password...' she pointed at the digits on the screen, 'but now we need to get into her pc, see what we can find... I'm using a program called rockyou which will go through lists of potential passwords until it finds one that matches.'

'How many passwords are in that file?'

'About fourteen million, but we can refine the search slightly. She probably won't have a long password so I can reduce the parameters, shouldn't take too long.'

She was right, it didn't.

About two minutes later we had her computer password and Jess entered it and there on Jess's laptop was Mel Craig's home screen.

Jess clicked on an icon. 'Let's check her mail.'

Almost immediately we struck gold. Without going too far back in her mail history we found five letters from five different restaurants within the past six months. All of them had been targeted with her scam. She had helpfully created a folder in which to store her blackmail correspondence called 'Catering'. All the paper trail was there.

Four had paid up: one had believed her story and offered profuse apologies, two had sent aggrieved replies but had confirmed payment and one had paid and told her in no uncertain terms what they thought of her. Only one had been brave enough to call her bluff.

'Wow,' I said, 'that's an eighty per cent success rate.'

If each restaurant had paid her five grand she was making a tidy income from her extortion.

'Let's have a look at her browsing history,' I said.

Mel was not a woman for computer housekeeping. Jess pressed control h and up it came. 'Do the search for salmonella,' I said. Sure enough she had visited seven sites to check on the symptoms of salmonella, four on how to fake salmonella and three on how to give yourself salmonella.

My God. I thought of the medical report. She'd probably gone as far as actually giving herself the illness so she could blame me. There was no end to the lengths that woman would go to.

We looked at each other.

'That's enough for now,' I said. 'Have you copied all that?'

'Oh, yes,' Jess said smugly, 'it's all done.'

'Jess,' I said with feeling, 'you're wonderful and I shall never complain about students ever again.'

'I'm pleased to hear it,' she said complacently. Then she frowned. 'You realise none of this will be admissible in court? It'll be classed as unlawfully obtained evidence.'

That was a blow, but she was probably correct. 'Oh, I guess you're right, but "know thine enemy" as they say. So before we go, let's see what else we can learn about Mel Craig.'

In a remarkably short period of time from the information she had stored for easy access on her pc, we learnt that she was mostly vegetarian but ate fish, that on YouTube she had subscriptions to yoga and diet channels as well as a plethora of YouTubers who did stuff on witchcraft. She was also a subscriber to the Horror Channel.

'Well, that's a bit unexpected,' Jess said.

'No it's not. Aside from the fact that she writes horror fiction and is an assiduous copycat, I can easily see her in league with Satan. She's obviously one of his acolytes. Look at the Rupert Bear doll. She's got a twisted mind. Jess, I think we've seen enough.'

I clambered into the front seat of the van and drove home. As we did so I thought about poppet dolls. Had she put the doll in Lance's flower bed, not for any reason other than general malice? Ditto the Rupert Bear doll in my dry-store? Was she perhaps mad as well as evil?

A few days passed and we reached the evening of the eighteenth and the talk by Dr Young on patriarchy and superstition. I had absolutely no doubt that it was going to be a swingeing attack on everything that Esther held sacred. That would fall under the superstition bit.

I had given Jess the evening off to go and see her. So I was very surprised when she walked into the kitchen at 8 o'clock looking both irritated and worried.

'Is there a problem?' I said.

Katie, one of the other waitresses came in at that point and read out an order.

'Cheque on, one chicken liver pâté, one soup – one guinea fowl and one salmon with Hasselback potatoes, lovage sauce.'

'Thank you, Katie.' I took the cheque from her and put it up next to the other three on the cheque grabber above the pass. I called the order back to her and turned to Francis.

'Francis, one pâté, one soup, please.'

I put a pan on for the guinea fowl, checked the state of the sirloin steak on the chargrill; it was nearly ready.

'Chips for the steak, please Francis and a Béarnaise in a ramekin... hang on a sec, Katie, this steak can go out.' I plated the steak, garnished it, put the steel container of chips next to it on the plate, checked the ticket, 'One medium rare sirloin, Béarnaise, table three,' and spiked the ticket.

'Sorry, Jess, was there a problem with the talk?'

'Yeah, she never showed up,' Jess's face expressed concern. 'There are quite a few disappointed people... but I had a word with one of the organisers, she was pretty worried. Dr Young isn't answering her phone, it goes straight to voicemail.'

'Well,' I said, 'I'm sure it's nothing...'

'Hang on a moment.' It was Francis, he was frowning at his phone. 'I've got a text from my cousin. The police have closed the road near Barracks Hill school... they're swarming around like flies at a picnic...'

'Well,' I said, 'I'm sure it's not related. Anyway, Francis, soup and a pâté please.'

But it was related. On the news on Beech Tree FM that evening it was revealed that the body of a sixty-three year old woman had been recovered from Swithins Lane. Later she was named as Dr Susannah Young.

Chapter Twenty

The following morning I had an unofficial visit from the police. DI Slattery, the policeman who lived in a house across the green from my restaurant, drank down his espresso. He pushed a large, muscular hand through his thick, dark hair and his cold grey eyes rested on mine.

'She had been stabbed,' he said, 'a single blow to the heart. There was no trace of the weapon in the vicinity of her car so the killer obviously took it away with them. Dr Young probably knew her killer, they were in the passenger seat when the fatal blow was struck.'

'That's terrible,' I said. 'Have you got any idea who might have done it?'

Part of me longed to blurt out, 'Arrest Mel Craig, she's a criminal nut-case.'

But I didn't.

Slattery shook his head. 'I am assuming it was probably the same person who tried to kill her when she was shot in that field a few weeks back. That person had good local knowledge, they knew where she would be at the time and they also knew the surrounding area well enough to work out where to shoot from and make good their escape.' He frowned. 'This attack shows a similar knowledge of local geography. The vehicle was in that layby near the school and as you know, it's partly screened by a hedge and trees and it is also next to a footpath. We assume that the attack occurred around about six in the evening, the killer making off down said footpath.'

'So, a local person then, or someone living in this area who knows it reasonably well.' I was thinking again of Mel Craig. Wishful thinking I daresay, but if she were hauled off to prison for murder it would keep her from trying to extort money from me.

'Exactly.'

'Why are you telling me all this, DI Slattery?'

'What do you think of Lance Thurston?' he abruptly changed the subject.

'Lance?' I repeated, surprised.

'Yes. You worked for him, did he strike you as the kind of man likely to commit murder?'

I shook my head. 'No. Then again, I've met a couple of killers and they didn't strike me either as the kind of people to commit murder. But he certainly wasn't going around complaining that Dr Young had ruined his life or his livelihood.'

I thought the thing that was worrying him most was being cursed but I wasn't sure if I should bring this to the attention of the police. Besides, I was sort of sorry for Lance. It sounds ridiculous but he struck me as a kind of sad figure. To many he was a huge success. His audience was measured in the hundreds of thousands, he was influential, he was

162

famous – not as famous as he would like to be but still pretty well-known, nevertheless. To me, though, he was like the kid at school whom nobody liked, forever trying to prove himself in ways that would always prove futile because whatever he did was never going to be good enough. He was never going to be part of the gang, he would always be last to be picked for the football team, he would never get the girl at the prom, he would never be asked to the parties that he wanted to be invited to. He would always have his nose pressed up against the glass of other people's houses watching them have good times while he remained outside.

Slattery stood up, he was a big guy, maybe six three, and powerfully built. He seemed to dwarf me and at five nine, I'm not particularly short. He also had a powerful personality that seemed to emit a kind of force-field that made you notice him. I reflected that was a quality totally missing in Lance. Slattery was like an anti-Thurston. And deep down, Lance would have known it. Self-awareness, that was his tragedy.

'Well, I'd best be off. I gather Dr Young knew Esther Bartlett well. Would you say that they were friends?'

This was a bit tricky. I would have to say that they were very definitely not friends, but equally I did not want to drop Esther in it. But the thought of her being a suspect in a murder inquiry was so ridiculous I couldn't see any harm in letting DI Slattery know what had been happening between them.

'They were friends, but they had a bit of a falling out of late,' I said, diplomatically.

'What happened?' asked Slattery. He spoke with an alacrity that I found a bit alarming. I suddenly thought, maybe the head of a group of witches does not sound unlikely as a murder suspect.

I explained the situation as best I understood it. Slattery made some notes.

'Thank you, Charlie,' he murmured, 'that's all very interesting. I'll see you later.'

I saw him out and a few moments later, Jess arrived.

'Was that Slattery?' she asked.

'Yeah, he was round here asking me about Lance and Esther,' I said. 'He seems very keen on my opinions.'

'He's very keen on you,' Jess said, raising her dark eyebrows emphatically.

'What!' I could hardly believe what she had just said. 'Slattery?'

'Yes.' She was smiling now. 'Don't tell me you haven't noticed.'

I could honestly say I hadn't and I was sure she was wrong. 'What do you mean?'

'I've seen the way that he looks at you.'

'No, Jess, you've got it all wrong,' I said with conviction. 'Besides, I'm kind of spoken for.'

'Kind of?' She looked almost shocked. I knew she was an Andrea fan. 'What do you mean, "kind of"?'

'I don't know Jess…' This was all getting a bit confusing. I didn't want to have to explain how I was beginning to feel backed into a corner by Andrea. I'm not sure I understood how I felt myself. Now, mystifyingly, I had seemingly managed to attract both Slattery and Roland. Jess looked at me expectantly. The look said, I'm waiting for an answer. Then rescue came.

I could hear the tramp of Murdo's feet as he walked down the stairs from the flat above to the kitchen. I certainly didn't want to discuss my emotional life in front of him.

'Good morning, Murdo!' I said brightly, 'and how are we today?'

Jess frowned darkly as she walked past me to get some milk out of the walk-in fridge. 'You can run from things, Charlie Hunter,' she muttered at me, 'but you can't hide.'

Murdo had the evening off and I asked him what he was going to do.

'I'm going up to Oxford,' he said. 'Could you give me a lift to Wycombe railway station? I can get a train from there.'

'Sure. We'll go after service. What are you going to do there?'

He blushed. He was red-headed and pale-skinned, he blushed easily, as do I come to that, his colouring is similar to mine. My hair went reddish-brown as I got older rather than staying red and my skin is not as milky as Murdo's but not far off.

'I ken a lassie who works in one of the colleges...'

'A chef?' I thought the chances of Murdo dating an Oxford University student or lecturer were slim. It wouldn't be a meeting of minds, unless, of course, she had a passion for Death Metal. Maybe a renegade theology lecturer with a taste for the dark side of things.

'Aye, she's the head chef at St Anselm's college, it's a women's college. Or was, anyway...'

I thought, that's the same college that Dr Young worked at.

'The head chef!' I marvelled. 'How old is she, Murdo, if you don't mind me asking?' I didn't want Murdo to be the victim of some kind of cradle snatcher.

He blushed again. 'She's a wee bit auld, twenty-seven.'

'Young to be a head chef.'

'She's very good,' he said, defensively.

'I'm sure she is.'

And we got down to our prep for the Friday lunchtime which I knew was going to be busy. Murdo had asked if he could stay on for another few days, the cruise ship was delayed, something to do with COVID. Fine by me, I thought.

Towards the beginning of service, about half past eleven, I saw Murdo check his phone and swear.

'What's the matter?' I asked. 'Problem?'

'Aye, I cannae stay at Lucy's tonight after all.'

'Why?'

'She lives in a shared flat in Cowley. It's surprisingly shite. One of the lassies has already made arrangements tae huv a whole muckle of friends staying, female japery, so there's no room for me.'

'Well, you could always ask her if she wanted to come here instead.'

He looked joyful. 'Are you sure? It's nae a bother?'

'Absolutely not. You can both eat here for free as well, if you want.'

'That's great. Thanks, Charlie.'

'Not at all, Murdo. The pleasure's all mine. We'll go

and pick her up from the station in the afternoon, if she comes by train.'

We started working together again over the deafening row that was Murdo's choice of music. At quarter to twelve Francis came in. I'd agreed he could come in late today, he had to help his uncle (the same one who had lent me and Jess the van, so I could hardly refuse). He beamed happily at the two of us.

'Have you heard the news?' he said, humming good-naturedly as he filled the huge washing-up sink with water.

'The news? No.'

'Esther Bartlett'

'What about her?' I asked.

'She's been arrested after confessing to the murder of Dr Young.'

Chapter Twenty-One

'What!' I said. 'Are you sure?'

The very idea that Esther could be arrested for anything was outlandish, that it should be for murder was utterly unbelievable. As always, Francis looked maddeningly cheerful.

'Are you sure?' I asked again. Just to check.

'Yes,' he confirmed, grinning from ear to ear.

'How do you know?'

'As you know, my auntie works at the police station in Wycombe, everyone's talking about it down there,' he answered. Well, that seemed to be that. In stunned silence I went back to work.

It was only later that day that I discovered via Jess whose father was a friend of Roy Bartlett that Esther was out of the police station. She hadn't actually been arrested as I had imagined, cars screeching to a halt, police bursting through the door, Esther handcuffed. She had gone to the local police station in Wycombe and confessed to the murder. She had been interviewed and then had been released under investigation. RUI'ed I believe it's called.

I texted her immediately, arranged with Jess that she would pick Lucy up from the station and at 4 o'clock I was sitting down with my friend Esther in her spacious living room with its military prints on the wall overlooking their immaculate lawn and flower beds. Her husband was ex-army and it certainly showed in the meticulous cleanliness of the house and the perfect order that everything was kept in, ditto the garden, as well as the choice of pictures.

Esther, resplendent in a blue and white striped caftan like the embodiment of the Greek national flag, sat under a picture of a Spitfire downing a Dornier bomber over the south coast.

'So what happened?' I asked.

'Well, the problem started when you showed me that poppet doll…'

'How so?' I asked, slightly bemused.

'Well, I'm sure you've had the experience when you've gone to a restaurant, Charlie, and you've ordered something and it's been okay but you think to yourself, you know what, this is a good idea, but it could be done so much better, so you go home and you improve it beyond all recognition…'

'Yes.' All too often, it was a very frequent occurrence.

'Well, that is what happened with the poppet doll. When I saw the way it had been done, it gave me ideas. Then when Susannah wrote that horrible article and was so mean to me, I decided to get my own back.' She held up the palms of her hands as if forestalling or warding off any criticism. 'I know, I know, I should never have done it, but

170

I did. I bought a child's doll, but I bought it thinking malicious thoughts. I did a naming ceremony. I hadn't got round to a towel wash so I still had a bath towel with a couple of hairs from Susannah's head from when she had stayed here – that was useful. I got some soil from a freshly dug grave... that's not everything by a long chalk but...'

'That's okay,' I said, hurriedly. I most certainly didn't want to know where the blood had come from. 'I get the picture...'

'And I cursed her, and it worked.' Her face was unusually solemn. 'I killed her.'

'Did you put the knife in her?' I asked. 'Because that's what killed her, not your curse.'

'You say that...' she was scornful, 'but that was only the means by which death arrived. Not the causation. She was killed by all accounts in her car, at least that's what I gathered during the police interview.' God, I wish I'd been there to watch that, I thought. I wonder what Esther's solicitor made of her confession.

'If I hadn't done what I did anything could have happened to prevent it, a dog-walker could have surprised them.' I immediately thought of Della, she'd almost certainly have intervened. 'She might have fought back... there are endless possibilities.'

I could see that she was determined to take responsibility for the murder and nothing I could say would alter that. I suppose it was expiation after the tsunami of hatred for her erstwhile friend that had engulfed her. Misplaced guilt together with a firm belief in her own power as a sorceress.

171

'Or,' she carried on, borne away on a tidal wave of remorse, 'the murderer might never have thought of killing her in the first place... I have a lot to be forgiven for,' she concluded dramatically.

'Well, you're out of the hands of the justice system,' I said, 'at least the sharp end of it anyway. Let's be thankful for small mercies.'

In the late afternoon I went for a run before work and started to shake off the cares of the day. My run took me past Marlow House, the home of the Earl, and in the path through one of the woods nearby I smelled weed and shortly afterwards, as I anticipated, I bumped into Bryony. She was wearing anatomically revealing tight leggings and a crop top that looked like it had been sprayed on to her. Her short blonde hair glinted in the sun. As always, she looked delighted to see me.

'Charlie, what's all this about Esther killing someone?'

I stopped and we talked. I explained Esther's guilt feelings. Bryony nodded.

'Yeah, she's right, those dolls are really heavy shit... they can kill you know, it all depends on your intention...'

I was surprised by this knowledge of the occult from Bryony. She obviously noticed this. 'Yeah, I know a lot about it. I used to go out with this dealer who was into black magic... he'd seen the devil on an acid trip, that set him off... Once he made one of, like, this rival guy who was muscling in on his territory.'

'Did it work?' I asked.

'Well, he got shot,' Bryony said, matter-of-factly, 'but

then, a lot of dealers get shot, don't they, it's sort of an occupational work-related hazard.'

I wasn't sure what to make of that. Well, I wasn't going to mock the efficacy of the dark arts. I felt that I myself was now the victim of sympathetic magic, courtesy of the Bear doll. I'm an agnostic on magic. In my view it was a lot less effective than being clubbed over the head with a baseball bat and shoved in a freezer by the real thing. But I wasn't going to split hairs.

'So how are you, Charlie?' she asked.

'I'm stressed, Bryony.' I poured out my story about the blackmail attempt by Mel Craig. Bryony frowned. 'What a bitch... and to someone as nice as you, Charlie... I'm sure she'll get what's coming to her, karma you know.'

'Well, I hope you're right, Bryony. She's taking me to court, she could bankrupt me.'

'You'll be okay, Charlie... you've got friends who care for you.' She smiled at me in an unfocused way. She was extraordinarily pretty. No wonder the Earl was so smitten with her. 'Do you want to see a photo of a baby orangutan having a bath?'

'God yes.' I absolutely did.

She got her phone out and we watched a tiny ginger orangutan being bathed in a washing up bowl. It was entrancing.

'Thank you, Bryony, I feel a lot better now.' The funny thing was, I did. And Bryony was right, I did have friends, and that was consoling. Unlike Mel Craig. All she had to keep her company was the Horror Channel.

She put her phone away and held my hands, looking

deep into my eyes, her own eyes unfocused and stoned, very bright blue. 'It'll be all right, Charlie, you just see.'

I bloody well hope so, I thought, as I ran off down the footpath.

Chapter Twenty-Two

That evening I met Murdo's girlfriend. They say that opposites attract and this was certainly the case with Lucy. Murdo was built like a beanpole, tall and skinny with his mop of curly red hair perched on top like it was roosting there. Lucy was a big girl, hefty. She had a very pretty face, light grey eyes, startlingly so, a big chest and powerful shoulders and forearms. Her thighs were sizeable, she could have crushed Murdo like an eggshell if she'd wanted to.

Murdo had offered to help me out in the kitchen until she arrived. There had been some crisis at the college that had necessitated her presence and she wouldn't get into the station at Wycombe until about eight. So Murdo and I were working when Jess dropped her off. She knocked on the kitchen door and Francis let her in and she stood on the far side of the pass while I said hello and she watched Murdo in action, critically evaluating him as he cooked.

Murdo, maybe unsurprisingly given his long limbs, was kind of jerky and ungainly in his movements, it was like watching a baby giraffe walk. But it was deceptive, he had that ability of perfect timing and memory that good chefs have to have, remembering how long each of the seven or eight pans that covered the stove had been cooking for and the cooking times for what was in them.

'How's he shaping up?' Lucy asked me.

'He's a joy to work with.'

'What was that?' Murdo shouted to us over the roar of the fans.

Lucy leaned forward and bellowed, 'She says you're shite, Murdo. You couldn't find yer arse if it was handed to you on a plate.'

Murdo laughed and stuck his middle finger up at his girlfriend.

Jess came in with some empty plates and gave them to Francis. She called out to me, 'That's table six ready...'

'Mains for table six,' I said to Murdo. 'One chicken chasseur, two salmon, lovage sauce.'

'Coming right up.'

He brought the food over to me and I probed the chicken. I knew it would be cooked perfectly but I take three or four random food temperature readings per service and log them, just in case the EHO, the environmental health officer, comes calling. In view of Mel Craig's attempted blackmail it seemed a very wise precautionary move.

Lucy turned to me. 'Should I give him a job in my college, Chef?'

Murdo laughed. 'You could never afford me.'

I looked at the cheques on the pass, there were only three there. 'You can go now, Murdo, there's just these few to do. Thanks so much for volunteering to help on your night off. Take Lucy upstairs, that's you done for the night.'

A couple of hours later, I had finished cooking for the evening, cleaned the kitchen down and checked the mise en place list for the following day. I yawned and stretched. It was half past ten. I'd been working since eight in the morning and I still had the ordering to do. By the time I'd finished everything and had a drink with Jess it was half past eleven. I went upstairs to my bed, undressed and crawled beneath the duvet, ignoring the squeals and groans and rhythmic thudding that emanated from the guest bedroom down the hall. You're only young once, I guess. Maybe I was a bit envious too of the passion that they had for each other. Eventually I fell asleep.

Saturday lunch was oddly stress-free. Sometimes you can be busy but everything goes smoothly. The cheques are nicely spaced, nothing goes wrong. Francis was weirdly on form.

The evening service was easy too. I cooked about thirty-five covers, again, they were all neatly spaced out and no large tables, which was good. Two of my customers were Murdo and Lucy. I gave them their free three course meal and, as we'd been quiet, I made a couple of amuse bouche for them, smoked salmon pinwheels with a chive oil dip – it was an almost hallucinatory deep green colour, quite amazing – and some deep-fried brie, très retro, it had been popular when I was a girl and starting out in cooking. Note to self, put it back on the menu.

I had the kitchen cleaned down by half past ten and Francis and I changed and we headed off to the Three Bells.

The pub was quiet, and playing pool were Murdo and Lucy. Esther's arrest had piqued my interest in the murder of Dr Young. I wondered if the killer was someone I knew (please God, let it be Mel Craig, I prayed again). The fact that the murder had happened around here made it seem possible. And of course, Dr Young had complained about Mel Craig's plagiarism. Maybe Satan had ordered her demise.

Still on the dead academic's legacy, it was interesting that she'd been at the same college as Murdo's girlfriend. I had asked him if Lucy wouldn't mind answering a few questions I had about Dr Young; he had put it to her and she'd said it would be fine.

I watched the two of them at the table. It made me think about my own love life. Andrea's offer had really spooked me. It was strange, it's what I had kind of dreamed of in the past, security with a man I loved – but now I realised it's not what I wanted. I looked at Murdo's young, excited face – that wasn't me either. I couldn't imagine being infatuated. I was beyond that.

I gave up on this introspection, stupid psychic frottage, and watched the game. I know absolutely nothing about pool and care even less, but it was obvious even to me that Lucy was infinitely better than Murdo. Every time she hit a ball, one seemed to go in the pocket. When she did miss, I kind of suspected it was deliberate so Murdo had a chance to have a go.

'She's bloody good,' said Francis admiringly, then wistfully, sotto voce, 'if I had a girlfriend, I'd like one like her.'

There are times when Francis could break my heart. That reminded me, I still owed him a suit.

They finished their game and came and joined me.

'Dinner was blinding, Charlie,' said Lucy cheerfully, 'thank you so much. That chive dip... wow... Murdo said you wanted to ask me some questions about Dr Young.'

'That's right, Lucy.'

'Murdo, darling, go and play pool with Francis,' Lucy commanded, turning to him, 'we're going to have a serious conversation, okay.'

'Sure,' Murdo said. The two of them moved off to the pool table. Lucy took a swig from her pint of lager and looked around the grotty, nondescript bar.

'Nice pub you've got here, Charlie.' She belched gently. 'Pardon me,' she said mechanically.

Lucy was probably the only person I had ever heard praise the Three Bells. I looked around the place wondering what on earth she had found to like. The carpet was threadbare and stained from innumerable spilt drinks and had burn marks from back in the day when you were allowed to smoke in public places. The lighting was unflatteringly bright and would remain so until eleven when the lock-in began and the curtains would be drawn and the overhead lights turned off so it was like being in a war zone in the blackout. The beer was suspect, you wouldn't get any real ale enthusiasts coming here. And behind the bar stood Malcolm, the red-faced, taciturn, monosyllabic landlord.

'Thank you, Lucy,' I said. On behalf of the pub, surprise winner of an accolade. 'So you knew Dr Young well?'

'Very well,' Lucy said, 'I'm bi, Charlie, and the good doctor and me, we were an item for a bit.'

I stared at her in surprise. This was unexpected.

179

'Are members of staff allowed to...?' I asked.

'Have sex with each other?' Lucy finished my question. She shrugged. 'Who cares, probably not. I never read my contract, except for the bit that mentioned salary. I only went with her for a bit of a laugh, maybe so I could just say I'd shagged a don. She's not my type, quite a bit older than me of course, but she'd kept her looks and her body, it was always understood it was just a fling. But then I found out what a bitch she was.' She drank some more lager. 'Word to the wise, Charlie, never fuck a bitch.'

'In what way was she a bitch?' I was interested now, there was certainly a pattern with Dr Young of biting the hand that fed her.

'Tried to have me fired.'

I blinked. 'Seriously?'

She nodded. 'Seriously. When we split up, she was a moody cow and I got fed up with it, plus she didn't approve of me seeing men. I told her it was none of her business, which it wasn't. She tried to get me the sack by complaining about my food to the Master of the college, well, that didn't go down too well. He'd seen through her long before anyone else did. She was going to get fired herself, well, her contract wasn't being renewed... I, on the other hand...' she bent her fingers over and breathed on them and rubbed them against her blouse in a show of triumph. 'Easy to find a feminist academic, there's shitloads with degrees coming out their arses, less easy to find a good reliable chef,' she said. She drained her pint and I fetched her another one.

'Cheers, Charlie.'

'Did she have any enemies at the college?'

180

'What, besides me? Yeah, there was a lecturer called Sam Hickocks, she got him sacked. He was having an affair with a student, a kid called Paul Whitten and she got to hear of it and grassed him up to the Master. But basically, she was a nasty piece of work; to know her was to dislike her.' She drank some more lager. 'If there's a large crowd at her funeral it'll be of people eager to see her buried or wanting to know where her grave is so they can piss on it.'

'Where does Sam Hickocks teach these days?' I asked out of curiosity.

'He doesn't. Not only did she accuse him of shagging a student and implying coercion, she got hold of an article he'd written that she claimed was racist. I dunno if it was or it wasn't, I'd say probably not, but she whipped it up into a real shitstorm and Hickocks got the hump and opened up a deli, said he'd had enough of the Nazification of tertiary education. Well, as you can imagine, that went down like a shit sandwich at a picnic.'

She opened a packet of nuts and tipped them into her mouth. 'Tell you another thing about her, that coercion thing. I reckon she'd tried that on with more than a few students herself. I heard rumours. I reckon that's where she got off accusing Sam of it, he was not the sort to do that kind of thing, he was quite shy, he wasn't the kind to intimidate anyone.'

'Where is his deli?' I asked.

'Near the college. It's called "The Freedom Deli"' – she turned to the pool table – 'have those two clowns finished?'

They had indeed. They were both standing by the bar and there were now a couple of kids playing on the table.

Lucy watched them. 'The blond one's good,' she said, judiciously, 'but I'm much better.' She put her pint down and stood up, then she winked at me.

I watched as she walked over to the table and stood staring at them playing.

The blond kid looked up at her. 'You all right, darling?' he said with an air of condescension.

Lucy smiled at him. 'You're a good player,' she said.

The boy smirked cockily. 'Know much about pool, do you?'

Patronising, I thought.

'Enough to know I can beat you,' Lucy bragged. 'Bet you twenty quid I can.'

The kid's smirk broadened. 'Make that fifty and we're talking.'

'Done,' she said and shook his hand.

Murdo brought me over a Diet Coke as they tossed a coin for the break.

'She grew up in a pool hall,' he said confidently, 'she'll slaughter him.'

Five minutes later, flushed with success Lucy sat down heavily next to us and kissed Murdo. She handed him a folded note. 'Go and buy me a drink, darling...'

Murdo obediently stood up and went to the bar.

The two of us looked fondly at him and the chastened kid and his friend slunk out of the pub. Lucy watched them go.

'Fucking muppets,' she said with conviction.

Chapter Twenty-Three

News of Lance's arrest travelled fast. I heard about it second-hand, courtesy of Francis's aunt, the cleaner at the police station in Wycombe. Further details were provided by Slattery. He turned up at the restaurant late on Monday as I was finishing a business meeting with Jess.

I made him his habitual espresso as Jess shrugged herself into her coat and I let her out the front door.

'Told you so,' she murmured to me smugly and winked as I closed the door behind her. I sat opposite Slattery at a table and poured myself a glass of Sancerre.

'So, what brings you round here?' I asked, casually. His first name was Michael but I rarely used it, to me he was DI Slattery. After Jess's claim that he fancied me, I was wary about anything that might encourage this. It's hardly a come-on to call someone by their first name but I felt it might have encouraged an intimacy that I could well do without. He considered the question carefully. You do not have to say anything, I thought to myself, but anything that you do will be taken down and may be used against you at a later date. He was wearing jeans and a white polo shirt which emphasised his tanned, muscular arms. He pushed a hand through his thick, dark hair flecked with grey as he considered the question. I suddenly, slightly unexpectedly, found myself considering him as boyfriend material in an objective way. He was undoubtedly an attractive guy, if somewhat grim of demeanour, but I suppose that kind of went with the job. And I did like his toughness. He didn't make a song and dance about it, it was just there. Unlike Lance, you just knew he would walk the walk. That was a given. Total self-assurance is a very attractive quality in a person.

'Did you know that we arrested Lance earlier today?' he asked.

'Yeah, I had heard.' I thought it highly unlikely that Lance was a killer; it was a step up from Esther Bartlett in the credibility stakes, but I did not believe it for a moment.

'Thought you would, that'll be Leonora telling Francis, I suppose.'

'Leonora?'

He nodded. 'Leonora Turner.' He smiled unexpectedly. It transformed his face, he suddenly looked years younger. 'I know, it's not really a name you associate with a Bucks cleaning lady who's about sixty-five but there you are.'

So that's Francis's aunt, I thought.

'So, what made you arrest him?' I asked.

Slattery frowned. 'Well, we went round to his house. We felt we had to speak to him because of his history of enmity, not to mention threats, that he had with Dr Young. He had no alibi for the time of the murder and his demeanour was suspicious, it was as if he was hiding something...'

'Do you really think Lance killed Dr Young?' I interrupted. It was obvious that Lance disliked Dr Young, maybe even hated her, but lots of people did. I could imagine half her colleagues did; there was Esther and her curse, there was the guy she had driven out of the college, Lucy didn't like her. The Master of St Anselm's who wasn't renewing her contract didn't like her. By the sound of it there were a fair few students too who might have reasons to have disliked the good doctor. It was a lengthy list.

Slattery drank half his coffee. 'I don't know,' he said, 'there is a lot of evidence against him.'

'What kind of evidence?'

'In the gun cabinet Lance had a couple of rifles of the same calibre that was used to shoot at Dr Young. They were checked at the time, and given the all clear but we're re-examining them. Just in case one of them was "missing" the first time around and has reappeared. He has quite a collection.'

'Lance is a gun nut,' I objected. 'It's hardly surprising he has got a few rifles, it's part of his masculinity thing. He wants people to think he's big and tough, like Jason Statham. I think you'll have to do a bit better than that.'

'How about the knife that was used to kill Dr Young?' he said. I opened my eyes wide in surprise. Slattery casually revealed this bombshell like a man putting down on the table a winning poker hand. Four aces.

'Seriously?' I was amazed. 'The actual murder weapon?'

He nodded. 'We found it when we searched his property, it was under the floorboards in his shed.'

'What did he say about that?' I thought someone must

have planted it there. Lance would almost certainly like to be regarded as the kind of man with whom it was dangerous to mess with, but underneath all those stupid, redundant muscles lurked a wimp. 'You'd better not mess with Lance, or you'll live to regret it', as no one had ever said. He'd no more knife someone than I would. I looked at Slattery. Not like him. I remembered that when I had first come to the village I had been told that he was not averse to beating suspects up. I disbelieved that, not because Slattery was not the sort, he most definitely was, but because these days it wouldn't help to get a conviction. I now knew Slattery to be a man of great integrity, but equally he was not someone you would like to face in a fight. He was as hard as nails.

'He claimed that someone must have put it there.' Slattery shook his head 'There's a lock on that shed with an electronic keypad. No signs of tampering. It's possible but unlikely. And he's got no alibi for the time when the murder happened. And he's on the record for having threatened her. So…'

He finished his coffee and got to his feet. 'I'd better go, I'm keeping you up.'

'I'll let you out.' I stood up too.

'I thought you'd like to know about Lance.'

'I appreciate it.' Our eyes met. I could smell the strong coffee that he had been drinking on his breath. I was aware that my heart was beating slightly faster than it should have done. I suddenly felt that something was very close to happening and I would be somehow powerless to help myself. Like in a dream.

The moment prolonged itself. Time seemed to stop.

There was a clock on the wall, an old-fashioned one with a pendulum that had belonged to my father. I could hear it tick. The noise seemed very loud indeed.

I walked over to the door and opened it, the cool evening air washed over me. The spell was broken.

'Good night, Detective Inspector.'

'Good night, Charlie.' He smiled again at me as he left. A rueful smile. Twice in one night.

I closed the door behind him and locked it. I leaned my back against it and stared at the ceiling. What was going on with me? Daydreaming about Roland and now nearly falling for Slattery.

I gently banged the back of my head against the cool glass panel behind me.

Christ, that was close.

Chapter Twenty-Four

The next day I had a visit from a Mr Hamilton. He arrived at half past nine. I'd already been up for two hours. I'd gone for a run, done some yoga and was now busy with my prep list. I'd decided to put gratin dauphinoise on the menu. It's a classic potato dish. To make it you slice potatoes very thinly, arrange them in a casserole dish, pour a mix of cream and milk over them and cook slowly in a low oven for about an hour and a half. It is slightly more complex than that, but not much.

I was slicing the potatoes thinly on a mandolin. I was smiling to myself as I did so. I still have some faded scars on the fingers of my right hand caused by that implement. The blade on a mandolin is like a razor.

When I was much younger I'd asked my then head chef, 'Chef, can you show me how to use the mandolin?' Its shape had fascinated me the moment I had set eyes on it. It was stainless steel, a long rectangle of smooth metal with a slit in it, like a pencil sharpener has. A metal strut folded out from underneath to support it so it formed a kind of triangle. You adjusted the height of the blade to the thickness you wanted, and slid whatever vegetable you were slicing down the slide of the smooth metal and it cut uniform, wafer thin slices out of things like potatoes and carrots. I so wanted to use it.

Marcus, the head chef at this hotel restaurant, was a lovely guy. Unflappable, good humoured, a joy to work with. He carried on working, ignoring my question.

'Chef, can you show me how to use the mandolin?' I pestered.

He glanced over at me.

'No.' Spoken with a finality that shut down any further conversation. And he went on with prepping meat.

Just a bald no. I felt hurt and continued doing whatever I was doing.

Later he came over to me.

'I'm sorry, Charlie, I was so short with you,' he apologised quietly. 'The thing is, in my time I've seen far too many mandolin-related accidents. I can't afford to take the time to drive you off to A&E to get sewn up.' He frowned. 'And besides that I hate the sight of blood.'

A while later I'd left his kitchen and was working somewhere else. I was feeling flush with money, I went online to Nisbets, the catering people, and bought my own mandolin. I was at home the first time I used it. I took it out of its box and set it up. It was so sleek and shiny. I peeled a couple of potatoes and took an exploratory swipe down the mandolin with one of them. It was effortless. It slid down past the recessed blade, leaving a wet, starchy patina on the smooth surface of the stainless steel and voila! I had a perfect slice. It was so thin it was practically translucent. I was so pleased with what I had achieved, it was almost magical. I could never have cut a perfect slice that thin with my knife. And I'm good.

Another deft movement of my wrist. The gleaming, silver metal was now slick with the juices leaching from the cut potato. It zoomed down the mandolin. Grinning now, like an idiot, I speeded up. Slice, slice, slice went the mandolin. In the back of my mind I seemed to hear someone saying, 'I've seen far too many mandolin-related accidents...' slice, slice, slice, it was such fun, slice AAAARGH!!!!

I looked down at my right hand. The tips of my first three fingers, index, middle and ring, were covered in blood, and then some. The potato had disappeared and instead of cutting root vegetable I'd sliced into myself. Red, red blood was everywhere. On the mandolin, the chopping board, the potato slices, me. It was horrible, incredibly painful and I felt incredibly stupid. It wasn't like I hadn't been warned. I wrapped my injured hand in a tea towel which rapidly turned red too and went in search of help.

Work for the next fortnight with my heavily bandaged hand was uncomfortable and problematic until the cuts had healed. Needless to say I had zero sympathy from my work colleagues, clumsy oaf was their attitude.

All of this passed through my head in the time it took Jess to inform me of the arrival of Mr Hamilton.

He was waiting for me in the restaurant. He was an oldish guy, thin and bald; what nature had started he'd finished himself with an electric razor. He was formally dressed in a dark, well-fitting suit. He looked quite formidable.

'I'm Nicholas Hamilton,' he said. 'I'm from Wykeham,

Harding and Anderson, the law firm, and we've been engaged to represent Lance Thurston.'

'And how might I be able to help you, Mr Hamilton?' I asked.

He smiled. It was a polite smile that did not reach the eyes. They remained hard, cold and evaluating. I thought he was rather frightening in a way. Maybe all those years of representing hard-core criminals in court.

'Please, call me Nicholas.'

'Okay, Nicholas, how can I help you?'

'My client wants to make you an offer.'

I wondered what on earth he was on about. Maybe he wanted his meals delivered to the prison. I'd heard that could be arranged, I didn't know how true it was.

'Mr Thurston has a high opinion of your abilities, Ms Hunter.'

Now it was my turn to say, 'Please, call me Charlie.'

'Well, Charlie,' that smile again, like the sun on a coffin handle, as I'd memorably heard it described once, 'my client feels that he needs someone to clear his name.'

'Isn't that your job?' I said.

'No,' he said as if talking to an idiot, 'no, it is not. My job is to represent my client in the judicial system. Mr Thurston wants someone actively working for him on the outside.'

'I see.'

'Like a private detective?' suggested Jess.

'Exactly,' he said with a wintry smile. 'I believe you've done it before.'

'How do you know?' I asked, astonished.

He smiled his wintry smile, 'I have my ear to the ground, Charlie.'

'That's true,' Jess said, butting in, 'she has. It's three hundred pounds a day, plus expenses.'

I stared at her in consternation. Was she my agent now? What she said may have been correct but I felt I was being railroaded by Jess.

Hamilton nodded. 'That sounds perfectly reasonable.' He stood up. 'I'll communicate to my client that you're willing to assist him and I'll call in tomorrow with a contract for you to sign.' He bent over and extended a hand which I shook in a bemused manner. He had a firm handshake and very cold hands.

'A pleasure to have met you, Charlie, I'll see you tomorrow.'

Chapter Twenty-Five

After he had gone, I glared at Jess. 'Are you crazy? I'm not a private investigator, I'm a chef, thank you very much.'

She looked at me levelly. 'Well, I'm your manager, aren't I?'

'Yes, of course you are.'

'Well, I'm also an MSc student at Warwick, aren't I? Not to mention dutiful daughter, and PA to Dr Siegfried Turner whom I have to walk on a daily basis. My point, Charlie, is that we all wear more than one hat these days. And let's face it, you've done this before.' She regarded me with calm eyes. 'I wasn't inventing anything when I said that, you've discovered a murderer and you've unmasked a blackmailer before now.'

'That's true.'

'So you are actually a PI, Charlie. Even if you refuse to recognise it. Like I said, this isn't the first time that you've done it – successfully I may add. If you walk like a duck, talk like a duck, then you probably are a duck.'

'I suppose you're right' – the money would come in very

handy – 'and I guess that I'll be able to afford to pay Murdo, assuming he's happy to stay on.'

'That's the spirit.' Jess looked around the restaurant. 'Well, I guess I had better get on with setting up, we've only got ten booked for lunch, so today shouldn't be too busy.'

I left her to it and went back to the kitchen. The money would come in extremely handy and Murdo was more than capable of taking my place. It would be nice to have a brief respite from cooking. It would also take my mind away from Rupert Bear and my dilemma with Andrea and the ghastly Mel Craig and her evil extortion attempts. If only it was she who had been stabbed.

My mind drifted back to Lance. Could he have killed her? I tried to imagine Lance as a ruthless murderer and failed. I could, however, imagine him panic-stricken with a blood-stained knife wondering how to get rid of it and stashing it in his shed while he tried to come up with a solution.

But right now, there was still cooking to be done. I took half a dozen cloves of garlic, smashed them with the flat of my knife and got rid of the skins, then chopped them finely. Leaning heavily on the blade, I crushed the garlic, adding a pinch of salt to make the mixture grittier, much easier to squish down into a smooth paste and then I mixed it with some butter at room temperature to make a garlic butter. That would go with the scallops that were on the lunchtime menu. I'd serve them garnished with chopped parsley and a little salad of chard and curly endive.

I checked on the potatoes that were still cooking away

in the oven, my gratin dauphinoise. When they were ready, in about half an hour, I would take out the heavy terrine that they were in, and when it was cool, place a weight on top to compress the potato and then I would be able to slice it up so I could portion it. I could then reheat it later. I was planning to serve it as an accompaniment to the lamb rump that I was going to put on the menu with a rosemary jus.

I started making a carrot cake next that was on as a dessert, when Murdo walked in.

'Murdo,' I said thoughtfully, 'if I could start paying you, could you work here for another month?'

He smiled. 'I'd be delighted tae work here for another month if that's okay with you.'

We shook hands solemnly and agreed on twenty pounds an hour plus tips, food and accommodation.

'I'm so glad, Charlie,' he said seriously, 'I love working with you. You're so calm in the kitchen.'

'I'm very flattered to hear it, but you're going to have to do quite a lot by yourself, I've taken on an outside job to pay for you.'

'Really? Who's that with, or is it more outside catering?'

I shook my head. 'Neither. You know Lance Thurston?'

'What, the loudmouth guy you did the catering for where you nearly got killed?'

'That's him.'

'What are you going to be doing for him this time? Personal chef?'

I shook my head. 'No, trying to keep him from being sentenced for a crime that he didn't commit.'

He looked at me wide-eyed. It was almost a perfect parody of surprise. 'And how do you do that?'

Good question. 'I really don't know, Murdo, I really don't know.' I put my knife down. 'But right now, I'm going to go for a walk. I need to think.'

I cleaned down, told Murdo to take the dauphinoise out when the timer went, ran upstairs, pulled my chef's whites off and threw on a T-shirt and some patterned running tights. I grabbed my running shoes from where they lived by the top of the stairs, trotted down them and out into the courtyard where I pulled them on. I slipped through the gate that was, as usual, unlocked. I still hadn't got round to beefing up security after the Rupert Bear doll incident. I made a mental note to check the packaging of the dry-store goods in case Mel had poisoned something the better to bolster her case against me.

I ran on to the common and saw Della with her dog walking in the opposite direction. She waved at me and threw a ball for the black animal who ran happily after it. It kind of reminded me of Francis in its carefree attitude to life.

At the crossroads at the top of the common I dithered and then took the road to Potter's Hill; I was going to go by Mel Craig's house. She'd passed my place the other day, maybe delivering Rupert. I had a sudden urge to do something similar, although in my case what I wanted to deliver was a brick through her window.

I ran past the layby where we'd hidden in the van when we had hacked into her computer, and there was her house. I thought of the information we had gleaned from her pc.

It had looked like the solution, but as Jess had pointed out I could hardly use it in court. It had after all been illegally obtained. If only we could make use of it somehow.

Mel's house was the last one before the village ended. The lair of the evil beast. There was a thick hawthorn hedge to one side. On the other side of the hedge, a field. The semi looked innocuous by day. Attached to the front door was a heavy old-fashioned knocker. I remembered a game we used to play when I was a young girl in North London, Knock Ginger Up. You'd ring a doorbell and run away. I ran up the path, lifted the knocker and slammed a quick tattoo, rat-a-tat-tat, then ran away. (I'm forty-four – I shouldn't be doing this). The noise had been incredibly loud, I'd put some serious welly into the banging. I hid round the corner of the hawthorn. Suck on that, I thought.

Nothing happened. No door opening, not a thing. She was obviously out. Then the noise of a van pulling up, the opening of doors, footsteps, a knock, I poked my head round the hedge. It was a delivery driver with a parcel.

'Hi,' I said.

He turned. 'Mel Craig?'

'Yeah.'

He handed me the cardboard parcel. 'Please sign.'

I squiggled something on his electronic pad, and he nodded thanks, got into his van and drove off. I ran a few metres along the road and disappeared up a footpath, clutching my stolen parcel. Petty revenge I know, but it felt so sweet.

Chapter Twenty-Six

Back home, I went upstairs with my parcel, well, technically Mel's parcel, but it was mine now. I opened it. Two books, both by someone called Aleister Crowley, *Magick in Theory and Practice* and *The Book of the Law*. A quick internet search confirmed the author's identity as a prominent black magician/Satanist/confidence trickster from the last century. It was more confirmation both of Mel Craig's horror/supernatural fascination, and quite probably whatever Mr Crowley had to say on Magick with a K would make its way into a Mel Craig novel like *Slave of Beelzebub* (that was another one of hers.) It also fed my own suspicion that I was being targeted by a woman with more than just a screw loose.

I put the books to one side. I certainly wasn't going to give them back. I toyed with the idea of giving them away. Would Help the Aged want them in their charity shop? I somewhat doubted it. Was demonology in vogue among the elderly? Eye of newt, toe of frog and a packet of Werther's Originals. You never know.

Anyway, fun as it had been to inconvenience Mel Craig,

I had work to do. I booted my laptop and started a new document labelled Suspects. Someone must have framed Lance, someone with access to either his house or his shed. Well, the first name that I wrote down was…

Well, who?

I couldn't believe Lance knew anyone who hated him enough that they might want to see him framed for murder. There were, however, two people who were local who may have wished him harm.

One was Mel Craig. Evil, blackmailing, devil-worshipping (?), horrible Mel. Ages ago she had threatened to sue Lance, maybe she had never forgiven him. What was it he had done? Bulldogs? That was right, he'd said she had a face like a bulldog licking piss off a nettle and she'd threatened to sue. Well, it seemed unlikely that she would kill someone purely to implicate him in the killing, but she was a possibility, however slim. Maybe all those horror movies had affected her brain. I have to say that there was quite a bit of wish fulfilment going on there; I really wanted her to be guilty, and, face it, it was possible. She had shown a great deal of ingenuity in gate-crashing his party solely to get some of my hair. Then there was the Rupert Bear voodoo doll thing, so maybe there was another agenda. I certainly wouldn't put anything past her.

Of course, there was the possibility that someone other than Mel had put the doll in my dry-store, but she was the only person around here who had it in for me. Someone else could have done it but the principle of Occam's razor, that the simpler explanation was the most likely, supported me.

Of course, it could also be revenge for Lance adding to her woes on the TherapyWhistleBlowers website. It was also possible that she had targeted Dr Young for the same reason. It would be very ingenious of her to have killed the academic and then pinned the blame on one of her enemies. In fact, the more I thought about it, the more I was beginning to like her as a suspect. And had she gate-crashed that party to decide on a possible future hiding place for a murder weapon? Thinking ahead?

Time for another suspect.

I wrote down the Bucks SOBs and their leader, Roland Sylvanus. The Save our Beeches group had put Lance at the top of their hit-list. Would they really have gone to all this trouble to silence Lance? I thought about Roland, dressed in his shorts and a T-shirt. Those sexy tattoos on his wiry arms. His... Stop it, Charlie, I said to myself, sternly. Concentrate.

If Mel Craig could infiltrate the birthday party in fancy dress, maybe he had too. I can remember thinking at the time he could slip into something, a costume – what about Rupert Bear? Rupert had been at Lance's shoulder at one stage of the evening. Had Roland also tried to kill me? Surely not. Would he murder someone to frame Lance to protect the beech trees? Then again, I recalled the demo he had organised outside Dr Young's talk. He had been gunning for her over somewhere called Priestfield Copse.

But, of course, it probably wasn't Roland in the bear suit. Roland fancied me, he wanted me hot and alive, not a frozen popsicle. I certainly didn't think it was Mel either. As well as the fact she would get nothing for me dead, she would have had to have somehow smuggled the costume in unnoticed, while dressed as a belly dancer, and changed into the costume somewhere. So I wrote down Rupert Bear. Rupert, whoever he was, had definitely tried to kill me at Lance's place, he had form as a homicidal ursine maniac. And if you can try to freeze an innocent woman to death in a chest freezer full of ice you're almost certainly capable of shooting and stabbing a lady academic and implicating Lance. Rupert must have known about the freezer, he had come prepared with a padlock, he obviously knew about Lance and his habits. He had either been invited to the party or had, like Mel Craig, gate-crashed it. He had taken the time to look around before attacking me, he could have done something that evening in advance to ensure he could gain access to the shed at a later date.

He was a bear who liked to think ahead.

I sighed and looked at what I had just written. Nothing screamed 'guilty'. The person I would most have suspected of framing Lance for murder would have been Dr Young, but she had ruled herself out by being killed. But her name set me thinking.

Now I had exhausted these possibilities, I came to what I thought was the most likely explanation. The killer had been someone who hated her and wanted to frame someone for the killing, that is, she was the intended victim all along, and the Lance-framing was entirely incidental, maybe opportunistic.

Sam Hickocks. He had reason to hate both Dr Susannah Young and Lance Thurston. He had been a victim of both of them. Directly, inasmuch as Dr Young had got him the sack, and indirectly, in that Lance was a notorious homo-phobe and had had a go at people like him on his podcast.

So, I had four people to consider.

I tapped my teeth with my pen. I suddenly thought of Della Peters, Lance's housekeeper. She might know some-thing. I added her down as another suspect. Quite what motive she might have had for framing Lance I didn't know, she seemed a huge fan, but she was in his house a great deal. I couldn't see why she would want to kill Dr Young either or think of how she could have got into her car to do so. I also found it hard to imagine her bypassing the keypad lock, she seemed hopeless with technology, but anything was possible.

Della was the easiest to reach. I thought I would run an appraising eye over her as a suspect and see if anything came up.

I had no contact number for her so on the off-chance I drove to Lance's house. Elmer's Pond was where wealthy people lived. In fairness, Hampden Green was hardly a poster boy for rural poverty (what with a Michelin star restaurant in it) but we did have social housing. Carefully hidden away. Elmer's Pond was forbiddingly exclusive. I rarely went there although once or twice I had run through it on my long runs.

I couldn't turn into the drive, the gate was shut. I parked my car in the road outside. It was fairly obvious I didn't live here, nobody who did would be driving an old Volvo estate. I walked up to the gate which was controlled by a keypad. There was an intercom next to it. I pressed it.

'Hello?' said a woman's voice.

'Della Peters? It's Charlie, Charlie Hunter the chef.'

'Oh, do come in.'

The gate swung open and I walked up the drive. Della was there to meet me at the front door.

'Hi, Charlie, come in.' She was dressed in jeans and a T-shirt, revealing her strong arms and was wearing pink Marigold gloves. There was her black cocker spaniel sitting at her heels with the breed's typical affectionate face and soulful eyes.

'It is Rand?' I asked, smiling at the dog; sometimes I'm bad with names and I wanted to make sure – dog owners can get upset if you forget their animal's name.

Della nodded proudly. 'That's her name.'

'Hello Rand,' I said and let her smell my hand which she started licking enthusiastically.

'I'm sorry, she's very friendly. What brings you here Charlie?'

I explained how Lance had hired me via his lawyer to clear his name. Della led me through to the kitchen and made me a cup of tea.

'Poor Lance,' she sighed. 'Of course he was framed, he wouldn't hurt a fly.'

'So you're still working for him?'

'Naturally.' She looked a bit shocked by the question. 'Lance needs his house looking after while he's away' – she made it sound like he was on holiday somewhere agreeable rather than banged up – 'he'll be out soon. I have every faith in British justice. They'll find out who killed that woman, just you wait and see.'

'You're very fond of Lance aren't you,' I remarked.

'Yes, he tells it like it is,' she said, emphatically, 'the country's going to the dogs but thank God we have someone prepared to stand up for decency... I think that's why he was framed, to hush him up. They didn't want to create a martyr so they tried to blacken his name. It stands to reason.'

'Who do you think might have done it? Who are "they"?'

To my relief, because I liked Della, she didn't blame Bill Gates or George Soros or even Big Pharma.

She shrugged. 'Lance has lots of enemies, any one of them could have done it but I think it was a man rather than a feminist. Probably the same man who shot at Dr Young in the field that time.'

'What makes you say that?'

'The method, shooting, stabbing, they are both very male, well, that's my opinion anyway. Probably these days I'd be laughed at, or arrested and put in prison for such old-fashioned thinking... but you asked me,' she said defiantly, as if I were going to report her to the thought police, 'and that's what I think.'

'How would a woman kill someone?' I asked, out of curiosity, 'in a way that's different from a man?'

'Poison,' Della said, with conviction. 'That's how women kill men, or run them over in their cars, or, if they were young and pretty, lure them to their deaths, like the mermaids do.'

'I see.' All that made sense. Dr Young hadn't been poisoned, crushed by a vehicle or died of misadventure panting after some hottie, aquatic or otherwise. Had to be a man then. 'Moving back to men, do you have anyone in mind particularly?'

Della nodded. 'Yes I do, two of them. One of them, I don't know the name, but I saw him on the camera doorbell. I took a screenshot of him on my phone.'

She took out her mobile and with maddening slowness – 'I'm sorry, I don't really understand technology' – found her Photos and then, 'here we are...'

She handed the old phone to me and I looked at a picture of a handsome, blond guy standing by the door. Then he disappeared inside.

'Do you know who it is?'

She shook her head. 'I bumped into him once before. I asked Lance about him then; Lance got a bit huffy, just said he was a business associate and then changed the subject, you know, really abruptly the way you do when you don't want to talk about something. And that, Charlie, is highly unlike Lance, the problem is usually to shut him up.'

'Was he at the party?' I was thinking of Rupert Bear once again.

'How would I know?' she said, pulling a face. 'It was fancy dress. If he was, I didn't see him. But he is someone who had access to the house and I think that makes him worth looking into. Maybe he has some kind of a hold over Lance. Blackmail,' she added dramatically.

Or maybe he was indeed a business adviser. Or, a thought struck me, Rupert Bear? He looked fairly bright, I had to say.

'He could have murdered the doctor and framed Lance, or at least shot her,' Della said.

'We could look through Lance's doorbell footage, to see if there are more pictures of him?'

Della shook her head. 'That camera only holds pictures for a fortnight, there won't be anything left.'

'Oh, well.' Then I asked, just to make sure, 'The police did check on Lance's guns didn't they?'

'Oh yes. The rifling didn't match the bullet that they found after Dr Young had been shot. If that's the right term... anyway, it wasn't his gun, but then why would it be? I wonder if maybe mystery man had something to do with it. Of course they've taken his guns away now for a second time.' She shook her head in disbelief. 'He didn't do it then, the situation won't have changed.'

'They think that the rifle used to shoot Dr Young may have been missing during the original check.'

Della snorted. 'What, and replaced later? How could that have happened? I'm sure I'd have noticed.'

Well, maybe, I thought. My mind drifted back to mystery man.

'Can you send me a copy of the man in the photo?' I asked.

'Sure...' she frowned at the phone, 'ummm, how...?'

'Can I have it?' I said. What was it with old people and technology? It wasn't exactly hard. 'I'll do it.'

I did so and gave her back the phone. 'You mentioned two men that you suspected?'

She nodded. 'There's that activist kid, the one who was demonstrating outside Lance's party. According to people I know in the village he's got a reputation for violence. He's involved with the hunt saboteurs and people say he was linked with an arson campaign against four-by-fours in Oxford, but, in fairness to him, I don't know if the arson bit's true. Also, whoever got into Lance's shed to plant that knife had to be able to deactivate his keypad, there's quite a few techy people, eco-nerds, in the SoBs. So, if you put together the violence and the know-how I think you've got a reasonable case for him as a suspect.'

She finished her tea. 'I hope that's been of help.'

I don't think it's Roland, I thought, he's too nice. 'Yes it has, thank you.'

As I left the house I thought I now have a plan. Tomorrow I would have to take Lucy to the station. I decided I would drive her to Oxford and visit Sam Hickocks.

It took about an hour to drive from my place to the Park and Ride car park on the outskirts of Oxford. I enjoyed chatting to Lucy on the way down, she was fun to be with and had a scabrous sense of humour which occasionally left me, veteran of years in a kitchen, slightly shocked at times. She was still on holiday but wanted to check up on the college kitchen to make sure everything was running okay during her absence. She asked me if I wanted to come along and I accepted with alacrity.

I'd never been to an Oxford college before, it was more or less as I had imagined it. There was an arched gateway that you went through, a Porter's Lodge where a guy in a uniform kept a vague eye on the comings and goings past a window, there was a space inside where students could pick up mail. I can't imagine that would be used too much these days since it would mostly be electronic. Then we walked into the college itself.

St Anselm's was gratifyingly old. A typical college as seen

on TV. Honey-coloured stone, low-rise, green lawns and a quadrangle with low clipped box hedges surrounded by cloisters. It was very quiet.

'There's not many students around,' I said.

'Term doesn't begin until October,' Lucy said. 'Michaelmas Term they call it, one of their poncy names.' As we passed by numbered stairways, I suddenly wondered would we have wanted to go to university, as opposed to catering college. I put that question to Lucy.

'Nah, the students are all effing middle-class snobs.' She laughed. 'They don't want people like you and me, Charlie, they want their own kind. Like I said, they ain't working-class and I don't mean that they are rich kids with money from Eton, they don't want the proletariat like you and me effing and jeffing... we're the great unwashed... we're here to take orders and skivvy, not like them who can sit on their fat arses, work from home and rake in the dosh.'

'Do you mean we'd lower the tone?'

'I fucking would,' Lucy said proudly.

We reached the end of the cloisters and turned and walked past a chapel and towards a small red-brick building.

'This is the dining hall, we'll go in the students' entrance.'

We walked up some broad steps and through a large arched door, St Anselm's was big on arches, and into a large, oak-panelled refectory. There was a kind of dais, like a low stage, with a long table on it. Lucy pointed at it.

'That's High Table where the dons eat. Evening meals here are a bit like posh school dinners but waiter service. You get what you're given basically. At lunch we set up trestle tables and serve it canteen style. There's a separate

211

dons' dining room that's used for formal dinners. Restaurant quality. It's pretty good food though I say so myself.'

She led me behind the scenes through a swing door into the kitchens where half a dozen chefs were hard at work. I could see them jump to attention as Lucy came into sight, but there were a lot of smiles, they were genuinely pleased to see her. You can sense loyalty in a brigade, it's generally a good sign. I've worked in some kitchens where the head chef was hated, universally reviled; they were terrible places to have to work in.

Lucy showed me her walk-in fridge (not as nice as mine, I was pleased to note) and was leading me over to her office when one of the chefs came over.

'Excuse me, Chef, the Master would like a word.'

Lucy frowned. 'What the fuck does he want?'

'I dunno' – the girl shrugged – 'he didn't say, he's out there in the dining room.'

There was silence as we digested this information.

'Oh well, better go and see what he wants before I go.' She asked the girl, 'How many have we got for lunch?'

'There's only nineteen students booked in,' she said, 'and six faculty.'

'What are you giving them?'

'Hunter's chicken, rice or mash and the veg option is roasted cauli steak with barbecue sauce.'

'Fine,' Lucy turned to me, 'that sound okay to you?'

'Yeah,' I said. 'Hunter's chicken, is that chicken in tomatoes and red wine?'

'Sure is,' said the young chef, grinning.

I nodded. Personally I'd have called the dish Chicken

Cacciatore. Odd that you wouldn't I thought, in a place where the clientele were middle-class students, but it wasn't my menu. Perhaps that's what the Master wanted to discuss. Nomenclature.

'Come on Charlie,' said Lucy, 'you can meet my boss.'

I can't say that meeting her boss was high on my wish list, but I really had no say in the matter and I could hardly refuse. We walked out of the kitchen back into the dining room. There was a tall, bald friendly looking man in a two piece suit and next to him a slim, commanding looking woman with short white hair.

'Hello, Charlie,' said Anna Bruce, smiling.

Chapter Twenty-Seven

'Hello, Anna,' I said. She was dressed for business in a black power suit and a white blouse with a gold necklace and matching earrings. As always she looked very much in control, as if she were in charge of the college and not the man next to her. An effortless projection of power.

The Master proffered his hand. 'I'm Richard Houseman, Master of this college.'

'Pleased to meet you,' I said. Lucy, standing beside me, looked thoroughly baffled.

'Did you want to see me, Master?' she asked, almost plaintively.

'Just to confirm that you're back tomorrow,' Houseman said, placatingly. 'We've got that alumni dinner and I just wanted to make sure that everything was in order for it. The menu looks great...'

'Oh yeah, it's all in hand,' Lucy said, looking relieved now that she knew why he wanted a word and not that there had been some unforeseen calamity. 'I'll be in from breakfast time onwards if you want to check on any details...'

'I'm sure it will be fine,' he said, 'knowing it's in your capable hands. Now, can I borrow your guest for an hour or so?'

'Sure.' Lucy looked totally mystified now, it was a feeling that I shared too. Why did he want to see me?

'I'm going home in a minute or two, Charlie,' Lucy smiled. 'It was nice to have met you. Keep an eye on Murdo for me.'

'Bye, Lucy, anytime you want to stay…'

Lucy's broad back turned to us as she disappeared through the swing door into the kitchen. Richard Houseman turned to me. 'Can I offer you a coffee and an explanation?'

'By all means.'

The three of us walked back out of the refectory and across to a porch at the corner of the Inner Quad where a sign read, 'Master's Residence'. Houseman opened the door and ushered us in.

We sat drinking coffee (not as good as mine I was pleased to note) and looking out at the pleasant view of the college lawns which were clipped, manicured and mown (in that clever, stripy way) to an almost manic degree of perfection. We had a plate of Jaffa cakes. Sophistication, I thought, biting into one. It had been ages since I'd had a Jaffa cake.

'Anna tells me that you're here investigating the murder of Dr Susannah Young, Charlie, is that correct?' he asked, with interest.

I nodded, chewing vigorously to mask my surprise that Anna Bruce knew what I was up to. 'That's correct,' I said, just about managing to avoid spluttering.

216

He sipped his coffee. 'Well, Anna has asked that I help you, so ask me anything you want.'

This was unexpected. My mind went blank. In desperation I asked, 'What did you make of her?'

He smiled. 'De mortuis nil nisi bonum, et cetera...'

'I'm sorry?' What was he on about?

Anna came to my rescue. 'He means you shouldn't speak ill of the dead, Charlie.'

'Ah... But?' I had sensed a definite 'but' camouflaged behind the Latin.

'But I couldn't stand her,' he said. 'She was given a three year contract by my predecessor and, quite frankly, she didn't deserve it.'

'Why not?' I asked.

'Her work was sloppy,' he said. Then he frowned. 'Mind you, we could say the same about several other dons but she was really a media person who used academia to boost her career. Rather than the other way round, which is more usual here. There was also a whiff of the casting couch about her appointment.'

'She used sex to get the job?' I asked. Dr Young may have been entering her seventh decade but she most certainly was not going gently into that good night. She'd been a hottie at twenty, still going strong apparently.

'It was one theory,' said the Master, 'it didn't really matter. What did matter was, when I let it be known we weren't going to be extending her contract, she threatened me with legal action, that she would take me to court over sexual discrimination and ageism. I was up for the fight but unfortunately we have a particularly spineless HR department, supine bastards, and they were leaning on me to either renew her contract or authorise a massive pay-off, neither of which I was prepared to do. But as she had excellent media connections the HR Department, probably rightly, said we'd be flayed alive in the court of public opinion...'

'You didn't kill her, did you, Richard?' I asked. His tone was light-hearted but I could sense real vitriol behind those words.

'No,' he shook his head, 'but part of me was shamefully relieved that she was gone. To be honest, the timing of her murder couldn't have been better as far as I was concerned.'

I have to admit, I'd felt that way myself. Shamefully relieved. I'd seen the predatory way that she had looked at Jess, the horrible way that she had betrayed Esther and maybe the disdainful way she had treated me, the intellectual's scorn of the manual worker, yes that had rankled too.

'I kind of know what you mean,' I said.

Richard looked at me gratefully. I think his conscience had been, if not tormented, at least pricked, by his reaction to her death.

'Tell me about Priestfield Copse,' I said, remembering Roland and the SOBs' protest outside the village hall at Hampden Green.

'One of the things about Oxford colleges are bequests.' Richard sighed. 'Don't get me wrong,' he hastened to assure me, just in case, 'but if you decide to leave St Anselm's a legacy, please do it by all means, but in cash... we get stuff like fossils bequeathed to us, or property, which while we're very grateful, can cause headaches.'

'Don't worry,' I said, 'Cancer Research are the main

beneficiary of my will.' It was true, they would get the lion's share, and a small legacy for Francis; he drove me crazy, but he was kind of lovable. That reminded me, I still hadn't bought him that suit I'd promised him.

'Anyway,' Richard carried on, 'Priestfield Copse is a small area of woodland in the north of Oxford and it's of very little significance. I moved a motion to sell it to developers, for community, low-income housing. The motion to sell was supported by faculty and then Dr Young said we were underselling it, financially, and all but accused me of taking a bung to accept the low bid. She said that she'd done research and we could get more money for the college.'

'Was that true?'

'Yes it was, but that plan was for a luxury development with ten per cent rather than eighty per cent of homes marked for low-income families. The rich are well enough served in Oxford with houses already.'

'And how did this go down?'

He sighed. 'The faculty aren't saints. Some were persuaded by the increased revenue, some by the fact that she was an effective lobbyist, one or two because they don't like me as a person and a couple she bullied or blackmailed into supporting her. Then a student called Roland Woods claimed that she was being bribed by the developers and it became a thing. He was particularly incensed because these developers had destroyed local woodland on the outskirts of Oxford last year in a separate housing project. It was very controversial'

Things clicked in my head. 'Is Roland Woods also known as Roland Sylvanus?'

'Exactly; he graduated last summer.' Well, that explained the demo outside her meeting.

'So was Dr Young being bribed by the developers, in your opinion?' I asked.

'Yes, I believe she was. Woods said she had been promised a house on the development and that he could prove it. Now, things get interesting here because he also claimed, according to sources of mine, there was never an official complaint, that she tried to coerce him into a sexual relationship.'

Anna Bruce had hitherto remained silent, now she remarked drily, 'The very charge that she levelled against Sam Hickocks. It would not surprise me if that's what motivated her accusation, it's very common to accuse other people of the very crime you're guilty of yourself, it's called projection.'

Richard Houseman put his cup down; it was with a kind of definitive flourish that I knew marked the end of the meeting.

'Indeed, Anna,' he nodded. 'So there you have it, Charlie, that's what I can tell you about Susannah. I hope it will help.'

'I'm sure it will,' I said. The more I learned about Dr Young the more unsavoury she seemed. It wouldn't have surprised me to learn that she had accepted the invite from Esther specifically to fuel an article to ridicule her and her beliefs.

'I'm afraid that we'll have to leave it there,' the Master said. 'I've got a faculty meeting starting soon.'

We stood up and he showed us to his door. He turned

to Anna Bruce. 'Anna, thank you so much for coming, I look forward to your recommendations.'

'A pleasure, Richard, I'll be in touch.'

We walked back through the college grounds to the gate and the main road.

'Did you know I was coming here?' I asked her.

Anna smiled. 'Kind of. I had a premonition that you would be here, and Richard had invited me a while ago because he wanted my advice on choosing a successor to a member of staff who's leaving; he had a shortlist and wanted my input. He wants to avoid appointing someone as problematic as Dr Young. Richard's off to pastures new, Australia to be precise, he's had enough of Oxford, but he's very conscientious. He wants to choose a good person for the job before he leaves. So I killed two birds with one stone.'

I looked at the self-contained woman walking beside me. I was always slightly envious of Anna Bruce, I admired her poise and her self-confidence hugely. She was the kind of woman I aspired to be. She seemed wise, self-confident, beholden to no one, a person in her own right who did not need to define herself by any role in society. I suppose in her own way she was a kind of seer, or shaman. She seemed to make her own rules and her own fate. Unlike me, I felt buffeted by events. Rudderless in the sea of life.

'How did you know to look for me in the kitchen?'

She laughed and shook her head, frowning at me in amused disbelief. 'You're you, Charlie, where else would I find you? In the college library?'

She stopped on the pavement and pointed across the

street. 'Sam Hickocks' shop is over there,' she said, 'good luck.'

She waved goodbye and I watched her with affection as she turned away and walked confidently down the street towards the city centre.

Chapter Twenty-Eight

The Freedom Deli was a lovely shop, no two ways about it. I'm a bit of a connoisseur of food shops, obviously I suppose given my job, but some are truly memorable. I remember a fish shop, a rough stone floor, breeze-block walls, a roller door open to the elements, in a small fishing village in the west coast of Scotland under dreich, grey skies. The fresh fish, still bright-eyed and odourless from the boats in the harbour below, lying in boxes of ice, while the two guys who ran it cleansed and filleted the fish at a trough of running water. I remember a superb bakery in Avignon in baking sunshine, spitting distance from the ancient walls of the town of the Popes, where Andrea and I eschewed the ridiculously priced breakfast available in our boutique hotel and bought croissants, rolls, pain aux raisins and beignets, several thousand calories' worth probably, but I was younger and slimmer and more reckless in those days and didn't need to care, and ate them in the early morning heat of a local park. I remember a fantastic covered market somewhere in Turin, the most incredible selection of charcuterie I had ever seen in Italy. A street in

Tokyo that sold nothing but stuff for catering; plates and ceramics (if only I had the money), mouth-watering displays of knives, hardware and plastic recreations of food that you could display outside your restaurant to lure customers in.

Sam's place was like that inasmuch as it was a delight on the eye and balm to the soul. It was clearly divided into sections, vegan, vegetarian, cheese and meat products. There was a small selection of expertly baked bread available and a bijou dining area consisting of four tables. This was presided over by a sensible looking girl who had shoulder length braided hair with coloured beads worked into it, standing behind a counter, making filled sandwiches; rare roast beef with horseradish and cornichons, brie and fig chutney, beetroot gravadlax on rye and a small side of homemade piccalilli, were the specials of the day chalked on a board.

She smiled at me, came out from behind the counter and sat me down at the only unoccupied table near the counter. I had the brie with the fig chutney on a half baguette with butter from Somerset. It was excellent as was the espresso.

When I was finished and she was clearing my table I asked if Sam was about.

'Yeah, he's in the back, who's asking?'

'Me,' I said and gave her one of my business cards that I use for catering. She glanced at it and said, 'I'll go and see if he's free.'

A little while later she returned.

'He's free.' She led me round the back of the counter and into the rear of the shop. There, behind a desk in a small office, was a good-looking guy in his thirties. If I were a film director and had to make a war movie very quickly I would have snapped Sam Hickocks up as a Nazi tank commander immediately. He was theatrically handsome with swept back blond hair and piercing blue eyes. But that wasn't what made me stare at him so intently. Sam Hickocks was the mystery man from the camera footage of Lance's house. And, just maybe, Rupert Bear.

'Charlie Hunter?'

'Indeed,' I said.

'I'll get back to the shop,' the girl said.

'Thanks, Hannah...' he turned his attention back to me. 'How can I help you?'

'I'm a chef by trade,' I began, I thought that might soften his heart as we both worked in the food trade. Kindred spirits and all. 'But I'm investigating the death of Dr Susannah Young.'

He gave me a thin smile, he looked seriously unimpressed. Maybe he didn't feel we were kindred spirits after all.

'Why would you want to do that?' he asked. 'If you think I did it, you're wasting your time, I was doing a cheese and wine party at St John's the night she died.' He frowned, 'surely finding the killer is the police's job.'

'It is,' I said. 'They've arrested the podcaster Lance Thurston. I don't think he did it.'

'Do you know him?' he asked, surprised.

I nodded. 'I've worked for him, I catered his birthday party.'

'Then you'll know that Lance is no friend of the gay community. He's quite homophobic.'

Well, I wondered, and what were you doing ringing his doorbell? That sounded very double-entendre even as I thought it. Roland rose to my mind. As did Anita Ward singing 'You can ring my bell'. I pushed these thoughts away and re-phrased it in my mind. Why were you at his house then?

'Do you know Lance?' I asked.

There was a beat, a momentary pause in the conversation. Then, 'No, I can't say that I do.'

Liar, I thought.

'Well, leaving him out of the picture,' I said, 'I was wondering if you had any idea who might have killed Dr Young? I believe you knew her quite well.'

'Like who?' he asked. An air of hostility had mysteriously appeared, like gas seeping in from somewhere. It was obvious he had no wish to talk about Lance or anything connected with him, such as the death of Susannah Young.

'Like, oh I don't know, one of her colleagues, a student... I was just wondering...'

'I'm sure you were, dear,' he said, sarcastically, emphasising the 'dear'. 'Now, why don't you get back to your pots and pans, and leave the crime-solving to the professionals.'

I looked at him sadly. Before I had arrived, I had been so sure we were going to be on the same wavelength. Both of us had been treated with contempt by Dr Young, (maybe I was being oversensitive in my recollection of the way she had looked at me, coloured as it was by what I had subsequently learned about her), both of us worked in the food business. I'd felt, mistakenly, we would have things in common. Now, not only had he lied to me, here I was now being rudely patronised. I was going to turn on my heels with a crushing remark, but to be honest I couldn't think of one.

I decided to leave with what dignity I could.

'I'm sorry you feel that way,' I said, haughtily, 'I'll see myself out.'

I walked down a couple of side streets away from the deli and found myself in front of a beautiful, ornate circular building that my phone identified as the Radcliffe Camera. I got my phone out and called Lucy.

'Hi, Lucy, do you know a gay bar in the centre of town?'

She laughed down the phone. 'Getting itchy feet are you, Charlie, want to see how the other half live?'

'No,' I said without elaborating.

'Okay, then, where are you?'

'The Radcliffe Camera.'

'You won't find any action there, darling. Good job you called me. What kind of gay bar are you looking for?'

'The kind that Sam Hickocks' boyfriend that you told me about drinks in. That kind of gay bar.'

'Paul Whitten, yeah, well, there's a pub called the Blacksmiths just off the High Street, near St Peter's College, you could try there. I know Sam used it, so you never know. But if not, I'll ask around for you.'

I found the pub easily enough and looked at my watch. I walked in. It was nearly 2 o'clock and it was quiet, there were just a few men inside drinking. They looked at me curiously and then turned back to their conversations or phones.

I bought myself a Diet Coke and sat by the window looking out at the tourists walking by. I thought about my morning. I thought about Lance. Then, at half past two, Hannah walked in.

She didn't notice me; she walked up to the bar and got a white wine. She chatted to the barman, they obviously knew each other. She turned around, saw me and did a double take. She came over to my table,

'It's you, isn't it, from the shop?'

'It is,' I said, 'Charlie Hunter.'

'You're a chef aren't you?' she smiled, she had a great smile. I admired her looks. Great hair too, some of the braids in different colours contrasted well with her very dark skin.

I nodded. 'That's right, chef proprietor.'

Her face softened. 'That must be wonderful.'

'It has its moments,' I said, drily.

'Mind if I join you?' she asked.

'Please do...' I said, making a by all means gesture with my left hand.

She sat down opposite me and leaned forward so I could see down her cleavage, which was impressive. She had a great body.

'So,' she said, 'how do you like my local?'

I smiled. 'It's very nice...'

'So are you, Charlie...' I felt a slight pressure on my ankle from her foot. I sighed; Hannah was nothing if not direct.

'I'm sorry, Hannah,' I said, 'I'm not available.' Which I suppose was true.

'Pity,' she said, leaning back in her seat, and eyeing me speculatively. 'So what are you doing here?'

'Right now I'm looking for Paul Whitten.'

'Paul, what, Sam's ex!' she sounded incredulous. 'Why?'

The real reason was that I wanted more information on Sam. I was now very suspicious of Sam Hickocks and his refusal to engage with me. I guess, too, I was resentful at him turfing me out of his shop the way he had.

'I think he might be able to shed some light on the death of a woman called Susannah Young,' I explained. 'Do you know Paul?'

'Yes I do. We used to share a flat. He introduced me to Sam when they were together.'

'They're not anymore?'

'No.' She shook her head.

'Do you know his address?'

'Yeah. So you're really going to visit him?' she laughed incredulously. 'You'd better take some drugs with you then.'

'Why's that?'

'That's Paul's main interest in life. I moved out because he never lifted a finger around the house and they split up because Sam couldn't stand his addictions anymore. But yeah, I'll give you his address.'

I got my phone out and she sent me his telephone number and flat address.

'Give me fifty quid,' she said, quite bluntly. I sighed, got out my purse and gave her two twenties and a ten. I was a bit disappointed in Hannah, it seemed kind of cheap to be taking money from me for information. I had expected better from her.

She walked over to the bar and spoke to the barman who nodded and then she came back. She handed me a small rectangular piece of folded white paper, about five by two cm.

'What's this?' I asked.

'Coke,' she said. 'Paul will talk to you now. Your only problem will be shutting him up.'

She stood up and gave me another piece of paper with a number written on it.

'What's this?'

She smiled. 'That's my number, just in case you change your mind about your availability.'

She looked deep into my eyes, raised her eyebrows meaningfully and turned and left the pub.

Chapter Twenty-Nine

Paul Whitten lived in the kind of street where someone with a drug problem might be expected to live. It was a street of terraced houses in urgent need of attention. The woodwork on windows was peeling or rotting, the tiny front gardens were a mess. Gates sagged on hinges, weeds grew in the gutters. I suspected that the owners of the houses were buy-to-let landlords whose tenants were students and they had zero interest in looking after the houses. They were bad enough on the outside, I shuddered to think what they were like inside. Well, I would find out soon enough.

I'd texted him earlier to say I would be around. I'd described myself as a friend of Sam's and I had something that I thought belonged to him. I hoped that would be enough to pique his interest. I was also relying on the fact that people with big drug problems tend to have significant lacunae in their memories. Jess had taught me the meaning of the word 'lacuna' –gap – and I was determined to use it more often. In this intellectual town where the deli owner had a doctorate and Lucy's boss quoted Latin, I was determined to use it. If only I had thought to trot it out at St Anselm's. During a lacuna in conversation.

Number forty-eight was particularly egregious, another posh word for shocking. One of the panes of glass in the door was broken and replaced with cardboard. The front garden was a tangled mass of unhealthy shrubs and plants in a Darwinian fight with each other for space and light. The curtains in the front room window were drawn, the glass filthy.

I texted I was here and banged on the door. I heard footsteps coming down the stairs and the door opened.

'Hi, do you want to come in?'

I followed Paul Whitten into the front room. It wasn't quite as bad as I had feared. It was untidy but not squalid. Paul himself looked in surprisingly reasonable condition. I was expecting some sort of tottering junkie. This was far from the case. He was small and lean, sharp featured and good-looking, with pierced ears and fine blond hair, slightly floppy and in need of a wash. He had thin lips and very blue eyes. There was a kind of mischievous, humorous glint in them. I could see why maybe Hannah had put up with him as a flatmate and Sam as a boyfriend, until his drug-fuelled behaviour made them both throw in the towel. He waved me to a grotty looking sofa and I sat down, he followed suit opposite.

'So, you're a friend of Sam's and you've got something that belongs to me?' he said brightly.

'Yeah,' I nodded, 'this...'

I handed him the package containing the coke, he looked at me suspiciously and opened it, wetted a finger, tasted it and grinned.

'Oh yeah, come to daddy,' he said softly. The coffee-table in front of us had a drawer which he opened and, ignoring me, he pulled out a mirror and a razor blade and chopped himself out a line which he snorted up, blinked several times then sniffed loudly.

'Oh, my days, that's much better… where do I know you from?'

Now that I was assured of his good humour I explained what had brought me to him. He had another line and said, 'Yeah, I knew Dr Young and Roland too, come to that. He's a nice guy, bit obsessed with Green issues, you know, saving the planet, trees, all that shit… quite a sexy guy too and he's as strong as fuck…'

Roland hadn't impressed me as being 'strong as fuck' when I had met him.

'Really?' my voice registering my doubt.

'Oh, yeah.' He paused to do some more coke then raised his eyes from the mirror. 'You should see him with his shirt off, he does calisthenics…'

'What on earth is calisthenics?' I asked.

'It's like gymnastics, using your body-weight to exercise. There's loads of it on Instagram'

A wistful, faraway look came into his eyes. I recognised the look, it was more or less how I felt when I thought of Roland. He continued, 'He and the Cal Soc, the calisthenics society gave a display on the college lawn. I think that's when Dr Young creamed her pants and became obsessed with him.'

'So they were having an affair?' This would have been what Richard Houseman had been talking about.

233

'In her dreams,' he laughed. 'She was a real bunny boiler, like I said, obsessive, and when persuasion failed, coercion took over, real example of tooth and claw capitalism.'

'So what happened?'

Paul lit a cigarette and squinted at me through the smoke. 'Do you know Roland?'

'Well,' I said cautiously, 'I've met him a couple of times, but, no, I don't really know him.'

'You know how it is with people, they say shit like, "I'll kill him", or, "if I'd been there I would have hit him", well, Roland actually does stuff like that. In freshers' week I saw him start a bar fight, I couldn't believe it... he hit this guy smack in the face' – his own was a mix of excitement and concern – 'I'd never seen such a thing in real life.'

I nodded, I knew what he meant. People like that have a huge advantage over the majority of non-violent people, they actually follow through on threats which the majority don't. For most people a threat is just an item on a wish list, seemingly not for Roland.

'And that all started over a remark about Just Stop Oil being a pain in the arse. So,' Paul said, 'when he joined the Hunt Saboteurs and Extinction Rebellion I wasn't that surprised. He had to leave Extinction Rebellion because he slapped a girl leader. He accused her of being a middle-class, Mummy's girl, Tik-Tok influencer who'd joined the movement to gain likes on her page. I think everyone agreed he had a point, Jemima was a huge pain the arse, but he hit her.'

'Whoa,' I said, slightly incredulously, 'Roland actually hit her?'

'That's what I heard,' Paul said, confidently. 'Then, coming back to your original question, I don't know what happened. I'm guessing Dr Young made a pass at him and he refused but she bragged she'd had him. Anyway, when he'd heard she was claiming she'd slept with him, he stormed round there, put the boot into her front door and read the riot act to her. I don't think he actually used violence but the threat was certainly there, she must have been shitting herself...'

'What happened after that?' I asked.

'Well, it worked. Dr Young backed down on the claims that she'd made, said it had been a misunderstanding, words had been misconstrued... the usual bullshit. She didn't want to go to the police about the threats and the damage, she was worried it would come out what she'd been up to.'

'So Roland is violent towards women?' I wanted to get this clear.

Another line, another insight from Paul.

'No, that would be unfair.' He shook his head. 'I think Roland is prepared to use violence if you get in his way, and what's wrong with that? Nietzsche would have approved, and other political thinkers.' He smiled. '"Not a single problem of the class struggle has ever been solved in history, except by violence", as Lenin said.' He added complacently, 'Maybe you can tell I did PPE.'

I was now seriously beginning to wonder if maybe Roland had killed Dr Young and then framed Lance for it as a way to stop him from building his helipad. As Lenin had suggested. It would have killed two birds with one stone, revenge for Priestfield Copse and preventing an eco-crime.

It would have been easy for him to have got to Dr Young. She would almost certainly have stopped the car if he'd flagged her down. I could imagine him leaning in the car window, 'Susannah, I want to apologise for my behaviour...' then the murder followed by planting the knife at Lance's.

Well, Paul had certainly given me something to think about.

'One last question,' I said. 'Lance Thurston.'

'That bastard,' Paul said with feeling.

'You don't like him?' I wasn't that surprised. Lance being quite publicly homophobic.

'Of course I don't bloody like him! That opinionated, bald, knobhead stole my boyfriend!'

'Sorry?' I said, thinking I'd misheard. Had he just said what I thought he'd just said? Lance, gay?

'I mean,' Paul said, slowly, with emphasis, 'Lance was sleeping with my boyfriend.'

I stared at him in a pantomime of disbelief. Had the world gone mad?

'Oh yeah, believe it babes,' Paul confided to me, 'our Lance is secretly gay.'

Chapter Thirty

I drove thoughtfully and slowly home from Oxford. Later that evening I went out for a drink in the Three Bells with Jess to discuss my day. I felt that by telling her about events it might click things into perspective in my own head. It certainly had been an eventful Wednesday.

First of all I confessed my theft of the books from the previous day. Jess rolled her eyes in disbelief.

'What if she'd caught you?' she groaned.

'Jess, I think I would have been delighted. At the time I was spoiling for a fight...'

'Well, thank God nothing came of it,' she said, relieved. We moved on to other things and I told her about what I had learned concerning Dr Young and her background.

'So, Dr Young is not the woman I thought she was,' Jess said with a certain amount of sadness.

'I'm afraid not, Jess. Our idols have got feet of clay.' I was thinking of the mindfulness woman, Melanie Craig, or Doctor Melanie Thomas as she had first appeared to me in her guise of spiritual guru.

'I suppose it's not entirely surprising,' Jess said, 'people are complicated aren't they? I mean, just because you're a good person politically doesn't necessarily make you a good person morally.'

'Well, that is of course true,' I said. I think we've all had enough of judging people's worth by the opinions they profess on social media. The trouble is it's hard to ignore your reviews on the social media outlets. Back in the day your restaurant review would be from the local paper and if you were very lucky a magazine or newspaper. Now you're only a click away from a one star review from someone who might not like your car park, the font of your menu or the way your waiter looks.

'So I guess you're going to make Roland a suspect for her death?'

'I'll have to, Jess.' I thought of his curly, dark hair, his boyish features, his full lips. God, I hoped it wasn't him. 'I've learnt he's capable of violence to women and seemingly he is very strong, so he could easily have overpowered her and stabbed her.'

'And what about Lance?' She shook her head in disbelief. 'Being secretly gay, who could have seen that coming?'

'Oh, I don't know, Jess, people always say, don't they, that people who moan about gay people are secretly gay themselves…'

'Well, they might say that,' she said, dubiously, 'who knows how true it is though.'

'The curious thing is,' I mused, 'that if anything, this gives him a reason for killing her, more than one actually. It could be that he wanted revenge for the way that she treated Sam Hickocks, driving him out of the college, or it could be that she had found out his dirty little secret and was going to out him as gay.'

'Would that have mattered,' Jess asked, disbelievingly, 'in this day and age?'

'I don't know. I think that most of his fans are reactionary old fogeys so maybe it would.'

'Or it might gain him a new group of fans,' Jess said. 'Face it, the old ones must all be dying off from natural causes.' Don't let Della hear you say that, I thought. She carried on. 'What are you going to do anyway?'

'Ask him,' I said. I continued, 'And then there is Paul Whitten. Maybe he framed Lance for running off with his boyfriend?'

'From what you told me about him that seems most unlikely; you may as well suspect the Master of the College for wanting to get rid of a potential embarrassment.'

I smiled. 'I guess I would have done if he hadn't been about to leave to take up a job somewhere else, so I don't think he was that invested in the college.'

Just then Bryony came in and headed over to us. 'Oh God,' muttered Jess. She was no fan of Bryony. She stood up.

'Hello, Bryony, I'm afraid I'm just going…'

Bryony's face fell. 'Oh, that's a shame, can't you…' she was obviously very disappointed.

'No, I've got to drive my mum to the vet's, Siegfried's not well.' Siegfried was the Turner family's Giant Schnauzer; it was not only a trump card in the game of excuses, it was a stroke of genius on Jess's part to think of it.

Bryony's face softened. 'Oh God, I hope he's okay.'

'I'm sure he is,' Jess was pulling on her coat, 'but we don't want to take any chances. Even though he is a Doctor himself. Dr Siegfried Turner.'

Bryony watched with concern as she left the pub, 'I hope he's okay, he's a lovely dog.' She frowned. 'What did she mean by saying he's a Doctor? I don't understand.'

'It's...' it seemed overly complicated to explain. 'It's a thing...' I said somewhat lamely.

She nodded. 'Cool. Anyway, how are you, Charlie?'

'I'm fine... do you want a drink?'

'Mmm, lager please.'

I went to the bar and got her a half and came back to our table. Bryony was wearing low cut jeans so I could see her pierced navel, with a silk blouse thrown over a scoop top. She had large, hooped silver earrings on and an expensive looking pearl necklace.

I thought I would find out a little more on Roland.

'The other day I was talking to someone who knew Roland. He told me that he has a history of violence towards women.'

'Well, that's rubbish,' she said, emphatically.

'He said he slapped an Extinction Rebellion supporter...'

'Oh my God,' she said, angrily for Bryony, 'that's such bollocks. I was there. That privileged cow, Jemima – what kind of a name is that! – attacked him, at a policy meeting. Not the other way round. She was giving it all this about how wonderful she was, and Roland was like, that's a load of bullshit, and she was like, no it's not, you dick, and he was like, well it's true and then she went ballistic and went for him, he was trying to defend himself.'

'Oh,' I said. Bryony's cheeks were flushed, she was very cross.

'The long and the short of it was that she was asked to leave the meeting, not him...' she angrily drank some lager. 'He's been misrepresented badly.'

'I see.'

'Who told you that rubbish anyway?' she demanded.

'Oh, just some guy...'

'Well,' Bryony snorted, 'he's full of shit, Charlie.'

We talked some more and she calmed down. I wondered if Paul Whitten was a reliable narrator of events. Was what he said about Lance true?

We left together and said goodbye in the road. We went our separate ways and as I walked home I reflected that although I was sad to lose Roland as a very obvious suspect, I was pleased that I wasn't secretly pining for a man who hit women.

Two days later on Friday I was queuing with predominantly females to go through security checks at HMP Burnham, the category one prison that was holding Lance on remand. As I drove down the lanes to the prison I noticed that the leaves on the trees were turning yellow and starting to fall. There was a chill to the morning air and that indefinable feeling you get when you know that whatever the calendar may tell you, summer is ending and autumn beginning.

I went through to my designated table in the Visitors' Hall and after a short wait, Lance came over to join me.

He sat down opposite me dressed in his prison denims. I studied him closely. Lance had lost weight and oddly, since he'd arrived in prison, he looked more confident than he had when he had been outside. Incarceration seemed to suit him.

'How are you, Lance?'

'I'm not too bad...' He looked around and waved at a couple of fellow prisoners at other tables. 'They listen to my podcast, they're real fans,' he said, proudly. 'I can't wait to get out, I've got so many ideas to broadcast it's not true, this place is a godsend.'

I sat there marvelling at him.

'I'm glad you're happy here, Lance.' I wondered if he realised how much trouble he was actually in.

'What have you found out so far?' he asked.

'That you're gay,' I said, just tossing that into the conversation.

Nobody was in ear-shot but he suddenly looked very uncomfortable.

'Shhh! Keep your voice down,' he hissed. So, Paul had been right there.

'Well, personally I don't think it will be a secret too long, Lance. Paul Whitten told me, he was Sam's boyfriend before you came along in case you'd forgotten, and he seemed delighted to give me the news. Sooner rather than later I think he will realise that there might be some money in it for him and he'll tip the media off.'

'Shit... How did you find Paul Whitten?'

'Does it really matter? You hired me to investigate, Lance, well, that's what I'm doing, investigating. Now, are there any other bombshells you might like to share with me?'

'I don't know... I don't even know if I am...' he looked

around to make sure nobody was eavesdropping and then whispered, 'gay. I went round to see Sam in secret, I wanted to get some ammo to use against Susannah Young, I wanted him to dish the dirt, but then, I can't really explain it, our eyes met and then... There's an expression in French, un coup de foudre, it means, I think, a thunderbolt, and that's just what it was. I doubt it will last, it's still ongoing but I just don't know... I'm not the kind of man who falls in love, Charlie, I'm not sure how to deal with it.'

'I'm not sure anyone is.'

'I tell you what though,' he laughed bitterly, 'when I started getting famous, I used to fantasise that I'd fall for a supermodel or a Hollywood actress. I never imagined, not even in my wildest dreams, that I would fall for a deli owner, and a male deli owner to boot.'

He stood up. 'Life's full of surprises, Charlie. Get in touch with me when you've proved my innocence.'

He turned and walked away.

Chapter Thirty-One

The weekend came and went in a blur of activity. Andrea came up to see me on Saturday night. He asked me how my investigation was going; I told him. He was very impressed by my uncovering Lance's affair.

'Who do you think killed her?' he asked.

'I have no idea.' Unhelpful but true.

'I think it was Esther,' Andrea said. That certainly took me by surprise. I frowned, considering this. If Andrea said something it was well worth listening to his opinion. He was rarely wrong about things, which although an admirable quality is also a bloody annoying one.

'Why on earth would you think that?' I asked.

'When she went to the police and confessed, and it all turned out to be a load of old hooey, I think that was like a double bluff designed to throw people off the scent. Now the police think she's off her rocker, even if some evidence implicating her arises, they won't follow up on it.'

'Motive?' I asked.

'Hatred, the strongest there is...'

Later he repeated his offer to me to pay for someone to run my business. The M word, marriage, wasn't specifically mentioned, but it was lurking. I'd live with him in London, run the Old Forge Café from there, visit it two or three times a week, install a head and sous chef in the accommodation above the restaurant which would offset a lot of the wages. It wasn't so much an offer as a powerpoint demonstration.

We lay next to each other in the bed that he'd bought me ages ago (he'd got tired of sleeping on a mattress on the floor, 'we're not students, Charlie'). It was a very Andrea kind of bed, stylish, expensive, Italian. I hadn't bought one as any money I made I tended to plough back into the business. I'd spent my own bed money on a blast chiller. A blast chiller (mine looked a bit like a microwave) cools hot food down quickly so you can refrigerate it, which reduces the risk of bacterial growth and contamination. It also sends the Environmental Health Officer into a kind of swoony ecstasy, at least that was the effect on Sandra Burke, my local EHO, when she saw it.

Andrea had made all his points again, backed up with his laptop, with helpful graphs and he'd added little animated lady chefs to his images to excite my curiosity. I was unmoved, emotionally and physically.

'Charlie, we can't go on leading separate lives like this, seeing each other what, twice a week?' he caressed my back, 'if we're lucky.' I was sitting next to him checking my mise en place list for the morning on my laptop with one hand on the keypad, stroking Andrea's body absent-mindedly with the other. Multi-tasking I suppose.

'What's wrong with that, Andrea?' I asked, yawning. 'What would we do with all that time together?'

He said something about talking more, I wasn't really listening. I looked at the time, it was midnight. I saved my work, turned the laptop and the bedside light off and rolled on top of him.

'I'm not a talker, Andrea,' I whispered, 'I'm a doer and this is what I want to do right now...' I began to show him. 'And Andrea,' I brought my mouth close to his as I straddled him, 'I can't do this seven days a week...'

He was too busy to reply.

I think I had made my point.

On the Monday I awoke. Andrea had gone back to London on Sunday, right now he would be on a flight to Singapore for some kind of investment conference that they were having out there. Murdo was up in Oxford, so I was completely alone savouring my solitude as I lay in bed upstairs at the Old Forge Café.

All was quiet in the kitchen below, it was wonderful. I stretched my limbs out under the duvet, luxuriating in the freedom of a day when I didn't have to do anything at all.

I spent the day in my pyjamas. I did an hour's yoga, had a weirdly unhealthy lunch of a couple of jumbo sausage rolls followed by a crisp roll. Here's the recipe. Buy a white crusty roll, hollow it out and then stuff it with a packet of crisps of your choice. I like cheese and onion flavour. Eat with head bowed over plate to catch the shower of crumbs. For dessert, a supermarket apple turnover with cream. I added extra cream. Then I went back to bed and slept.

By half past six at night I felt the walls closing in on me. I also felt slightly nauseous from eating so much crap. I changed into my running gear and headed out through the door. My plan was to run for about an hour and a half, a long run for me, and be home no later than eight when it would be starting to get quite dark; I didn't want to stumble and trip and injure myself.

I ran across the common and then down the footpath across the adjacent field, the same field that, what felt like ages ago, Dr Young had been shot in. Over a month had gone by since then. I can remember thinking when she got shot that it was a thirteenth, unlucky for some.

Thinking about the academic set off a train of thought that, as I ran, led inexorably to Lance, languishing or possibly flourishing in his prison setting. I ran across the field where the Earl had his opera festival every year, that's where I had met Murdo, then across his drive that led from the main road at the bottom of the hill up to his house. I glanced down at the drive as I ran. It was flanked by twin rows of enormous horse chestnut trees, their green foliage fading now as autumn approached. He wouldn't cut them down for a stupid helicopter.

A while later I crossed the main road and was now headed along the valley that ran below the sight line of Lance's garden. Looking up the steep slope towards the ridge which marked the boundary of Elmer's Pond, I could see the large houses that had been built on the outskirts of the village whose lucky owners enjoyed a vista over the fields below and the woods beyond.

There was a footpath that led up along the edge of the

field and I took it as far as the main road and then walked along to the gated entrance of Lance's property.

I squeezed through the gap where the hedge met the gate pillar into the front garden and looked up at the house. It wasn't yet dark, I guessed there would be smart lighting that would kick in soon to make the place look occupied. One of Lance's cars, a Mercedes, not the Maserati, was parked near the door. A burglar alarm flashed ominously.

I skirted the side of the house into the back garden, walked up to the shed where the murder weapon had been discovered and peered at it closely, wondering how easy it would have been for someone to have gained access to plant evidence and incriminate Lance.

Not easy, was the immediate answer. The shed was in very good repair, practically new. It had a proper door with a touch keypad, not the kind of thing that you could get through without knowing the combination.

I checked the window, it was barred. Well, so much for that idea.

I walked round into the front garden, the lawn, immaculately cut but sprinkled here and there with leaves, ran down to the row of beeches at the bottom, earmarked for destruction by Lance's absurd idea for a helipad. Hopefully his prison experience would rid him of this folly. The trees were lovely, to cut them down a kind of eco-crime.

Then I froze. I could see a figure at the bottom of the garden. I immediately thought, it has to be a burglar, then I wondered if maybe it was something more sinister. I had no doubt Lance had been framed for a murder that he did not commit. I wondered if maybe this was the guilty party.

I crouched behind a hydrangea bush that grew next to the shed and peered round. The figure had disappeared. I scratched my head in frustration. I wanted to get closer to the trees but to cross the lawn I would be clearly visible from the bushes at the bottom where I assumed the person had gone to ground.

Maybe if I waited a bit they would break cover and come up to the house. That had to be why they were there. I looked at the Garmin running watch on my wrist, it was 7.15. I'd give them twenty minutes and then go and look.

Ten minutes passed slowly. A couple of blackbirds came and hunted for worms in the grass on the lawn. A jet passed overhead on its way to Heathrow. It was getting quite dark now. Then I was aware of a presence behind me.

I froze. I scarcely breathed, my heart was beating like a jack-hammer. The hunter had become the hunted.

There was a cough behind me, a deliberate sound, the noise you make to get someone's attention. I slowly stood up and then turned round.

All I could see was eyes in a black ski mask. A black tracksuit, black gloved hands. I felt terrified. Then one hand reached up to the top of the mask and pulled it off, and I saw his face.

Chapter Thirty-Two

'Charlie, what the hell are you doing here?' he asked.

It was Roland.

'Why are you dressed like that?' I demanded. What I meant was, why are you dressed like some kind of burglar/rapist?

'Badgers,' he replied. Badgers yourself Roland, I thought. What the hell was he on about? I wondered but I let it pass.

We stared at each other some more.

'What are you doing here, Roland?' I asked. 'Lance asked me to keep an eye on the place while he was away.' This wasn't true, but it's the kind of thing he might well have asked me to do.

'Come with me and I'll show you,' he said, with a grin that lit his face up. I couldn't refuse. 'Okay,' I found myself saying. I hoped I wasn't going to regret this.

We walked slowly to the end of the garden, towards the beech trees.

'You'll have to keep very still and be very quiet,' he whispered.

Slowly we crept to the base of one of the trees. Roland turned and looked at me, he put a finger to his lips. His eyes were alive with excitement.

A couple of metres from the trunk of the tree the ground fell away steeply like it had been cut with a knife and then the grassy slope of the valley began. Roland dropped to his knees and signalled I do the same, and then on to his stomach. I followed suit. Together we inched our way forward on our bellies until we were right at the edge of the bank.

There was a stiff breeze now blowing straight towards us. Roland put his mouth close to my ear. I could hear his breathing, feel his warm breath on me, I trembled, but not from cold.

'Now we wait,' he whispered. 'Don't make a sound.'

I wondered what we were waiting for. I looked down the valley. On this side as the slope fell down steeply, there was nothing but grass with the odd clump of yellow ragwort. Down below, on the floor of the valley was the footpath that I had run along earlier; to my left there was a fence that ran down to that self-same path. That marked the way I had run up, then the track carried on up the other side of the valley to the tree line that marked the start of a small wood, its trees silhouetted against the evening sky, now turning dark.

There was nobody around. Soon, in about half an hour, it would be dark.

Then suddenly, to my amazed delight, a badger appeared from the bank below, followed by another one. Their sett must have been excavated into the side of the bank. The two animals stood on the grass below us, their long snouts kind of whiffling as they tested the air. Their black and white striped faces moved side to side, their short, flat, stubby tails kind of wagging. They were absolutely entrancing. I guessed they couldn't smell us, we were downwind of them, our scent blown away from them by the breeze and we were invisible from where we were lying.

We watched them for about five minutes or so, as they shook themselves briskly, as if getting down to business and trotted off out of sight.

I rolled over and looked at Roland.

'Thank you so much,' I whispered, 'that was absolutely fantastic.'

He grinned and sat up. 'Aren't they amazing. They have a sett they've excavated into the bank.' It was as I had thought then. 'They've got incredibly sensitive noses and good eyesight, that's why I was wearing the mask.'

'I've only ever seen them dead by the side of the road.'

'It's hard to see them, you have to be with someone who knows what they're doing.'

'Well you obviously do.'

He nodded. 'I do indeed.'

We got to our feet and walked back across Lance's grounds to the main road. He pointed at the house. 'And that arsehole wants to drive them out with his fucking helipad.' He shook his head in angry disbelief. 'Selfish bastard. I don't think he killed that woman but if they keep him in for thirty years I'll be absolutely delighted.'

Well, I thought, thinking of the badgers, you've got a point Roland.

'How did you get here?' he asked me.

'I ran.' I indicated my running gear.

'Do you want a lift home,' he offered, 'my car's just down the road.'

I didn't fancy going home in the dark. I had no torch and although I knew the path well enough, it would be difficult to make my way through the woods in the dark. I did not want to trip over a tree root and twist my ankle or pull a muscle.

'Yes please,' I said.

Together we walked back along the road through the gathering gloom to his car, an old Subaru.

'I live in Hampden Green,' I said.

He laughed. 'I know where you live, Charlie.'

His choice of music for the short drive home was classical. That didn't entirely surprise me. I had Roland marked down as a bit of an intellectual. I tried not to let that cloud my judgement. I often find people like that, for example Dr Susannah Young, tend to look down their noses at people who did not go to university. Ironic really, as they are often left-wing but despise the working classes whose causes they affect to champion. I could never really figure that one out.

He drove into my car park and I looked at him. 'Want to come in for a coffee?' I said.

'Sure.'

I'm not quite sure when the words, 'want to come in for a coffee', in my mind metamorphosed into a meaning, an invitation, that did not really include the concept of coffee. Maybe it was when we had been watching the badgers, but really I think it went back to that first meeting in the field

254

when I had seen him with Bryony. Tonight's the night, I thought, one of my dad's favourite songs.

I unlocked the door, silenced the alarm and switched on the lights and the coffee machine.

'Have a seat,' I said. 'Table three appears to be free, what would you like?'

'Espresso.'

He smiled and sat down, watching me as I made us both an espresso.

'It's a nice restaurant,' he said.

'Sure, but I think we'll go upstairs,' I said. 'We'll be more comfortable. It's this way.'

I led him through the swing doors into the silent kitchen and up the stairs to my flat.

We sat down in my lounge and looked at each other.

Then I stood up slowly and moved over to the sofa that he was sitting on and I sat down next to him. I drew him to me as I removed the coffee cup from his hand. His arms were now around me and he buried his face against my chest, kissing me. We stood up and embraced, he felt hard and muscular as I held him against me. I lowered my head pressing my face into his jumper. The wool was against my nostrils. I could smell the fabric and feel his warmth. He smelled good.

'This way,' I said, quietly as I led him down the hall to my room. We pulled our clothes off with feverish haste. Roland's body was every bit as great as I had imagined it to be.

Afterwards as I lay half on top of him, my hand travelling over his shoulder and biceps and his amazingly toned stomach, I murmured, 'So calisthenics did all this?'

He looked at me startled. 'How did you know that?'

'Oh,' I said, 'a girl can tell these things.'

Later I cooked him dinner. I had some quiche left over from the day before and I made a potato salad with fresh chives, flavoured with crushed garlic and some rye bread and a small garnish of red cabbage salad with dates.

We went back to bed, it seemed a shame to let that toned body of his not have any exercise and then we fell asleep in each other's arms.

I'd left the hall light on in case Murdo came back early although I wasn't expecting him until Tuesday morning. I am a light sleeper and I was woken by the bedroom door opening.

Murdo? I thought. What did he want in my room? I pushed some hair out of my eyes and squinted at the door.

Andrea was standing there framed against the hall light. Our gazes met. I saw his lips tighten as he took in the scene. Me, Roland's head cradled in my right arm, the tattoo of the Green Man vivid against his skin on his arm, free of the duvet, thrown over me.

Andrea said nothing. He stood there as if frozen, his face registering shock, then he shook his head slowly, with infinite sadness and closed the door behind him gently.

I heard his footsteps as he walked back down the hall and the creak of the stairs as he descended them.

Roland stirred in his sleep and I stroked his hair,

'Sssh, darling, you go back to sleep,' I whispered.

Sleep for me was a long time coming.

Chapter Thirty-Three

I woke Roland early the next morning and sent him on his way. I walked into the kitchen. Things immediately got worse. If you like putting a figure on these things I would say about ten times worse. I felt shittier by a factor of ten.

Sitting in water in a steel mixing jug on a workbench were a dozen beautiful red roses. No prizes for guessing who had brought them. If Andrea had angrily stuffed them in the bin or jumped up and down on them on the floor and left them there as testament to his feelings, it wouldn't have been quite so bad somehow.

I felt physically sick, in the pit of my stomach, like I was going to throw up with misery and guilt. I stared around my kitchen at the comforting familiarity of the big six burner stove, the gleaming work-surfaces, the fridges, the blast chiller. I walked around in a kind of haze, flipping switches as I turned the fans on and tried to calm my mind.

What have I done, I kept thinking. I looked at my MEP list and made two cheesecake bases and put them in the fridge to set. What have I done... The veg order arrived and I put that away, ditto the fish. I was very short with

Kenneth the posh fish guy, he looked hurt as he got back into his van. I couldn't concentrate.

Just after eight, Murdo arrived back from Oxford where he'd spent Sunday and Monday with Lucy. He looked a bit bleary and worse for wear but after he'd had a shower and changed into his whites he looked a little more alert.

'You okay, Charlie?' he asked. 'You seem a bit out of sorts today?'

'I'm fine,' I lied, 'I just slept badly, that's all.'

My phone was propped up on the windowsill by the kitchen door; it started ringing.

Murdo looked at it. 'It's your boyfriend, Charlie.'

Repressing the urge to say 'which one?', I walked over and glanced at the screen, it was Andrea. I let it go to messages.

During the next hour he tried once more to get in touch with me. Again I ignored him. Then at ten Francis arrived. He flung open the kitchen door with an ear-splitting crash and stood there, beaming at me and Murdo with immense good nature.

'Do you want to hear a joke, Chef?'

His bad-timing was impeccable.

'Not really,' I said, unhappily.

'It's brilliant,' he said confidently, utterly unaware of the atmosphere in the kitchen, 'I'll tell you anyway... Why did the scarecrow win an award?' Murdo and I looked at each other blankly.

Francis continued, 'Because he was outstanding in his field.' He stood there waiting for us to laugh.

'That's very good, Francis,' Murdo said, eventually.

'Didn't you like it, Chef?' Francis asked me anxiously as

he rolled his sleeves up and pulled an apron on. 'You did get it didn't you? Field? It's got more than one meaning.'

'Yes, I did, it was great,' I said through gritted teeth.

The phone rang again. Guess who. This time I switched it off. I felt reminded of Sunday school, Peter denying Christ thrice. Later Jess arrived.

'Can I have a quiet word, Charlie,' she said. The way she said it, ominously quiet and level-toned made my heart sink. I knew what was coming.

'I'll be back in a minute,' I said to Murdo and Francis as I followed her into the restaurant. My heart was no longer located where it usually was. I felt it descend. To the pit of my stomach.

'I've just had a call from Andrea,' she said. The look in her eyes was not one of friendly camaraderie.

'And?' I said brightly. As if I didn't know. I looked around the small restaurant, the chairs and tables seemed to look back at me in more or less the same accusing manner as Jess was doing.

'He says his flight to Singapore was cancelled due to industrial action so he thought he would visit you, surprise you...'

'Oh.' So that explained that then.

'I gather he did surprise you.'

I nodded. 'Surprise' was possibly inadequate to convey what had transpired. In the same way as passengers on the *Titanic* were surprised when it hit the iceberg and sank.

'You could say that.'

She shook her head angrily. 'I mean what the fuck, Charlie... seriously, what were you thinking?'

259

I felt like saying, whose bloody restaurant is this? Also, I'm not a child. And, I think, madam, you'll find I'm the boss here. And, whose side are you on, Judas.

But I didn't. I mumbled something, as if I were the student and she were a forty-something successful career woman, enraged by my childish behaviour.

Jess was not on my side at all. No doubt whose side she was on. She was furious. 'You're having an affair with Roland' – she broke off and gesticulating with her arms described a kind of circle – 'with bloody Roland! He's an over-privileged nepo-baby and he's half your age, what kind of dumb shit is this?'

'Nepo-baby?' What was she on about?

'His dad owns Farfalla Productions, they're a massive TV company. If Mr Woods senior isn't in the *Sunday Times* top one hundred rich list it's because he's bribed someone to keep his name out of it.'

I thought of Roland's old Subaru. He'd certainly made the effort.

Jess wasn't done yet. 'He knows Bryony Mogg because his dad's on the same board as the Earl in that investment company... Jesus, Charlie...'

'Have you quite finished?' I said, as haughtily as I could.

Jess looked away from me out of the window and when she turned back to face me I saw her eyes were wet with tears.

'I'm sorry, Charlie,' she said, 'the only reason I'm cross is because I care for you... that's all.'

'I'll be in the kitchen,' I said. It came out coldly but inside I was touched by her feelings for me.

I went back into the kitchen and went over to Murdo.

'Could you hold the fort for me for an hour or so, I need to go and see someone.'

'Sure.' I could see concern for me in his eyes but he didn't question me and for that I was profoundly grateful. At least Murdo was non-judgemental. Jess's reaction had severely affected me.

I suppose I was lucky I had people who cared about me who were close, but it sure didn't feel that way.

I went upstairs, changed into jeans and a shirt and an old pair of cherry-red high sided Doc Martens that never failed to cheer me up, and left. Half an hour later I was pulling into a car park in central Wycombe. I walked along the road by the station until I came to the block I wanted and I took the lift up to the top floor, the penthouse.

I rang the bell and the door opened.

'Hello, Charlie,' Anna Bruce said, 'I was wondering when you'd come.'

Chapter Thirty-Four

'Take a seat,' she said. Her apartment, minimalist chic, Bauhaus furniture – like Anna Bruce herself – was elegant and expensive looking. She was old but mature, like a really good building with great, classic, timeless lines, St Pauls or Moray Place in Edinburgh. The structure didn't need ornamentation and the façade didn't need tarting up. There would be no slipping into a push-up leather basque or inappropriate youth fashion for Anna Bruce.

'Tea?'

'Please.'

She left the room and I stared out of the window at the roof-tops of High Wycombe and the hills flanking it as the town snaked away in a valley of bricks and concrete westwards. Far in the distance I could see the elaborate mausoleum that crowned the hill that had been hollowed out a couple of centuries ago to create the Hellfire Caves.

I could also see the housing estate where she had been born. She had told me once that she liked to look down on it and remember where she had come from, how far she had risen. Quite literally, as well as metaphorically, given how high up we were.

She came back into the room and gave me a cup of Earl Grey, in a kind of Japanese cup without a handle on a matching saucer. It was thin, grey, almost translucent, very beautiful.

'Lovely cup.' Something stirred in my memory, 'haven't I seen it before?'

'You have indeed,' She nodded. 'I got it back in the summer when I was in Japan.'

'Holiday?'

She smiled. 'I don't really do holidays, Charlie. I was there for work, but, yes, I did add a few days on for myself.'

'How was Japan?'

'Humid.' She sipped her own tea. 'And how are you?'

I told her about Andrea and Roland. She listened with a faint smile on her face which I found slightly irritating.

'Well, you've answered your own question, it seems to me,' she said. 'You don't want to be Mrs di Stefano and you obviously have no future as Roland's long-term girl-friend. I can't see you chaining yourself to trees or gluing yourself to roads. And the reason that you don't want to move in with Andrea is that you don't want to lose your independence and the reason Roland finds you so attractive, or at least one of the reasons aside from your undoubted good looks, is that quality of independence. So embrace it. That's my advice.'

I felt a bit cheated. I had wanted her to get her tarot cards out and give me a more detailed road-map to follow, I didn't want sensible psychological guidance.

'Oh,' I said. You wouldn't need to be psychic to recognise the disappointment in my tone. Pull yourself together, was the gist of Anna's advice.

'I'm sorry,' she said, unapologetically, 'not what you wanted to hear? Well, that's what people pay me for, Charlie, my version of things, not theirs. You're a tough, independent woman, if you want to have a meaningless affair for the sheer hell of it, why not.'

I finished my tea and Anna Bruce stood up.

'Don't feel guilty. One of the reasons Andrea loves you is you're passionate about things, but that obviously has a dark side to it. If he's serious about you, maybe he'll realise that. If not, that's his loss.'

'Thank you,' I said, and I meant it. I did feel better, slightly more in control.

'It was nice to see you again,' she said. My time was obviously up. I stood up too.

'By the way,' she said as she led me to the door, 'there is still danger surrounding you from that woman I warned you about. She hasn't gone away.'

Damn it, I thought, what with everything that had been going on I had totally forgotten Mel Craig and her court case against me. 12 October was the due date, just under a fortnight away. If I was found guilty the evil cow would succeed in her wish to destroy me and my business.

'Don't get distracted by all this, you need to watch your back, Charlie.'

'Thanks, Anna. I'll take what you said on board.'

'You do that,' she said and the door closed behind her.

As I walked back to the car I got a message on my phone from Roland.

'When can I see you again?'

I thought for about a second, maybe less.

'Now.'

Send.

Chapter Thirty-Five

The cottage where Roland was living was at the edge of a village called Frampton End, which was one of the neighbouring villages to Hampden Green. It had once been a farm labourer's cottage. It stood on the opposite side of the wide entrance to a still working farm that faced onto the main road.

I parked my car on the far side of the house so it would be invisible to passing traffic, knocked on the door and went inside.

Roland was waiting for me wearing just a pair of jeans. The waist was unbuttoned. I kicked my shoes off, put my arms around his naked torso and felt his hard, lithe, muscular body pressing into mine. My hands travelled down his chest, I loved his flat, ridged, stomach. We kissed and, kind of fused together, we made our way up the narrow, winding staircase to his bedroom, Roland walking backwards, our mouths still glued to each other's and fell upon his bed.

Later I looked at my phone, it was 11.45.

'Roland, I'm going to have to go soon, I need to be back at work. Can I use your shower?'

'Yeah, it's in the bathroom, that's downstairs. I'll join you soon, give me a shout when you're finished.'

I picked my clothes up from the floor where I'd let them fall and draped them over one arm and walked back down the stairs. It was a small cottage. Upstairs there were the two rooms, the other bedroom I could see he had converted into a study.

The staircase led into the area between the kitchen space and the living room. I walked into it and looked around. It was beautifully tidy; I nodded approvingly, I'm not keen on messy people. Not that I had any intention of having any kind of long-term relationship with Roland, but I was pleased to see he was a neat person.

The small bathroom had obviously been built as an extension to the house. There was a door into it opposite the foot of the stairs. When the cottage was constructed, baths for working people were made of tin and put in front of the fire and toilets were at the bottom of the garden. I was pleased to note that the bathroom was almost surgically clean. I showered, dried myself, and put my clothes back on. I was missing a sock.

'Roland...' I called. I was going to ask him to bring down the errant sock but he was coming down the stairs before I got a chance to speak. Damn, he looked good naked, I thought to myself.

'Can you do a pistol squat?' I asked him when he was standing in front of me.

He looked at me in surprise, then he extended his right leg so it was straight, held his arms out parallel to it for balance and sank on his left knee so his backside nearly touched the floor and then straightened the bent leg so he was standing again. It was essentially a one legged squat. Then he did it on the other side.

'Like that?'

'That's so impressive,' I said. And it was.

'I'll just be a couple of minutes,' he said, smiling and pointing at the shower.

'I'll just get my sock,' I said.

He nodded and went into the bathroom, closing the door behind him. I ran back up the stairs and found my sock hiding under the bed. I sat down and pulled it on. I walked out on to the landing, I wondered what his study was like, if it were as tidy as the living room.

I walked in. In front of me was his desk under a window overlooking the farmyard and beyond that Monklands wood that lay between our two villages. I knew the wood well; a footpath that I often ran down went through it. It crossed my mind that I must have passed his house dozens of times unknowingly. It also struck me that in the future I could pop in either before or after a run on the way home for a bit more exercise should I so desire. I smiled, lost in an erotic reverie when I suddenly had the uncomfortable feeling I was being watched. I knew somehow, there was someone behind me. Staring at me.

I turned around and nearly screamed.

I was being watched, by Rupert fucking Bear.

Chapter Thirty-Six

He was standing in the corner, staring at me with his cruel, piggy eyes. I flinched and backed away, heart beating wildly and then I realised I was looking at the untenanted costume.

Rupert was naked and two dimensional. He was pinned to an upright folding clothes horse about head height, giving the illusion he was standing up through his own agency. On the same rack were his trademark clothes, red jumper, yellow check trousers and matching scarf.

My thoughts then turned immediately to Roland. He was Rupert Bear, so it was he who had tried to kill me in that freezer. Now he was downstairs. And I had stupidly wandered into his den. I ran down the stairs; thank God, he was still in the bathroom, I could hear water running. I pulled on my shoes by the back door where I'd left them and ran to my car.

It took all of three minutes to drive back to the Old Forge Café. I pulled into the car park and took my phone out. I texted Roland.

'Work emergency, xx Charlie.'

I didn't want him to know that I knew. I sat in the car

271

taking in deep lungfuls of air. I wondered what I'd done to deserve all this stress going on in my life. Running a restaurant was hard enough, trying to prove Lance's innocence difficult, my love life was an absolute shambles, and of all the people I could have picked to go to bed with I had managed to choose the one person who had tried not that long ago, and almost successfully, to kill me. If there were an award going for Stupid Woman of the Year I would ace it.

I walked into the kitchen.

Murdo was at the stove, he turned round and smiled at me.

'Had a nice morning, Chef?'

I smiled thinly and walked towards the stairs to go upstairs and change.

'I've had better, Murdo,' I said. 'I've definitely had better.'

Rarely have I enjoyed the hurly-burly turmoil of service more than during the next couple of hours. We were crazily busy; I didn't care, I was on fire. Murdo, relegated to a secondary role of doing the starters and desserts was practically open-mouthed with admiration. Everything I touched was cooked to perfection. That's unusual in a small kitchen when there's only one chef doing mains; something gets forgotten or remembered last minute and has to be disguised with artful presentation (the culinary equivalent of a conjuring trick, distracting the eye) or sent out with fingers crossed; a surprising number of people don't seem to notice what they're eating. I once worked with a chef who sent out thirty portions of Christmas pudding one December and suddenly realised as the last one went out, that he'd been sprinkling salt, not sugar, on top of each one. As the bowls came back to the kitchen twenty minutes later he asked the waiter with anguish if anyone had said anything about them. The waiter frowned. 'No, why?'

'And everyone was quite happy?' the chef said disbelievingly.

A shrug. 'Seemed to be... oh yeah, I heard one guy say to his wife that his pudding tasted salty...'

'What did she say?' worried look.

'That it was probably supposed to taste like that, and to shut up and eat it.'

'Oh.'

All the while Jess had studiously refused to speak to me. The last cheque came at two thirty and as Murdo dealt with it, Jess said, 'Can I have a word?'

'Sure. Upstairs.'

We stood facing each other and Jess said, 'I just want to apologise...'

'No,' I said. I threw my arms around her. 'I want to apologise, and I'll go first cos I'm the boss and you have to do what I tell you... you were quite right...'

I released her from my grasp and poured about the story of Rupert Bear. Jess's eyes widened. 'Oh, my God, oh no, Charlie, what are you going to do?'

'I have no idea,' I said. That was certainly true. 'I don't see there's any point in going to the police with this.'

'Well, I guess you're right, but I suppose at least you now know who tried to kill you that night and who put that scary bear doll in the dry-store.' Her face darkened. 'That bastard!'

'Hang on a minute...' A thought had just struck me. 'What if he's in league with Mel Craig? That's how she knew I'd been attacked by Rupert and it was she, as we originally thought, who sneaked into the dry-store...'

We looked at each other as we pondered this. Then I said, 'Well, whatever or whoever or whyever. I'm going to have to deal with it myself somehow.'

'How?' asked Jess.

'I shall fight fire with fire,' I said, grimly. 'Roland Woods will find he's made a big mistake.'

I took my phone out of my pocket and sent a message to my godfather, Cliff Yeats.

'I need help xx.'

He replied immediately.

'Where and when?'

'Three Bells, tonight. 10.' A thumbs up emoji was the reply.

'That's that sorted, Jess,' I said. 'Now we have to deal with bloody Mel Craig.'

'What are you going to do about her?'

For one thing I was going to let her know that I knew she had worked her scam on a number of other people, that she was making a living by blackmail, fraud and deceit. Please God, let her give me an excuse to hit her. I remembered Paul Whitten's Lenin quote, 'Not a single problem of the class struggle has ever been solved in history, except by violence.' Right on, comrade, I thought, balling my fist.

I looked at her grimly. 'I've had enough of being other people's punching bags. Time to dish it out for a change.'

Chapter Thirty-Seven

We came down to find the kitchen tidied and deserted. Murdo had gone up to his room for a lie down and Francis had returned home until he was due back at 7 o'clock in the evening. I started making a list of all the things we were short of that needed replacing after the lunchtime spanking we'd received.

There was a knock on the back door, it was Della.

'Hi Charlie, I was just passing and I thought I'd pop in and see how you were?'

'I'm fine,' I said, lying through my teeth. I was actually feeling terrible. The sight of the Rupert Bear costume had badly rattled me. It had brought back all those memories of being trapped in that icy blackness feeling my body shut down, and then, like a grotesque cherry on the cake of humiliation, I'd been to bed with my would-be killer.

My godfather, Cliff, had always maintained I had a terrible taste in men, well, this had to be a new low. It was all so humiliating I felt like howling. I was pleased to see Della, her homely, pleasant face a beacon of normality in a world that seemed to be increasingly hostile and downright strange.

I went outside into the yard where she was standing, waiting for me, her dog, Rand (was that short for Randy? But she was a bitch. Krugerrand?). It was a lovely sunny autumn afternoon. I noticed that the mint growing in a couple of the tubs outside needed cutting back, it was getting long and straggly.

'I've been to see Lance,' she said.

'How is he? He seemed very well the last time I saw him.'

'He always puts a brave face on things,' she said. I remembered how anguished he'd been at the poppet doll and how upset he'd been at not being recognised in the pub. Really, Della? I thought to myself. Still, you couldn't fault her loyalty.

'Oh, I do miss him,' she said, with feeling. 'He thinks it might be mainstream media and their puppet-masters orchestrating a campaign against him to silence him.'

I thought, well, that's highly unlikely. I couldn't see Bill Gates making a poppet doll and Sharpieing the name Lance on an Action Man toy, nor could I imagine George Soros ordering a hit on Dr Young and instructing the assassin to hide the murder weapon in Lance's shed to implicate him.

'What do you think, Charlie?' she asked, eager for support.

'I'd certainly be surprised, Della,' I said.

'Lance just wants the best for everyone,' she said sadly, 'a return to how things used to be.'

'Sure.'

We contemplated St Lance, the altruist, in silence, then Della said, 'He's a very noble man, and a great thinker... he tells things how they are.'

I reflected, you simply can't buy loyalty like that. Lance

was very lucky in his choice of a cleaner. She continued, 'When I was going round the house yesterday, making sure it was all in order for his return,' don't hold your breath, I thought, 'I remembered the poppet doll.'

'Go on?'

'All the terrible things that happened after it was discovered, do you think it could somehow have triggered all of this?' she asked.

'Do you mean that the curse really worked?' I immediately thought of Esther's own theory.

'Exactly.' She looked very sure of herself.

'I don't know,' I said.

'Well, he discovered the doll about a month ago, maybe six weeks…'

'It was just before the party certainly,' I said. 'I remember, he brought me the doll to look at.' No point bringing Esther into this.

'That sounds right. Well, when you think about it all of this, the attack on you, the murder, Lance being arrested… it all happened after the poppet doll.'

'True, could just be a coincidence, though.'

'Coincidences don't exist.' Della shook her head pityingly. 'You're a lovely woman, Charlie, but you're a townie, you're not a country person. We know things like this work… I've seen things… such things… you'd be surprised…' she sighed. 'Never mind. I think it was the shot that started the avalanche. But I think even you'll agree that whoever made the doll had it in for Lance, that's indisputable, isn't it?'

'Absolutely, Della.' I could agree with that. 'I saw the doll, it was an evil looking thing.'

'Well, I've got this.' She handed me a piece of paper with the name of a website, a login name and a password code.

I took it. 'What's this?'

'Before Lance moved in last December, the house belonged to a Mr Pereira, I was his housekeeper too. I kind of came with the house, Lance kept me on. Anyway, Mr Pereira had a security system, including cameras. Lance took that on as well, but he didn't see the need for the ones covering the side and rear of the house, so he had those taken down. So there's just the one covering the drive left.'

'I see.'

'But the guy who took away the side cameras, I was the one who let him in and showed him where they were, couldn't reach the one on the left of the house, it's way up in the eaves. The cabling it's attached to feeds through into the loft. Anyway, he said if we wanted it done it would cost another grand; he'd have to bring in a scaffolding tower, it was too high up to work on with a ladder. I said, it's small, you can't see it unless you squint up at the guttering, just leave it, do the others.'

'I see.' I wondered where this was going.

'I paid all of Mr Pereira's household bills for him, I do the same for Lance, and I remembered I'd paid the fee to store the images in the cloud.' She frowned. 'I wonder how they do that… in the clouds? Weird.' She looked up at the sky and sighed. 'Anyway, it was for a year. That camera should still be active and still sending its photos up to those clouds. I can't work computers, maybe you can. If it's still working, and there's no reason it shouldn't be as far as I can see, it should have filmed whoever put the poppet jar where Lance found it. The flower bed where it was discovered is in the area that should be covered by the camera. Maybe you can have a look.'

'Thank you,' I said. 'I'll give it a try.'

'Well, the details are on that piece of paper. I'm glad I didn't get rid of the accounts books, I'm a terrible hoarder.'

'Thank, you, Della.'

'I'll see you around, Charlie,' she said and walked out of my yard, through the gate towards the common.

I looked at the piece of paper in my hand; maybe this held the key to who had framed Lance.

I opened the kitchen door and went in.

'Jess,' I called.

She came into the kitchen, she'd changed back into her shorts and a T-shirt and was obviously about to go home.

'Yes, Charlie, what is it?'

'I need your help.'

'To do what?'

'To find a witch.'

Chapter Thirty-Eight

We went upstairs to my living room. I explained to Jess what Della had told me. She nodded and we logged on to my pc. The account was still current and the images were still being stored and we had access to them.

Soon we were looking at a picture of a reasonably clear view of the side path by the edge of Lance's house. The camera offered only a fairly restricted view but I could see a flower border where I assumed the poppet doll had been found. Today's date, year, month and day, was on the display. Jess clicked on this and a calendar popped up.

'Go to twenty-ninth September,' I said.

Jess did. The view remained the same but the quality of light seemed different.

'Now go to 18.40.'

She moved a slide at the bottom of the screen and the picture darkened as we moved forward into the evening,

'Keep going until I appear.'

Then, as if by magic, there I was, moving purposefully and somehow furtively alongside the house. I felt childishly excited by this. Look, there's me, I thought.

'Okay, now go back to the twenty-first of August... that was the evening I met Lance in the pub and he brought me the poppet doll. Keep going back from there.'

'This could take a while...'

'It's important, Jess.'

'Okay,' sighing deeply.

She started slowly scrolling backwards through the camera footage. It took forty-five minutes but then we found it.

On 18 August at half past five in the morning a figure dressed in black made their way along the path to the blue hydrangea bush. They crouched down and then stood up, surveying their handiwork. Their back was to the camera, but I knew who it was.

'Turn round, you bastard,' I heard Jess say.

They did so and raised their head to look around.

It was Roland.

'Gotcha!' I muttered.

Chapter Thirty-Nine

We looked at each other.

'What gives?' Jess asked.

'What gives is this, Jess,' I said, 'I think it's fairly obvious that Roland is either very superstitious and thought that he could stop Lance killing those trees using magic...'

'Killing the trees,' Jess said, 'that's very Roland language, Charlie.'

I was about to contradict her but weirdly, although he had tried to kill me, I was a convert to Roland's Save our Beeches cause. That and the genuine love he obviously had for the badgers. I had seen the reverence in his eyes and heard it in his voice, that hadn't been fake.

I finished my sentence, 'Or he thought Lance would be too afraid to do it because he would be afraid of a witch's curse.'

That had indeed almost worked. Lance had been badly rattled by the idea that supernatural forces were after him, unfortunately not rattled enough that he would give up on his plans of housing his stupid helicopter at the bottom of the garden rather than wherever it was normally garaged.

'If Roland's responsible for the doll, do you think he's responsible for Dr Young's murder?' Jess said.

'I don't know.' Yes I thought, that's exactly what I think; I hated Roland with a passion. Roland had to be semi-insane. He'd tried to kill me, he was more than capable of killing a woman he suspected of ecocide, or arboricide, tree-killing. But I wanted to sound rational. 'I don't know how far he would go to protect the countryside,' I said. 'It's one thing to fashion a doll, no matter how evil, another to knife a woman to death simply to frame Lance and stop his depredations.'

But even as I said that I wasn't too sure. He was Rupert Bear, a furry would-be murderer. He put voodoo dolls in people's hydrangeas. He had toyed with my heart. Did he have a screw loose, I wondered, was he genuinely crazy, or was he just misogynistic. And Dr Young had tried to seduce him by all accounts. Another horrible thought occurred to me. Had she tried to seduce him, or had it been the other way round and when she rejected him, had he then killed her? Had he put out the 'I was molested by Dr Young' story just to either discredit her or to disguise the truth?

My phone buzzed. I looked down. My heart sank, it was him. They say revenge is a dish best served cold. I needed to make sure that the instrument of my vengeance, Cliff Yeats, was on board, and until then I couldn't afford to let Roland know that I knew any of his secrets. That, like Bluebeard's wife, I had gone into the forbidden chamber.

'When can we see each other?' Roland's text was mercifully free of emojis, memes and GIFs.

'V busy at work, fully booked out, will contact you tomorrow xc.'

That would hold him, I thought. If he came to the Three Bells, which was not a habitual hangout of his, I'd never seen him there, I would get Cliff to act. I knew the problem wouldn't be firing him up, it would be restraining him. Roland might be a hard nut when it came to frightening elderly, out of condition huntsmen; slapping Extinction Rebellion girls for their lack of commitment, or hitting me with a baseball bat – he might be able to do pistol squats but Cliff Yeats broke bones for a living, had done time for GBH, had been a bare-knuckle fighter, collected debts from hardened criminals and chucked thugs out of night-clubs. I knew who I'd bet on in a fight.

And he didn't have a degree.

'Love you, miss you...' he replied.

I frowned. Well, matey, love is going to break a lot more than your heart, I promised myself grimly. Say bye-bye to the current shape of your nose, and I hope those expensive looking very white teeth of yours are insured.

I worked with Murdo that evening until about eight, then I left him and Francis to it, went upstairs and showered and changed.

I left the restaurant by the tradesman's entrance, via the gate that opened into my yard where the kitchen door was, rather than the front door of the restaurant. It was now completely dark. There were only a couple of street lights in the village and I felt comfortably invisible in the darkness.

I walked down the road to Mel Craig's house which was almost bang on the edge of Hampden Green. There was a hedge beside it and then fields. The next village along was Potter's Hill.

I was fuming with rage. Roland wanted to take my life, she wanted to take my hard-earned money. I was surrounded by pond life. I opened the gate and walked up the path. The curtains in the front room were drawn. I could see a light was on and I could hear the sound of a TV playing. Whatever was on involved a lot of anguished, terrified shouting and full on screaming. Not *Bake Off* then. Unless it was the final and someone's show-stopper had gone terribly wrong.

I rang the bell. The noise stopped and the hall light came on, I could see a figure through the opaque glass. There was the sound of a bolt being drawn and then the door opened a few centimetres; I could see a safety chain stretched taut.

Her eyes fixed on me. I frowned, menacingly I hope.

'Yes?' She obviously didn't recognise me in the gloom. I doubt she had ever really noticed my features ever, I was just a cash cow to be milked.

'I'm Charlie Hunter.'

That got her attention. She stepped backwards, alarm, more than alarm, fear on her face. I wondered why. Then I thought, who cares, fear was good. Cower, you horrid woman!

'I know what you've been up to, you blackmailing bitch,' I said, threateningly, 'and I'm going to make you suffer... I know I'm not the only innocent person you've had your claws into.'

'And I know what you've been up to!' she countered.

She spoke very loudly and there was a hysterical edge to her voice. I held my scowl but behind it I suddenly wondered, did she know I'd stolen her parcel or hacked into her pc?

She carried on. 'I know about you and your witch friends, but I'm not backing down, I'll see you in court.'

I wondered what Esther had got to do with this. Then I thought, so she doesn't know about the theft or the hacking. A wave of relief travelled over me. Then I remembered her Horror Channel addiction.

'And I'll see you in Hell,' I said, dramatically. She looked stricken then she slammed the door in my face.

I walked back down the darkened path and gently closed the gate behind me. I felt cheerful for the first time all day. I'd had enough of being the victim, it was nice to dish it out for once.

'That went well,' I said to myself. I had achieved nothing, but I felt better, it had been cathartic. I headed off to the Three Bells.

Chapter Forty

'So, how badly do you want me to hurt this toe rag?' Cliff asked pleasantly.

Cliff Yeats had been my dad's best friend and was also my godfather. He was a conservative twenty stone of powerful weight-lifting muscle gone to seed. In his youth he'd been a medal winning heavyweight boxer, now he'd have to be hoisted into a ring by a crane. He smoothed the few strands of ginger, hair he had left over his gleaming scalp in a crazily pointless comb-over.

'I'm not quite sure,' I said, 'but I would be very grateful if you could come along as backup. I think we'll play it by ear.'

He looked at me affectionately. When my dad died Cliff had been grief-stricken, heart-broken. I think that's why he was so fond of me. No matter how old I got, or whatever I did, I was always, in his eyes, Barry's little girl. I could do no wrong in Cliff's eyes.

'Of course, Charlie, just let me know when and where, I'll be there.'

His hand, the size of a shovel, encircled his pint, the

large two sovereign rings on his middle fingers glinting in the light as he tipped three quarters of a pint of lager down his throat and put his empty glass down on the table.

'I'll get you another one, Cliff.'

'Cheers.'

As I reached the bar the pub door opened and, much to my surprise, Jess walked in accompanied by Bryony. Bryony looked insanely happy to be with her. I wondered what was going on. The two girls (women I suppose, but they were of a different generation from me) had been at school together, but they had drifted apart to the point where Jess, if not actively disliking Bryony, was not far from it. Bryony, on the other hand, it seemed to me, worshipped Jess from afar.

Well, whatever the reason, here they were.

They both smiled and nodded at me, but made no attempt to come over, whether because they didn't want to intrude on me and Cliff or, more likely, didn't want me involved in their conversation. Well, that was their business, not mine.

I went back and sat down opposite Cliff and handed him his pint.

'That's the girl who works for you isn't it? Jess?'

'That's right.'

Jess waved across the pub at Cliff, he saluted her gravely with his glass.

'Bright girl,' he observed. Then he turned his attention back to me. 'Look, you might as well grasp the nettle sharpish, Charlie. Let's get this over and done with regarding this Roland, no point prolonging things...'

'I suppose you're right.'

'I am,' he spoke with granite certainty. 'We don't want him to have another pop at you. Tell him you'll see him on Friday at five in the evening, his place. We'll sort everything out there and then, one way or another. Does that sound good?'

I nodded. Cliff was right, there would be absolutely no point in prolonging the agony. I was also tired of having to worry every time I got a miscall or a text. I wanted it over. I got my phone out of my pocket and messaged him. Roland replied immediately.

'Yes please!!!'

I sent him a thumbs up and switched my phone off.

'Done.'

Cliff nodded. 'Cheers.' He made the one word pregnant with menace and danger. I knew I would not like to be in Roland's shoes when Friday came along.

Chapter Forty-One

Cliff moved in the following day. The upstairs flat that I lived in was sizeable, it was the same size as the restaurant and kitchen downstairs and had three bedrooms, one was small, more like a box room. This is where I installed Cliff. He'd been there several times before, it was not unknown for Mrs Cliff, whom I had never met, to get the hump (as he put it) – making a tactical withdrawal from the marital home advisable. Cliff was afraid of no man, but he was very wary of his wife, that was for sure.

I was delighted he was there. I now had my very own bodyguard, I felt safe and secure. On Wednesday night I gave Cliff the best table in the restaurant, followed by a jumbo-sized prawn cocktail. Prawns are very good for you, high in protein, low in calories, the lettuce a good source of vitamin C. I piled his bread basket high with extra brown bread, provided him with extra butter. I thought I'd better counteract all this healthy food with a massive amount of carbs and fat in case his body went into toxic shock from ingesting healthy food. Then I gave him steak and a double portion of fries followed by plum tart and a cheese board.

This was washed down with G&T, a bottle of house red and several brandies. Then we went to the pub. Bang went the evening's profits.

The following day, I cooked him a huge breakfast (you didn't need to ask yourself, where did he put it, the answer was staring you in the face), his stomach straining his shirt buttons. Maybe I should buy him some kombucha I thought, boost his gut biome.

After breakfast he went upstairs for a lie down and to watch some TV. Murdo and I prepped the lunch. The lunchtime service was busy but relatively straightforward. About half two as we were winding down and starting to clear the kitchen up, my phone rang; it was Della Peters.

'Is that you, Charlie?'

'Yes.' (Who else would it be! Maybe one day Della would get the hang of tech).

'Something's happening,' she said excitedly.

'Like what?'

'You know the fair-haired man, the one I suspected, the one on the doorbell camera.'

Sam Hickocks.

'Yes.' She had my full attention now.

'I was walking Rand in the fields, between Hampden Green and Potter's Hill, and I saw him, walking with the eco-activist boy.'

'Oh.' That was interesting but less than enthralling.

'It was the way they were walking that was so weird, Charlie, it was like he was Roland's prisoner.'

Rupert Bear strikes again, I thought.

'Where was this exactly?' I asked.

'You know that field, the big field, near where the path is that goes down to the picnic area by the main road?'

I did indeed. 'Yes.'

'You know the copse there, in the middle of the field, there's a shed in it?'

'Yes I do.'

'Well, they both went in there and only one person came out.'

'Which one?'

'Roland.'

Chapter Forty-Two

I stared at the phone in my hand. 'I'll be right over,' I said. 'Are you there now?'

'No, there's no signal there,' she said. 'I had to go up to the village to get one.'

'Look, Della, you go home and wait for me there, I'll deal with this, okay?'

'Are you sure? Shouldn't we call the police?' Her voice sounded worried.

'No, what would we say? That you saw two men out for a walk, they wouldn't be interested. I'll deal with this.'

'Okay, Charlie, take care,' she warned.

'I will, bye.'

I ended the call. A wave of elation ran through me. I hadn't liked the thought of confronting Roland in his cottage with Cliff. It was an idea born of desperation. But the chance to catch Roland red-handed engaged in criminal activities, that was unexpected gold. And I had Cliff with me as backup, I'd be safe. God knows what Roland was doing with Sam Hickocks, but then again God knows what had gone through his mind when he had attacked me.

'Murdo, I've got to go,' I said.

'Aye, nae bother, chef, I'll be fine, ken.'

'Thanks Murdo.'

I sprinted up the stairs and into the living room. Cliff looked up surprised from his copy of the *Sun*.

'Wot's the excitement Charlie?'

'Get your boots on Cliff,' I said, 'it's party time.'

Chapter Forty-Three

The shed stood in a small copse in the middle of a large field that had been planted with wheat which had been harvested not that long ago so that most of the ground was covered in a kind of straw stubble. The farmer had left one large square patch of wheat which stood tall and golden a few metres away from the hut.

At first I wondered why it had been spared but then I noticed a large, blue plastic barrel on top of a kind of tripod standing in front of it. I recognised it as a feed barrel for pheasants. They had left this area uncut as cover for the birds to live in.

Landowners buy them in as chicks, poults they're called, and rear them up to be full-grown birds. Then they organise shoots and charge a huge amount of money, round about a thousand pounds per person per day, to kill them. I personally find the whole process distasteful, but since it means a cheap source of game and I profit from it, selling pheasant at my restaurant, I can't really criticise.

Cliff and I approached the hut. The door was closed and padlocked. I looked at Cliff questioningly.

'It's locked,' I said, somewhat stupidly, stating the obvious.

Cliff looked at me as if I was crazy. 'Really?' he said. He raised a knee, balanced balletically with a grace that I wouldn't have thought possible from such a ponderous guy and kicked hard with a booted foot caked in mud from the field.

The door burst inwards with a loud splintering crash.

'Not now it isn't,' he said.

I looked at him and shook my head in mute admiration. Cliff was one of those rare people who actually do the thing that you yourself wish somebody would do.

The door sagged on its hinges and we walked inside, Cliff leading the way. It wasn't a big place, I guess it was about five metres long and a couple of metres wide. It contained, as I had thought, sacks of feed for the pheasants, then I heard a strange moaning kind of noise. Cliff and I exchanged glances and we moved further inside.

It was dark inside. In the dim light that was filtering in through a filthy, fly-blown Perspex window, I could see a couple of legs sticking out from behind some of the feed bags. I moved closer to take a better look. Someone wearing jeans and deck shoes was sitting there on the floor, hands behind their backs, an old burlap sack covering their head and body. I pulled the sack off and to my astonishment saw the face of Sam Hickocks.

There was a blindfold over his eyes and one of those ball gags that I associate with bondage games in his mouth. I gently pulled the blindfold up and he squinted painfully up at me. I could see recognition in his eyes.

Cliff and I helped him to stand and I undid the gag from

around his mouth. I looked down at his wrists, they were secured with those plastic ties that you can buy. His ankles were also secured.

'Have you got a knife?' I asked Cliff.

He nodded and took a pen-knife out of his pocket and slowly cut through the bonds that held the ex-academic turned deli owner.

'Thank you,' Sam said. He looked closely at me. 'It's you isn't it? The chef, you were in my deli!'

'That's right,' I said, 'and still working for Lance.'

'How did you... ?' he rubbed his wrists and gestured at the shed.

'A tip-off. Who did this?' I asked.

'Rupert Bear,' he said.

'Of course, it would be.' I nodded.

He mistook my agreement for sarcasm. 'No, seriously, it was Rupert Bear,' he insisted.

'I believe you,' I said, reassuringly, 'tell me more.'

'Okay,' he said. 'I was at Lance's place collecting some of my stuff which I had left there, clothes and whatnot. We were an item, I never told you that before...'

'I knew,' I said, 'I found out.'

He raised his eyebrows in surprise. 'Oh, well, anyway, Lance dumped me. Said prison had made him rethink a lot of things about his future and it didn't include me. The housekeeper let me in and then she said she had to go and walk her dog. She told me to just close the door on my way out. The next thing, a guy dressed as Rupert Bear appeared and walked up to me, I was in the living room. I just kind of froze,' he shook his head in wonderment, 'it

301

was weird, cos it was funny. It's Rupert Bear, but it was kind of scary because he didn't say anything, just walked up to me in a kind of purposeful way...'

'I know,' I said, 'exactly the same thing happened to me... did he have a baseball bat?'

Sam nodded. 'I think so, he certainly had something in his hand, it was all a bit of a blur. He hit me with whatever it was, I went down. I was groggy. He tied my wrists and blindfolded me and dragged me into the back of a van. Then he drove me somewhere, near here I guess, I'd come round by then, untied my feet, marched me across some fields to here, tied me up again, and now you rescued me... what time is it?'

'Quarter past five,' Cliff said.

'And it's still Thursday? Isn't it?'

'It is indeed.'

He looked around at the hut. 'Where are we?'

'Christ alone knows, mate,' Cliff said cheerily shaking his head, 'we're in some poxy field, somewhere.'

'So, Rupert Bear's local then, is he?' asked Sam.

'Almost certainly,' I said. I thought of what had happened to me. I repressed a shudder. Della can't have noticed the blindfold from where she'd been watching.

'Can we go now?' Sam said, blushing, 'I really need the loo.'

'Sure,' I said, 'after you...'

I indicated the door with an upturned hand gesture. Sam walked to the door and two things happened. First there was the dry crack of a rifle and then Sam staggered back as if pushed by an invisible hand.

I stood there, as if rooted to the spot, Cliff however didn't. He shoved me out of the way. 'Get down!'

I dropped to the floor. He grabbed hold of Sam who was sitting in the doorway where his legs had given way and had a hand clamped to his left shoulder. Blood was welling from the top of his index finger and through the other three.

Cliff dragged him away from the open door. There was another loud report and as if by magic an irregular hole appeared in the dirty Perspex of the window.

'How bad is it?' whispered Sam, in terror and pain, looking up at Cliff who was crouched, studying his blood-soaked shoulder.

'You'll be okay mate,' he said gruffly, 'it's gone through the muscle at the top of yer shoulder, there's no artery in there, you'll live.'

Another shot.

'I think I'm going to faint,' Sam said, his voice was weak and he closed his eyes. Then I saw his head sag.

'Oh my God!' I said. I couldn't believe how badly all this was going. Triumph had turned to tragedy in seconds.

'He'll live,' Cliff said. The two of us crouched there, below the window ledge and looked at each other.

'He must be hiding in those trees at the top of the field.' He checked his phone. 'There's no signal,' he said, more in astonishment than anything else.

'No,' I said bitterly. It seemed clear now that Roland had used Sam as a lure to draw me here. That Della had seen him was just good fortune on his part. If she hadn't called me he would have found another way to let me know that Sam was here. He must be up there grinning like a maniac at his good fortune. Or possibly he knew her dog-walking habits and had arranged this so their paths would cross. That was more than likely.

'He'll have known that, that's why he chose this place to lure me here.'

'Sam was the bait?' Cliff asked.

I nodded. 'Yup, I don't know what the furry cos-playing bastard's got against me.'

I looked around the shed for inspiration.

Cliff said, 'We'll be okay if we keep behind these feed sacks. I don't know what calibre bullet it is he's using, it'll go through the wood and still kill, but we should be okay behind these.' He patted the pheasant food with the flat of his hand like you might a dog.

I looked up at the corner of the shed. Light was coming in from under the eaves. It was an old shed and had been poorly maintained. The planks that made up the walls were stained and mildewed from where water had seeped in from the roof. They looked in terrible condition.

I'm reasonably tall for a woman and quite slim. Against the far wall was a workbench.

'Cliff,' I said, 'those top planks look rotten. I think I can pull them off and squeeze out, I can go and get help.'

As if to underline the point there was another rifle shot and the front wall trembled as the bullet struck.

'Good girl,' he said. 'Best be quick about it. He won't be able to see you, those windows are filthy. He's firing blind, just don't hang around.'

I clambered up onto the bench and tugged at the top

plank of wood under the eaves. It wobbled like a loose tooth and then a piece came away in my hands. It was as soft and easy to break as I'd imagined. Fairly soon, no more than a couple of minutes, I had a hole big enough to take my shoulders and I slithered out of the back of the shed head first. I fell the last couple of feet, my jeans scraping against the jagged wood, my hands getting stung by the nettles that grew tall in the shade behind the building.

I picked myself up and looked around. I could sprint through the trees and across the large field on the far side. I knew this area from running the footpaths. Beyond the wheat field there was another row of trees and then a hedge and beyond that a grass meadow where horses usually grazed. That marked the edge of an adjoining village, Potter's Hill. That's where Della had called me from. There I would find a phone signal, failing that I could do it the old-fashioned way and bang on someone's door for help.

Then I heard another shot.

That was what triggered me. I felt a sudden surge of fury deep inside. I am a remarkably even-tempered woman but the fact that three innocent people had been lured to their deaths for no good reason at all suddenly made me furious, driving out any understandable fear of being shot. I think too that part of me worried the police would react by arriving with sirens blaring, lights flashing, giving the killer ample time to melt away. He had local knowledge of the terrain on his side, the cops didn't.

I would deal with this myself.

Propped against the shed was a bundle of cut timber. I selected a chunk of four by two wood, about the length of my arm, as my weapon of choice and walked through the trees until I came to the edge of the copse. From there to the patch of tall maize was about twenty metres. Once within it I would be invisible to the shooter in the woods beyond where he was hiding.

I waited. There was another shot. I dashed forward bent low, minimising my profile, across the stubble into the cover of the maize. Immediately there was a loud squawking and several startled pheasants zoomed upwards as if propelled on springs, uttering their weird, metallic sounding alarm call. Bloody birds, I thought. If Roland were looking this way he might guess what was happening. I dropped to my hands and knees and started crawling through the maize towards the trees where he was hiding.

Fortunately for me the crop had been sown in rows so I could move in a direct line towards my target rather than pushing my way through the lines of stalks. Occasionally the small brown heads of immature pheasant chicks would stick their beaks out from behind the foliage and stare at me nervously as I crept long but I made good progress without alarming too many of them.

I reached the end of the maize and peered out across the no-man's land of stubbled field. Ten or so metres away was the edge of the wood where the shooter was. From where I was the land fell away to the main road far below, invisible behind yet more trees and a hawthorn hedge.

Then I saw it, a sudden movement, barely perceptible. About fifty metres away. A casual observer or someone walking by might have mistaken it for a branch, but I knew differently. It was the barrel of a gun. There was the sound of another shot and while he was distracted reloading, I ran over the spiky ground into the shadow of the wood. I had reached safety.

Now I was the hunter. I had become my name.

I stood behind a tree, gripping my piece of wood, my heart hammering. I wished I was armed with something a little less primitive than what was essentially a stick. It wasn't even stone-age weaponry, wood age, was that even a thing? A piece of timber versus a rifle.

I very slowly crept forward, avoiding fallen twigs or small branches that would crack under my weight, and then I saw him. I froze and took in the scene in front of me.

Rupert Bear was lying full length on his stomach, fully costumed except for his paws which were lying by his side. Latex gloves covered the hands that held the rifle. I guess the paws wouldn't fit through the trigger guard. I watched as he ejected the spent cartridge and slid another bullet into the chamber.

Hardly daring to breathe I crept up on him from behind. He was totally absorbed in what he was doing and didn't hear me. I guess too the mask that covered his head would deaden all sound.

I stood over him like the Angel of Death with my piece of four by two. He fired again at the shed and I pounced. I lifted my arms above my head and brought the piece of wood down between his ears as hard as I could as if I were driving a stake into Dracula's heart. The end thunked down on the back of the furry skull, but it didn't incapacitate him as much as I had hoped. I thought it would knock him out. It didn't. He rolled over and momentarily stared up at me through the eyeholes in the bear's head, then I stamped down hard on the rifle to stop him picking it up and lifted my club again.

He scrambled to his feet, turned and ran. He headed out across the fields and I followed in pursuit. It was a very uneven contest.

Although I was wearing jeans, far from ideal to run in, I was wearing trail shoes and a T-shirt. Unlike a real bear, capable, I believe, of thirty-five miles an hour, Rupert, admittedly never an athlete in the comic books, was woefully slow. I had been expecting a great deal more from Roland. He must have been stunned from the blow to the skull. I ran behind him, he was visibly tiring now, his head was lolling, he turned to see how far away I was, that was a mistake. He tripped over a rut in the ground and went sprawling, face down. I guess he had restricted vision in the bear's head.

There was a blur of movement from the corner of my eye; I turned to see what it was. It was a sight worth seeing.

Cliff was running towards us from the doorway of the shed. His stomach bounced as he ran. There would be no mistaking him for Jakob Ingebrigtsen.

I raised my piece of wood like a sword, leaned forward and with one movement ripped the head off the bear lying at my feet. It came away cleanly in my hands and, to my astonishment, I found myself looking into the angry features, not of Roland Woods, but of Della Peters.

Chapter Forty-Four

It was Friday afternoon and I kept my appointment with Roland. I was alone. I didn't need Cliff to babysit me, anyway three would have been a crowd.

I ran my hand lightly over his muscular body as he lay beside me in bed, those abs, those shapely pecs. How I would miss them. I rolled over and we lay chest to chest as I looked into his dark eyes,

'Why the hell do you own a Rupert Bear costume?' I had been silent up to now, but I really needed to know.

'I bought it when I was in sixth form,' he said. 'I had to go to a fancy dress party, I had so many compliments. Everyone loves Rupert. He's been on a rugby tour, two stag nights... some more fancy dress parties, demos when I didn't want my photo taken... it's been a bloody good buy. How was I to know my cleaning lady was a homicidal maniac and borrowed it when I wasn't looking?'

He gently moved me aside and poured himself a glass of the champagne I'd bought with me. I felt I owed him some kind of apology for thinking he was a murderer and for arranging to have him nearly beaten to a pulp for something he hadn't done. Vigilante violence seems to be frowned upon for a very sensible reason. I didn't think he needed to know my plans though. Some things are better left unsaid.

'Have you got any more questions for me, Charlie?'

'Yeah, can you show me those pistol squats again?'

He got out of bed and executed six on his left, followed by six on his right. I was open-mouthed with admiration.

I drank some more champagne, half a glass, I had to get back to work later.

'Charlie,' he said, his voice sounded deeply serious. Oh no, I thought. I leaned forward and kissed him. I deepened my kiss and felt his body respond, he really was in superb shape. We made love again and I broke the silence this time,

'God, is that the time, I've got to go, we've got forty-five booked in…'

'Charlie…'

I swung my legs out of bed and searched for my socks, they had to be around here somewhere. They can be very elusive sometimes.

'Charlie, I…' he couldn't finish the sentence – I had leaned forward and put a finger in a kind of shushing motion over his lips. I knew where his tongue was, resting behind his two front teeth, trying to form the letter 'l'.

'Sssh.' I removed my finger and started pulling on the rest of my clothes.

'When can I see you again?' he asked.

'You can't,' I said, buttoning my blouse up. 'This is goodbye.'

'But...' his face looked stricken.

'I know, I know,' I said gently, he looked like he was going to burst into tears, 'but you've got a life to live and I've got a business to run... it's been great, Roland, but it could never last.'

I leaned forward and kissed him on his mouth.

'Take care sweetheart,' I said, 'I'll miss you.'

And I left without a backward glance.

The following Tuesday morning I was prepping at half past eight when there was a knock on the kitchen door. It was DI Slattery. I let him in. I would be without a kp today, Francis was in London, at Savile Row no less, having measurements taken for a suit to be made. I wasn't paying the bill, a grateful Lance Thurston was. He'd also promised not to cut the beeches down. It was a sweet victory, my present to Roland and the badgers.

'It's good to see you, Detective Inspector,' I said. 'Coffee?'

'Please.'

I led him through into the restaurant and switched the machine on. Slattery sat down and looked at me. He smiled.

'So, why did she do it?' I asked Slattery. No need to say 'Della Peters.'

'That's a very good question. I doubt if anyone knows. Her legal team will be claiming that she was crazy, and personally I'm inclined to believe them. She's confessed to the whole thing, she really left them no choice.'

'I see.'

'From what she's said, and her statement reads like some nutty political manifesto, she started working with Lance

311

because she totally bought into his view of the world, that there was this big, woke conspiracy out there. All the usual suspects, as you can imagine.'

I ground his coffee and did the same for myself. He continued. 'Now, she first tried to kill Dr Young because she was Lance's avowed enemy, in league with the woke forces of evil, that kind of makes sense.' I suppose it did, but that didn't answer her attack on me.

'And what about me?' I asked.

'Well, at the party, Lance told her that he really fancied you but you were a horrible, ball-breaking woman, and a prick-teaser…'

'Can I be both simultaneously?' I wondered aloud. Bloody Lance, pissed as a newt, I thought, trying to come on as some good-time-seeking womaniser when he was secretly busy with a highly masculine deli owner.

Slattery grinned. 'Seemingly. Anyway, she had already decided that people like you, independent women, were part of the problem, you shouldn't be running companies, businesses et cetera, you should be married and at home. She told me that would solve the benefits and unemployment problem too. It was wokery of the worst sort: women should know their place, they were emasculating men, look at poor Lance. Turning to a gay lover because of people like you. Anyway, there you were… bingo.'

'And the costume?' I knew, obviously, but I asked anyway.

'She's Roland Sylvanus's cleaner. Or Roland Woods as he is formally known, the woodland activist. The costume belongs to him.'

'Oh,' I said. I was glad our brief affair was still secret, I certainly wasn't going to be spilling any beans. Slattery continued. 'The house is an Airbnb on a short-term let. She's the woman who does the changeover cleaning for it, and Roland hired her as his weekly cleaner. She borrowed the costume to use when she decided to kill you. It was a fancy dress party after all. Nobody saw Della follow you, a witness would have seen Rupert Bear.'

'And what about Lance?'

'When Della initially found out that Lance was having an affair with Sam, she was furious, she said she felt betrayed, she doesn't like homosexuals, "perverts" as she calls them. It was then that she hatched the plan to kill Dr Young and implicate Lance. She felt he had let the side down and betrayed her trust in him.'

'Whose gun did she use to shoot Dr Young?' I asked.

'I'll come back to that. Della called Dr Young and told her that Lance was having an affair with a man, would she like more details. You can imagine her response, yes she would. So, they arranged to meet, they did and she killed the doctor and placed the murder weapon in Lance's shed.'

'How did she get in?' I couldn't imagine Della breaking codes or anything clever like that, bypassing security systems. It was one reason why she'd never occurred to me as a suspect.

'Lance uses a password generator for all his logins,' Slattery explained, 'so they are secure, but for four digit combos, which is what that shed keypad is, he does what a lot of people do and uses a birthday, in his case his mother's, the seventeenth of September, that is, 1-7-0-9. Now Della knew that this number was the key to the gate,

Lance had also set it for the shed. She tried it and it worked. It was that easy.'

'And Sam?'

'She visited Lance in prison and he told her that he'd finished with Sam. She was at pains to exonerate Lance, she still adores him, she was adamant he knew nothing about her murderous activities.'

'Is that true?'

'I believe it is.'

'How did she know he was having an affair with Sam?'

Slattery looked at me like I was mad. 'She's a cleaner, Charlie, they know everything about you. Anyway. He also told her it was just a phase, that Sam had seduced him when he was weak and confused... she was delighted and determined to clear his name.'

'So, she'd framed him for a murder and now wanted to unframe him?'

Slattery nodded. 'That was her thinking: "anyone can make a mistake". That's how she put it. She felt that if she killed Sam and pinned it on Roland, the whole thing would exonerate Lance. Which, in fairness, it could well have done.'

I put his coffee in front of him and we clinked cups. He drank some, he nodded approvingly and continued. 'Now, Roland Woods has two rifles. They're in a gun safe in the cottage. He has a key, and so, of course, does Della. She had already used one rifle to shoot Dr Young, now she decided to use the other to kill you and Sam.'

I nodded; now I could see her thinking. And of course, Slattery didn't know about the poppet doll. After she'd killed me, Jess would have told him all about the attempt on my life at the party, the Rupert Bear suit, the poppet doll as seen on camera. Things would have looked terrible for Roland. Owner of the suit, owner of the murder weapon, placer of the poppet doll.

Slattery said, 'So when Sam came over to collect some of his things – he'd called in advance to arrange a time with her – she took the Rupert costume, changed into it, ambushed Sam and used him as bait to trap you. If anyone saw her, they would see Rupert. I think she was going to report her suspicions to the police, she was wearing one of Roland's T-shirts. I think she intended to get blood on it to further implicate him.'

'What will happen to her?'

'I think her legal team will claim she was suffering from a diagnosed mental illness, as defined by the DSM.'

'What's that?'

'I seem to remember it stands for the Diagnostic and Statistical Manual of Mental Disorders. Under the McNaughton rule I should think she will get at least thirty years.'

'How is Sam Hickocks?' I asked 'Do you know?'

He nodded. 'He's out of hospital and we've released Lance.'

'How is Lance?' He was a total bastard, but for some reason I liked him. He'd also transferred a lot of money into my bank account which made me like him even more. I'm shallow like that sometimes.

'He's a happy bunny,' Slattery said. He looked at me. 'And how are you?'

'I'm the same as ever, only more so.'

Slattery stood up. 'I was afraid of that.' He smiled sadly, sighed and gave me a kind of ironic salute. 'I'll see you around.'

I smiled. 'You know where to find me,' I said and showed him to the door.

Chapter Forty-Five

I took our cups into the kitchen and put them down by the dishwasher. I had enjoyed my chat with Slattery; I liked his company, he was kind of reassuring. Della Peters I thought, what a crazy bitch. At least I was free of mad women. But I was wrong.

And then as I looked out of the glass panel of the kitchen door, the gate opened and another mad woman walked into my life.

Oh, Jesus, I thought, not you. Like the Bogeyman, just like when you thought everything was okay, she had returned.

Mel Craig, stony faced and carrying something in her arms wrapped in a towel like she was holding a baby, marched up to the kitchen door.

I opened it.

'What do you want?' I demanded.

'You win,' she said, angrily, gracelessly. I did a double take. I hadn't expected that. Her face was haggard and lined. She'd put some make-up on but kind of badly. I could see big bags under bloodshot eyes. Did she have some kind of drink problem, I wondered. She looked awful.

'Take this,' she said, thrusting the towel forward, 'and promise you'll stop bothering me. I've dropped the proceedings against you. It's over.'

'What is it?' I couldn't see what the towel contained.

'You know what it is, you evil witch,' she said, 'take it, please…' to my alarm she was almost shaking with emotion, 'take it and say it's over.'

'Okay, it's over,' I said, taking the bundle from her.

'I'm leaving the village tomorrow,' she said stiffly. 'You'll never hear from me again.'

She turned and walked away. The gate closed behind her.

I opened the towel. It was a poppet doll, with a very faithful rendition of Mel Craig's face, eerily so, distorted in an agonising scream. It was amazingly terrifying. Such horrible artistry, a sinister masterpiece.

'What the fuck!' I said aloud.

'Amazing what you can do with a 3-D printer,' Jess's voice said behind me. I turned and there she was, a huge grin on her face.

She took the doll from my hands. 'Come to Mummy,' she cooed.

Another coffee.

'When I saw Roland with that doll,' Jess said, 'I went round and spoke to Bryony. You've probably forgotten but you told me that she had that boyfriend into black magic. That got me thinking about Roland and the poppet doll. He's friends with Bryony. She told me they'd hatched the idea to try and frighten Lance into abandoning the helipad

318

scheme. So I got her to make me one of Mel Craig; it was good, but I improved it. I had that photo of her from the doorbell. I've got a 3-D printer at home and I created the doll's face, it worked brilliantly.'

I stared at Jess, open-mouthed with admiration.

'You're so clever!'

'I know,' she said, 'I got a first, remember. Then I re-hacked into her computer. Mel Craig has been getting some pretty terrifying stuff online and on her phone over the past few days, makes *Saw* or *The Exorcist* look like Teletubbies.' She smiled. 'I got quite a lot of good ideas from those Aleister Crowley books, so they came in useful after all. It must have triggered all that latent fear and respect of the occult she had in her subconscious. It obviously worked quickly, better than I had hoped. I doubt if she's had any sleep whatsoever in the past week.'

'Thank you so much, Jess.'

She smiled again. 'It's what friends are for.' She hesitated. 'Andrea called me... he wants you back Charlie.'

I looked at Jess, I looked at my kitchen, out of the window I could see Francis peeling potatoes in the sunshine.

And I knew then that my decision to stay here was the right one.

'Tell him,' I hesitated, I don't know why, I finally knew my own mind, 'tell him, thanks but no thanks.'

Alea iacta est, as they would say at St Anselm's.

The die is cast.

Charlie Hunter was staying right here.

ABOUT THE AUTHOR

Photo credit © Alex Coombs

Alex Coombs was born in Lambeth in South London
and studied Arabic at Oxford and Edinburgh
Universities, and is a qualified chef. Alex lives
in the Chilterns.

www.alexcoombs.co.uk

NO EXIT PRESS

More than just the usual suspects

'A very smart, independent publisher delivering
the finest literary crime fiction' – *Big Issue*

MEET NO EXIT PRESS, the independent publisher bringing you the best in crime and noir fiction. From classic detective novels, to page-turning spy thrillers and singular writing that just grabs the attention. Our books are carefully crafted by some of the world's finest writers and delivered to you by a small, but mighty, team.

In our 30 years of business, we have published award-winning fiction and non-fiction including the work of a Pulitzer Prize winner, the British Crime Book of the Year, numerous CWA Dagger Awards, a British million copy bestselling author, the winner of the Canadian Governor General's Award for Fiction and the Scotiabank Giller Prize, to name but a few. We are the home of many crime and noir legends from the USA whose work includes iconic film adaptations and TV sensations. We pride ourselves in uncovering the most exciting new or undiscovered talents. New and not so new – you know who you are!!

We are a proactive team committed to delivering the very best, both for our authors and our readers.

Want to join the conversation and find out more about what we do?

Catch us on social media or sign up to our newsletter for all the latest news from No Exit Press HQ.

f fb.me/noexitpress **🐦** @noexitpress
noexit.co.uk/newsletter